The Gifts of Ghosts

A Musical Novel

"The Gifts of Ghosts" is a musical story sprawled across America from Montana to San Francisco.

Songs come from ghosts.

All the songs in this book may be found here:
https://thegiftsofghosts.bandcamp.com/album/the-gifts-of-ghosts-songs

or
if reading electronically, click below for access to all songs

<u>MUSIC</u>

or
wait for the song to appear in the story and click on the title.

Hope you enjoy "Skulk Rock".

Songs are
The Gifts of Ghosts

Published by Neckend Publications

ISBN 978-1-0685088-0-6 eBook.
ISBN 978-1-0685088-1-3 paperback

First published 2024

This edition published 2024

Original music: Robert T. Morrow, Andrew Cutts
© ANeckenderMusic 2014–2024

This is a work of fiction. Names, characters, businesses, places, events and
incidents are either the products of the author's imagination, or used in a
fictitious manner. Any resemblance to actual persons, living or dead, or
actual events is purely coincidental.

The publisher has no responsibility for the continued existence
or accuracy of URLs for external or third-party internet websites
referred to in this book, and does not guarantee that any content on
such websites is, or will remain, accurate or appropriate.

"Time is upon me like a pack of wolves
Gravity like an avalanche
I got sins I can't absolve
Just like everyone
The cinema in the back of my mind
Keeps replaying all of my crimes
Memories malinger
Like death's cold finger*

Lucy Smith
San Francisco
Star Date: 001586.34

The Gifts of Ghosts the 1st story of Skulk Rock. It hasn't happened yet – but it could. Who's to say where a story really begins? Everything depends on what has gone before? Or does it? Although, better not get lost in Philosophy or Physics right now. This story really orbits around the three originators of 'Skulk Rock'. There's Michael J Remo (upfront), there's The Thunderman (on the bass guitar) and there's TheGnome (at the drumkit).

These guys are uncompromising musician warriors operating in and around San Francisco, but it's strange how fate can tie certain people together and draw them into whirlpool destinies that no-one could really foretell. Is it random Butterfly Effects that instigate Event-Avalanches and draw fates together? Rogue-gravity-space-time-interlocks? As already advised, leave that to the laws of Philosophy and Physics.

So, we could start this story in San Francisco, or even Manchester England, but let's begin way up north in the Montana High Plains, at the boundaries of the land of Assiniboine, and Sioux, and sanctuary of the bald eagle.

Chapter 1
Moonlight Over Montana

"Don't lose the groove." She sings the phrase to herself, over her new chord discovery. Chords sound nice and full - but nothing without the groove. That's when it all clicked for her. It was her dad that told her. Bless his heart. She struggled with fingerings, but she wouldn't let go. "Guitar is a hard thing to get started on." He encouraged. "Sing it Lucy and, **'don't lose the groove. The groove is everything.'"** She remembers her room at home, on the day that advice clicked into place. She was singing "Dink's Blues". The version by Bob. It was like electricity suddenly filled the room and filled her. Charged. A ghost in the room. A dream shared. It clicked. Ghosts bring you songs. Gifts from ghosts.

****

How did she get here? She does love this line of poplar trees though. They are handsome and tall, in a totally straight line. Why is that? Someone must've planted them? Nature doesn't do straight lines? She looks out at the view over the high plains. *"What do you mean, nature doesn't do straight lines? Light travels in straight lines. That's pretty fundamental nature?"* The straight-line light of a Montana view fills her vision. Montana is vast for sure. The light from the distant sierras takes a fair amount of time to reach her. Vast is kind of lonely these days. It makes her feel small. It's no disenchantment; she felt small in the city too. Lucy is from suburban Illinois and beginning to revise her notions of the country life. Her Dad had warned her about becoming 'marooned out there', one time when he was rattling on, after she told him where she was going. She had politely ignored his advice, whilst thinking, *"What's he on about now?"*. But, "now", as she turns around and scans the land and sky and distant sierras, she begins to wonder if he had a point. Maybe there is something in what he was saying? He was right about 'the groove' after all? Oh well, here she is, in the vast vagueness of Montana, and feeling smaller every day. Maybe she is mistaking smaller for lonely? It has all been her choices. After all, she knows herself best, and fathers can be a little 'overprotective'. Hers was prone to talking in riddles, and trying to put his old head on her young shoulders, but maybe, just maybe, for once in her life, she was beginning to see what he had meant. "Marooned in Montana". She muses with the phrase and wonders if it could be the start of a song? May be like 'Anchored in Anchorage', that's a great song. Sometimes it happens like that, and one phrase hooks you in. Not a "hook line", as such, but more of a "hook thought", from which other lines will hang in some way. Other times, she really does feel that a ghost visits you and gives you the song. It just appears in your mind, and then on the paper in front of you. However, it works, there it is. A song. One of her favourite feelings. Offset by all the failed pages of drivel in her notepad, it is always so worth it when a song is born. Maybe they do come from ghosts?

Her Dad also used to say, "Lucy Smith, always fighting back, and she keeps coming at you, and she don't give up." In her mind, he was probably wrong about that too but, she does understand that you don't get gold without panning for it, and she isn't going to surrender and crawl. Not to nobody and not to no circumstance.

This all being so, she finds herself walking up this hill more and more often to offset the gradual darknesses that have crept into her life here. Her life with Seth has soured, little by little. Littles have become a lot, and she realises she has begun to welcome the solitude and distant view at the top this rise. These noble poplar trees also seem to provide quiet company and protection for her. That's dumb, but she does wonder who had planted them, and when, and even why?

The farm has seen better days, and Seth and she are not exactly moving it along. So many plans, and so much disappointment. Ambition is a form of greed. She carries on punching the chords on her faithful old Gibson "Nick Lucas" guitar, as these thoughts come together in her mind. The chords match the Montana key. Big and open, like the sky, and like the singing air across the old poplars.

The farmstead from up here looks like a painting. She often thinks of it like that, and how the painting can change during the day and evenings. If she was a painter, she would be like JMW Turner; the greatest of them all. You would surely need all his skills and visions to capture the Montana skies and sierras on a canvas. It will have to be a big canvas; that's for sure. JMW was famous for 'vagueness' and her life is certainly vague these days. She needs to end things and move on. There's a big but though; Seth can be scary these days. He's not the easy going guy she first met. Lucy Smith moves her nervousness to a closed cupboard in her mind. She'll sort it all out later.

The farm sits neatly in a green valley with distant hills, over which the moon often hold court. Is it some kind of optical effect in the Montana atmosphere that magnifies the moon? Or is it getting closer, its orbit diminishing? She sometimes figures she can see highways and houses on it. It seems so close. Look – see it ruined by roads – just like the earth. She mentally kicks herself. *"I really have been out here too long"*. None of which alters the fact that maybe there is a weird gravitational kink over Montana. Something Einstein missed. She will ask her dad next time; he does have a qualification in Physics, and maybe he doesn't talk total riddles after all? Gears click into place in her mind, and the Final Decision Office Department of her brain informs her that now is the time to leave this adventure behind. Now ... well, as soon as possible.

Decisions seem to relieve tension, and her elevated mood even generates a skip in her step as she walks back down the hill. Maybe it's having made her decision, or maybe it's the good feeling she gets when she knows she has found a new song. Maybe it's both?

This time, she's hit on some gorgeous chord sequences and melody to fit and a good start of lyrics. There's a threshold you cross when you know the song will appear, and it always lifts her mood. She wonders which ghost gave her this one. She sings more words to herself, over and over, until she reaches the dishevelled farmyard. She keeps her mind on the song, not wanting to forget any of the lines before she can write them down. Not wanting the problems of how to leave Seth to occupy her mind anymore. They do though; they rattle inside that cupboard. Has love turned to hate? So many songs out there, and she is stuck out here. The wide-open space of Montana suddenly claustrophobic. How upside-down crazy is that?

A shiver runs through her as she thinks of how she can tell him. Seth Snake, the acceptable face of The Snake family dynasty; but now it's not quite that way. Love isn't turning to hate yet, but it might, and now is the time to depart, before it does. She will tell him tonight when he returns from his gig.

**

Time flows inexorably, according to Lucy Smith's dad, although she seems to remember it's a quote from Sir Isaac; her Dad's hero. How much of it has flowed recently is something of a mystery to her at this moment, because she seems to be awakening from some kind of trance. A weird nasty dream. She hopes so. She is shaking, and cold, and hot, and confused, and lost. She is beginning to piece a memory framework back together and, once again today, she finds herself stood with the faithful poplar trees. This time it's night-time, and the trees silently sway in a light breeze, like wagging fingers admonishing her. The sky is moonlit but stars, many stars, are also visible this time. The distant mountain range is still there in the moonlight, as her eyes descend from the stars, swoop down the Sierra slopes and over the intervening high plains. She didn't really do that did she? Has to be a dream. She forces herself to look out over the lower land to the farmhouse, across the dry stream and in the middle distance. Her eyes then sink further to her hands and the neck of her faithful old Nick Lucas, which she now holds with trembling fingers. Splinters of wood dangle where the body was. Fragments, and a tangle of strings. She turns a tuning peg and runs a finger over the headstock. She thinks of her father and her 12th birthday, when he gave the guitar to her. Lucy was betrothed to Nick Lucas from that moment on. An arranged marriage. More tears run down the already marked tracks on her cheek.

Her gaze gradually, and reluctantly, moves upwards again from the guitar remnants, and slowly along the 'Eagle Meadow', towards the farmhouse. As her focus tightens on the building, she suddenly sees a fire flicker inside one of the windows. Her knuckles whiten even more, one hand gripping the guitar neck, the other in a tight clench by her side. As the flames become visible through the glass, her mind's camera moves inside. It sees the cooker ablaze and the whole kitchen begin to catch. She gazes upon the lifeless body of Seth, now grey skinned and slumped. A single bullet wound to the chest and, as the camera moves upwards, another bullet hole in the head. Suddenly, flames follow a liquid path from the kitchen to his body, and it takes light, doused in a flammable liquid. So ... it wasn't a dream. Oh fuck.

Lucy's mind-camera slowly backs out of the building, and gradually returns the viewpoint back to the raised ground and poplar trees, from where she still stares. She jumps back as flames suddenly blow out the windows and engulf the house. Vivid against the surrounding stillness of the night-time. She moves slowly forward again and watches impassively as the flames caress the buildings, until a gas cylinder flares high into the night sky.

She takes a deep breath and replays, in chronological sequence, as best she can, the events between the 'now' and her previous time here earlier today.

Flashback memories return, as if she's watching fragments of a movie that need splicing together. She sees Seth returning home late from his gig, and lurching into the room where she is singing her new song. She even remembers thinking to herself that maybe this wouldn't be a good time to tell him she is leaving. She winces, as she recalls his reaction to the new song. The drunken sneer as he grabs her guitar. The awful sound-tsunami as he smashes it against the sideboard. She sees her own face watching impassively, tears forming and silently running down her cheeks, for the first time that evening.

She sees herself stood as he slumps down onto the couch. She sees herself walk silently from the room as he fumbles with a whisky bottle. He takes a drink and lays his head back. She sees herself open the drawer in the kitchen, where he keeps a very large handgun, and then walking slowly back into the room, with the gun. How it had taken two hands to hold the gun. How, as he looks up, she sees herself shoot him in the chest. His face shocked; disbelief. She then shoots him in the head. Time stands still, except for the expanding clouds of blue smoke from the two gunshots. There are also two Lucy's in the room, one watching the other in disbelief, unable to stop her counterpart. She then sees herself pause for a dilated moment, before taking the half-drunk bottle from his grasp and, in a vexed act,  pouring the remaining whisky over him, and then in a trail back to the kitchen. Partway to the destination, the bottle empties and she throws it to one side in disgust. In frustration, defiance and determination to finish the job, she sees herself return with a can of paraffin. She overlays the trail of whisky and extends it into the kitchen, as far as the cooker.

Next, she diverges and packs a bag with clothes, boots, a sheaf of manuscripts. Appearing to lose patience with packing, she goes to a drawer and takes out some keys. She walks out to an inconsequential looking farm building. Opening several locks to reveal an older but well-kept Dodge pickup truck. The letters on the front of the bonnet are missing a "d" and "e" so that it's a 'Do_g '. She drives 'The Dog' to the front of the

farmhouse and walks back inside. Several repeat trips sees her throwing bags and belongings into the rear tool trunk. On the last trip, she loads a saucepan with cooking oil and walks slowly out, leaving the gas ring heating the oil on full. Finally, she remembers the panic as The Dog would not start again. She pauses and prays as the engine finally coughs and convulses into life. "Wake up Dog". Finally, she remembers driving The Dog, as if on auto-pilot, around the old road and up to the old poplars.

Standing with the poplars once more, she doesn't feel alone for some crazy reason. They all stand as still as the watching moon. Smoke and flames rise vertically into the indifferent night air. She bows her head, with weariness, or shame, or despair, and a curtain of hair falls in front of her face. She sings some opening lines of a song, without knowing where they came from. As she raises her head, the curtain of hair from across her vacant stare is suddenly gathered backwards by a misplaced gust of wind; it jolts her mind totally back into the present. She shudders, as she watches the farmhouse fall in on itself.

Santa Monica

So, I stand once again beneath the poplars
Thinking of life without you
Some of us are saved and some of us damned.
I remember the touch of your violent hands.
Talking to myself nobody heard me.
These long shadows disturb me.
Life is suddenly lonely.
But better than with you around me
And I'm leaving so you can't haunt me.

One bullet for your cold heart
One bullet for your evil mind
Who knows what I will find?
I got a brand new start.
One last look in your black eyes
The last time in this life
There's no teardrops – as I say goodbye

You made your big mistake.
When you found out how much I could take
And now you speak like silence.
You were my ideal of violence.
Say goodbye to the stars above me.
Is there anyone to judge me?
Surrounded by nature's beauty.
I bury something so ugly.
And the law won't catch me
Not tonight

One bullet for your cold heart
One bullet for your evil mind
Who knows what I will find?
I got a brand new start
One last look in your black eyes
The last time in this life
There's no teardrops – as I say goodbye

Even God won't understand yer
He'll send you back as a black mamba.
But you will be in Africa.
By the time I'm in Santa Monica

Shivering as the buildings now smoulder in the dawn light, still, she watches. How long has she been here? The film running in her mind now finally merging with the present, as she wakes up, and shakes herself back from the trance, and back into the reality of it all.

An old High Plains ghost is summoned, and he watches too. As far west as he ever got. This was the extent of his dream,s and now the embers of his old homestead rise as smoke into still air. All that remains are these poplar trees he planted with his wife. They would protect the cattle shelter that once stood here. How tall they have grown? How long has it been? He sings an old song to himself "My last heartbeat my first dream"*, as he watches the young woman stood next to him, and, as she raises her head once again, he runs a ghostly finger through the curtain of hair in front of her face.*

As the grey smoke, now turning black against the dawn light, rises higher, Lucy Smith gathers herself, breathes deep, and walks slowly back to The Dog. She carefully places her guitar remnants on the passenger seat. As she starts the engine, she is startled by a vision of the moon which seems closer than ever through the windscreen of The Dog. She freezes, as if the moon bears witness to her soul. She fights for control of her emotions. She wins, and drives off, away from the rising sun and swinging away from the moon. *"Use your last heartbeat chasing your first dream."* She sings the lyric fragment to herself, over and over and over. A mantra. Where did that line come from?

Songs play in Lucy's mind as miles, lonely trees, yellow highway lines, roadkill, and road signs pass. Power lines running next to her. Do they track her? Is the magnetic disturbance of The Dog enabling the law to track her? Please, please don't let anyone recognise The Dog. Maybe it's famous, a valuable antique? The sun rises over mountains to her left. The road is deserted. Eventually, she arrives at Saco. Her need of coffee wins out over her panic for anonymity and stealth, and she pulls into a deserted diner and sits in a secluded corner. The waitress seems to smile sympathetically as she takes Lucy's order. Lucy notices the waitress's pale and slim arms, as she tries to avoid face to face conversation. Even so, she is grateful for the friendly countenance. After her meal and coffee refill, she finds the phone booth, shuts the door tightly, and dials her mother's number. "Hi Mom."

She waits whilst her mother rambles.

Eventually. "You won't be hearing from me for a while."

Mrs Smith rambles more. Lucy becomes impatient and interrupts. "YESSS ... Mom, I'm ok, but I ended things with Seth."

There's a pause.

"I thought you might be pleased Mom?"

"No Mom, I'll be okay. I have a plan."

"I'm going to go to California."

"I have a truck."

"It was his ... but ... he never ever used it."

"No Mom, he doesn't mind."

"No, I don't think we'll hear much from him from here on in."

"No-one will miss me in Montana Mom. To be honest no-one really knew I was there."

"Was two years solitary."

"Yes, I love you too Mom."

"Mom, this is important though, I don't want Seth's family to know where I went so if ANYONE contacts you, you never heard from me in 2 years?"

"Yes Mom. Two years."

"It's important, Mom. Very important."

"Tell anyone that asks that you suspect I went to New York to be a singer. It always was an ambition of mine."

Lucy Smith coaches the witness that her mother might one day become. "You have to believe a lie yourself to be able to tell it. You did teach me how to lie Mom?"

"We're method actors, aren't we, Mom?"

"Tell Dad I love him."

Lucy sends a kiss down the phone line and hangs up. She looks wide-eyed through the glass of the booth, wide-eyed, as if in a trance. Her gaze piercing out through Diner glass, and along the highway. Across the high plains, there are distant mountains. The future, whatever it holds, is beyond those mountains, and under that distant sky. The way things are it might not hold very much at all, but she is not about to wait to find out. She needs distance. Distance between her and the Montana moon. Escape velocity from its gravitational pull. The moon sees everything.

As she climbs into the truck, she pats her guitar remnants on the adjacent seat and pulls away. Lucy Smith remembers one of her many 'Highway' songs. This is America, and the continent is crisscross with highway dreams. She sings to guide her dreams and invoke the highway spirits.

Highway

Use your last heartbeat chasing your first dream
Don't let it go it won't chase you
What did they do to the world you knew?
Time's a thief that much is true

Dream guitars that cry and sing
Dream movie stars in high heels
Dream visions that life can bring
Time's a thief and dreams are what it steals

Scatter me on a highway
Let the trucks take me away
But turn around and I will be there
In your dream or in your nightmare

Second glances in a rear view mirror
Missed chances of history
Circumstances can change your character
No defences to time's robbery

Scatter me on an ocean green
Dark and deep like my sleep
I'll never sleep with the fishes
This life is sweet and delicious

You've come so far – it's come to this
Teardrops running like piss

Lucy Smith stares ahead as she negotiates the bump and rise of America. She thinks of her youth and the excitement when her father gave her the guitar. The same one that his father had given him. A 1940s Gibson 'Nick Lucas', with a small but deep body, 13 frets to that body, and the sweetest tone you ever heard. The same guitar that now rests on the passenger seat. Sad, smashed, and smitten by evil. It has been avenged though? She remembers her first song. She remembers her first song notebook. She remembers singing her early songs to Seth. She remembers him smiling and laughing. She remembers his guitar embellishments. She remembers his smile, and how sweet their voices sounded together. She remembers her excitement at the notion of building up a life on the farm with him. The fantasies of youth. But now, the highway line hypnotises her. It marks her escape route, as it leads her and keeps her sane.

Still, she drives, as evening drops from the sky. She stares ahead. The highway is quiet. She likes it that way. Her nervousness increases with approaching cars and diminishes as they pass. Vehicles in her rear-view mirror make her more nervous, though. Much more nervous. She tunes into the sounds of The Dog. She dreads the tone and groove of The Dog changing or, even worse, any unevenness, which may be a sign of impending mechanical failure. As night falls her mind floats, up to stars above. They hover and sparkle over distant mountains. She gradually accelerates the truck, as the dawn chases her. She doesn't notice an eagle high in the sky as the first shafts of sunlight catch its wingspan as it glides over the truck below.

In dawn light, she tries to remember how many road junctions she has passed. A compass is stuck to The Dog's dashboard, and whenever she is undecided, she favours west or south. She figures that each junction makes it more difficult for anyone to follow her tracks. She longs for the state line. She wonders how many state lines will be required to escape the moon and 'The Snakes'? She tries to work out how many states are between her and the end of land. "C'mon Dog, we're gonna go see the ocean."

Chapter 2
She's Too Much

A young teenager sits in his room, somewhere in a cold grey industrial England. He strums a guitar and scribbles in a notebook. As he gazes vacantly through a frosted window, his mother enters. She sits quietly staring at him, before reaching out and touching his hand tenderly. "Highly unlikely you'll ever earn a living playing that thing, James."

"No Mum, let's be positive."

She smiles at his enthusiasm. She always did. Ever since he opened his eyes, he had seemed enthusiastic about whatever gained his attentions. The downside was, he was never interested in anything that didn't. As a toddler he never seemed to integrate with mainstream kids and now, at school, he would neglect his studies for the things that fired his imagination. Mostly the guitar.

"Mr Meadows – your illustrious music teacher at school, would agree with me?"

"We call him 'Flushing', Mum, you know why that is?"

"Of course. 'Flushing Meadows'? Where the Tennis Tournament is played?"

"No, Mum. Because he is so full of shit, he needs a good flushing."

Pause.

"James."

They look at each other, and then giggle.

The giggle subsides to silence and a sadness takes over. "You shouldn't have missed the exam, James?"

"I don't understand Biology, Mum. There's more to life than amoebas."

"Yes, but you have to start somewhere?"

"If you start at all, maybe? Mr Meadows has an amoeba for a brain, Mum."

She giggles again. "That's as maybe. Your father will not be pleased."

"He wants me to be an accountant. What good is biology for that shit?"

"James." She sounds a little more severe this time.

Another silence.

She continues. "Let's just hope he's had a good day at work? You know he just wants you to get to university."

"Another 3 years of not doing what I want, Mum."

"And what do you want?"

"I want to go to west coast USA and rock, Mum."

"Yes, James. And I want to open my back door to a nice country garden with flowers in bloom and an apple tree. We can't have everything we want?"

"Use your last heartbeat chasing your first dream, Mum."

Her face softens and she smiles at him. James returns a smile and begins to forget his transgression already. "I said I'd go to town tonight, with Pete Royle?" As if to ask permission.

Mrs Smith just stares at him smiling knowingly. "I bet you're going to that pub where the music bands play?"

"Well, yes. The Duke of York."

"And where the girls go?"

He looks at her smiling.

"Ohhhhhh." She smiles back. "Off you go. I'll deal with your father. Fridays are not usually a bad day for him."

**

A bright summer morning arrives and, as he wakes, he wishes he would've asked Annie Clark to dance last night. *"She sings for a band. I love her hair stacked up on top of her head. Real style. Her boyfriend is older, though? Works at the steelworks. He'd kick the shit out of me? Pete Royle would be no help."*

James giggles at the thought of him and Pete in a fight, as he watches a strange circle of light formed by his window and curtains. *"Why is it circular?"*

The globe of light tracks across his bedroom ceiling and down the wall. He thinks of it as the moon and its orbit, and physics lessons at school. He thinks how strange it is that he like Physics.

"Cos I fucking hate fucking biology."

He laughs inwardly and tries to work out where the 'moon' will end, as it moves on an orbit along and down his wall. And that was when he noticed his guitar wasn't in its usual place. He sits upright in bed and looks around the room. He suddenly stops mentally nursing his hangover, as the guitar's absence begins to dominate his mind. He dresses quickly and moves carefully downstairs. His father sits quietly at the breakfast table. His mother is in the small scullery, washing dishes. James speaks to her in a low voice. "Okay, Mum?"

His mother slowly turns her head, looks at him, and tries to smile. He sees snail-trail tear tracks down her cheeks and moist eyes. Jigsaw thoughts begin to come together.

"It turns out Friday wasn't a good day at all, James, and your father has to go to work this morning to catch up on things."

There's a pause.

"Where is it, Mum?"

Her tears run now. "It's in the bin outside."

James walks out into the backyard and immediately sees the headstock of his old acoustic guitar protruding from the dustbin. The dustbin lid resting precariously on it. As he pulls the neck from the bin, a tangle of strings and a broken body follow it. A strange blood circulates in him. His hangover evaporates. His brain crystal clear in its thought schemes. He walks back in and stares at his father and speaking calmly in a fake American accent that cannot disguise his own Manchester accent. "That's my Gibson Nick Lucas man."

His father stares straight ahead.

"I was going electric anyway. You superfluous old cunt."

James walks out and doesn't see the tear of regret running down his father's cheek.

****

Now, an older James Smith stands on stage, and waits for a count from a drummer who smiles at him over a Zildjian crash cymbal. An American flag with a small sewn-on Union Jack in the top left hangs raggedly at the back of the stage. The singer addresses the audience. "We're The Lowdown Dirtkickers and you have been our audience. Rowdy, drunken, desperate for life and, above all, dancing. That's just how we like it. We hope you have enjoyed some Skulk Rock. Sophistication and high art, here in Susanville – but – remember – The Groove is Everything."

An older audience member, with a cantilever belly above an ornate belt to his Levi's and an oil-stained Caterpillar cap, manifests a strange walk across the dance area as a show of appreciation.

Mike Remo smiles as he continues. "This is our first time in Susanville, and we are definitely going to migrate here. Probably after our case comes to court or when we bust on out of wherever they send us. Ain't no chains can hold our hearts – and – anyway - I still wanna meet Susan."

Female voices around the room shout in excited union. "I'm Susan."

Mike Remo laughs as he continues. "On the drums we have THE MetroGnome."

'TheGnome' plays a strange Captain Beefheart-esque drum lick and smiles at James, as he simultaneously lets his tongue lol out of the left side of his mouth. James laughs as his Stratotone barks alongside TheGnome's HiHat within a deep groove.

"THE Thunder from way down under is from El Thundero. The Thunderman."

Thunderman drags the lowest notes you ever heard from the flatwound strings along his '67 P-Bass and grows TheGnome's lick into a unique groove adventure. The groove is everything. 'The fucking groove is fucking everything'. 'TFG-IFE', The favourite war cry of TheGnome and The Thunderman.

Mike Remo, the one and only God of Skulk Rock, modestly introduces himself. "I'm Mike Reeeeeeemo ... the man the girls all wanna know ... we're gonna finish with a song by our tame limey on guitar."

He looks across at James and extends an arm and a smile. "Mr Jimmy English ..."

TheGnome crescendos and stops, as Thunderman lets a long low note hang so it can seek out every corner of the room. Four clicks and ...

Fall

I put my head out of an aeroplane window
I saw the face of god in his Heaven
Nowhere to be and nowhere to go
A single dice can't roll a 7

All I could do was fall fall fall fall

We'll be hitting the drop zone soon
And I don't want to take you down too
The moment has passed and time turned sour
Life could be over in half an hour

All I can do is fall fall fall fall

So now I only travel in dreams at night
I navigate by city lights
It's a little tricky with an ocean to cross
But I follow boats like an albatross

All I can do is fall fall fall fall

It's late Saturday evening and the bar clientele have been up for the gig. Mike Remo has drawn them into the world of "Skulk Rock", and now they dance with abandon and individuality. Their worldly cares are lifted by the relentless groove and poetry of the songs (assisted by the reduced bar prices, courtesy of the venue owner and gig promoter).

Partway through the song, a contrasting set of people enter at the back of the room. They are immediately incongruous in the context of the skulk rock audience. James' radar is alerted to them as the women in the group are striking and they all seem to circulate around one particular woman. She stands out amongst the group. The more James looks, the more he can't seem to take his eyes off her. She blesses him with a momentary eye contact; brief but significant. Massively significant, before she looks away to chat to her friends once again. James struggles to regain his stage self. He notices Mike Remo looking at him and shaking his head, smiling.

When James looks back to where she was standing, the whole group are already leaving. They exit through some rear doors. The stand-out girl is last to leave, and James watches her hair sway as it reflects the electric lights of the doorway. Did she look back there? She did.

**

After the gig James is packing equipment away and joking with bandmates. "Hey – that audience were locked to the groove? Correct me if I'm wrong?"

"Not wrong Jimmy Boy. Except for the guys at the back; they looked like they'd beamed onto the wrong planet."

"Did you see the girl in the red dress?"

Mike Remo pauses and looks admonishingly at James. "Jimmy English, your pussy radar was on red alert there – as usual." Mike smiles.

"She just caught my eye Mike. That's all."

Mike Remo affects his Cary Grant accent as he repeats. "She just caught my eye, Mike." (Well, he thinks he sounds like Cary Grant. James thinks he sounds like an American who thinks he can do an English accent.)

Thunderman joins in now. "She never took her eyes off the geetar player, Mike." And then, in a tone of disappointment. "It's always the guitar player. I should'a been a guitar player."

TheGnome cranks it on up. "I bet she's got a thing for English accents, Mike. What chance have we got?"

James looks up from putting his guitar in its case and sees the three Dirtkickers stood smiling at him. He tries to come up with a witty reply but fails miserably. He settles for giving them the finger. The three Dirtkickers smile and high five each other.

TheGnome engages his serious tone now, as if delivering a philosophical conclusion. "Women like that never stick around. Man, they are wired differently."

"You should know, pal." James smiles at his minor last word victory.

**

The Lowdown Dirtkickers are silent now. Weary as they carry equipment back to the van. This time it's a long carry from stage and through a lobby. James shivers as his sweat cools in the late northern California air.

After they pack the last amplifier neatly in its place, James decides he needs a bathroom call before the long journey ahead of them. He walks across the car park and into the foyer of the hotel, rather than back into the venue. His bandmates wait in the van and shake their heads. "Our Jimmy – always hopeful."

As James rushes out of the bathroom, his dreams are answered surprisingly quickly as he bumps into THE girl. "Oh shit. Sorry." He saves her from falling.

"It's okay." She smiles.

They look at each other in an embarrassing silence moment, although, in James' case, it's a dream-spell moment and he is struggling to catch up.

She breaks the dead air. "I enjoyed your music."

"Thanks, but we didn't manage to keep you all in the room."

She looks at the ceiling. "Peer groups. They wanted to go back to the wedding disco. I enjoy live music though."

He pauses. "Thanks. Glad you enjoyed it anyway."

She smiles again. "Where are you playing next?"

"We have a gig tomorrow night in Yuba City, and then a couple of bars in Napa. Then back to SF."

"What are you called?"

"The Lowdown Dirtkickers"

"Alluring name." She giggles, then adds. "Maybe I'll catch you back in San Francisco?"

"What's your name?"

"I'm James."

"I'm Felicia."

She lightly kisses him. He is spellbound. As she turns and walks away, she stops and turns back momentarily. "Love your accent too."

She turns the corner, and he pauses, his mind whirlpooling. He has no idea how much time has elapsed before he finds a flyer in his back pocket and walks quickly after her. Turning the corner, he sees a long, long corridor and a thousand doors. No Felicia, and no clues.

His bandmates are, by now, sounding the horn, and he reluctantly exits.

In the van he excitedly tells his bandmates of his encounter.

"Told you they love the Cary Grant accent." The Thunderman laughs.

Mike Remo momentarily wishes he had been the one deploying his own Cary Grant, before affecting an impatient tone. "Long piss, Jimmy English. We got miles to make, and you have been on another wild woman chase?"

"Wasn't like that Mike It was different."

"Where have I heard that before? Was it 'Veronica from Santa Monica'?"

James is quiet.

Thunderman makes a suggestion. "No Mike, it was 'Mona from Sedona' ... I think."

James stares sullenly through windscreen glass.

TheGnome has his own recollection. "What about 'The Giraffe from Flagstaff'?"

James speaks without moving his forward gaze. "She just liked wearing high heels."

"Bet she bumped her head a lot?"

James returns to a vow of silence.

Mike Remo's eyes sparkle as he speaks. "Then there was 'The Mover from Vancouver'. Now she really could dance?"

Thunderman adds detail. "More like gyrating Mike."

Mike Remo turns and smiles at TheGnome and Thunderman before resuming. "Hey, and then there was 'The Redwood from Deadwood'? Remind me why he was 'The Redwood' Jimmy?".

James is resolute in his hermit phase.

TheGnome demands forensic detail. "Was he a big boy Mike?"

"You'll have to ask Jimmy."

James' hermit crust is suddenly ruptured. "FUCK OFF Remo."

The Dirtkicker Van falls to silence. Thunderman is suddenly aware that no-one inside the band has ever spoken like that to Mike Remo. TheGnome is suddenly aware that no-one inside the band has ever spoken like that to Mike Remo. TheGnome and Thunderman look at each other wondering as to Mike's response. This could turn ugly.

Mike Remo lets the moment ride. Like a stop in a song. Thunderman and TheGnome wait for his count back in. Tense. Expectant. Mike stares at the side of James' face until James turns to face him down.

Mike face transforms into a broad smile erupting with laughter. "Limey on the line boys. Reel him in."

The Dirtkicker Van rocks with combined laughter as Thunderman mimes working a big fish from the stern of a luxury yacht on the deep blue of a Marin County rocky bay whilst surrounded by supermodels on sun-loungers watching his muscles ripple through their designer sunglasses.

As the laughter subsides James is defiant. "This was different."

Mike slowly shakes his head. "Jimmy English ... you're on this planet to write songs. Don't give me the 'this was different story'." A smile, lets James know he is still only semi-serious.

James mutters defiantly. "This WAS fuckin' different."

Mike Remo pulls out a CD, slots it into the car player as he guides the trusty Dirtkicker Van onto Highway 36. "Anyway, she'd be too much for you Jimmy English."

She's Too Much

She got a high class voice
And high class friends
She wawks the dawg
From her Mercedes Benz
She got a sun tan in winter
And she's cool in June
but if you don't flash cash
she don't notice you

She could be my babe and I swear it's true
and I could paddle to mars in my old canoe
She believes in love at first sight

The song plays as the Lowdown Dirtkicker van cruises out of Susanville on the starlight highway, surrounded by a pine forest. James' thoughts ascend high above the highway, high above the pines and on up to the Californian stars. He remembers the stars of Manchester England and his Dad telling him how they are made of electricity. *"Memories, feel like a disease"*. He wonders if this is a ghost giving him song lyrics. Whenever his songs arrive, that's what he thinks. You must welcome the ghost. Everyone has stories to tell. Write down the ideas. His Mum had told him that songs are "The Gifts of Ghosts". It's a truth he carries precious. He worries about her. It's been a while since he wrote.

TheGnome and Thunderman doze, dreaming of groove-riffs. Mike Remo stares ahead at the highway, keeping his thoughts to himself. James remains wide awake and watches the stars. He thinks about Felicia. He thinks about Felicia. And then, he thinks about Felicia.

<h1 style="text-align:center">Chapter 3
Resurrection</h1>

A golden eagle falls from a low-slung white cloud meandering across the Montana sky. Far below, Lucy Smith follows a deserted highway 243 rolling south. Fence posts mark distance and her nervous heartbeat marks time. The fields are bare until she passes a cemetery to her right. Isolated trees and gravestones sprout from the ground. Ghosts queuing up with songs for her, but she doesn't have the time right now. Her white-knuckles on the steering wheel turn a little whiter. She sings to The Dog. "I got ten forward gears and a Georgia Overdrive". Her dad's favourite trucking song.

Eventually, she meets Highway 2 at Saco. Again, it crosses her mind to turn left and east and maybe head home after all. She quickly discounts that idea. Her mind panicking a little as she wonders how much Seth had told his family about her. Did they even know her full name? Did they know she was from Illinois? When she had first met Seth, he had told her he was desperate to escape the gravitational pull of his family. Even he seemed scared by the rest of The Snake Family. One time only he had taken her to meet them, and the family had virtually ignored her. She hadn't been too worried by that though, having found his Dad and two brothers to be scary, bordering on evil. Inwardly Lucy had giggled at his father being called Jake Snake. She didn't giggle upon meeting him. Fortunately, he didn't seem much interested in her either. Maybe she made his skin crawl too? A strange thought, because he did seem to carry loose wrinkle-skin around his neck; she wondered if he could hood it like a King Cobra?

In contrast, Mrs Snake and his sister 'AJ' seemed so different, withdrawn, as if they didn't want to talk to her either, but for a different reason. A different breed of snake for sure. It had crossed Lucy's mind that they were as nervous as she was.

She had been so totally relieved to get out of the house. She still shivers as she remembers Jake slowly looking her up and down. She reminds herself of how she almost decided to end things with Seth at that point. She wishes she had now, but he had convinced her that he was also trying to distance himself from his family and make a life of his own.

So much was unexplained. How did Seth come to have a whole farm to himself, when he didn't seem to know anything much at all about farming? At first it was fun together, trying to work out what to do and when. Lucy had become enthusiastic, if not a little obsessed even, but most things they tried failed. Eventually, Seth would begin to go away for days telling her he had to help on Jake's farm and, when he did, he would always return with a bundle of cash. She banishes these thoughts, as best she can. For now.

From Saco she turns west on Highway 2, presently arriving in Malta and gassing the Dog, before stopping at a diner. Over a meal and coffee, she studies the old map book she had taken from the farmhouse and decides to head south on Highway 191. As she starts The Dog, she talks to it as if her only friend. "Okay Mr Dog, we're gonna be rollin' south on 191."

Leaving Malta, the country is dull and depressing, but her mood lifts as the sun breaks through and the bump and rise of America now becomes littered with fresh, spring-green trees. The Dog rolls obediently.

Lucy can't stop looking in the mirror. The Snakes slither into her mind and she dreads the sight of The Snake Family Van on the road behind her. Again, she fights hard to lock those thoughts away. She dials in the radio, and Morrissey's voice suddenly fills the Dog. *'I decree today that life is simply taking and not giving, England is mine and it owes me a living'.*

She thinks of England. What is it like over there? Maybe she'll go over there if San Francisco doesn't work out? She can't remember when she had decided to head for SF. Maybe sat in the diner in Malta? She has always had an ambition to see Santa Monica one day, and hoped music would take her there. Zuma Beach and passing Bob in the street. Who knows? Maybe there were too many people with that same idea? It crystallizes in her mind that SF may be a better option? Easier to blend? Easier to find casual work? Not so far? Yes. This was a good plan.

And so, at that moment her masterplan is formed as best she can figure. Head for San Francisco, and if that doesn't work, she'll go to England. She bangs the steering wheel and confirms it to herself. "Yes."

Clinging to positivity. A voice in her head is pessimistic and warns. "Not much of a plan, Lucy." She arrogantly overrules it. She glances in the mirror once more. No Snake Family. So far, so good. Surely, if she can get as far as San Francisco, she can lose herself? She daydreams of a flat on a hill overlooking the bay. She has had enough of wide-open spaces.

She cruises through Judith Gap now. Snow-capped

mountain ranges visible to the east and to the west. It feels like she is escaping. She takes a deep breath. She wonders about Morrissey? She knows he is from Manchester. She now also knows that if San Francisco isn't far enough, she will head for Manchester, England.

She crosses Highway 12 at Harlowtown and continues on 191. After

Melville, there are tall mountains to the west. Her first glimpse of the Rockies. She likes the thought of her insignificance. Her nightmares even begin to retreat. At Big Timber, she pulls over and gazes at the Yellowstone River. She sleeps in The Dog for a couple of hours. After Big Timber, 191 becomes an interstate and she nervously guides The Dog onto the westbound side. She gradually settles into a drive groove as the landscapes and clouds pass. Every mile eases her nerves as she heads due west now.

As she hits Bozeman, she suddenly remembers Seth telling her that Gibson Guitars are now made there, and she decides to detour into the town for coffee and food. She pulls off and finds herself on Highway 191 once again. This time it's Main Street. She finds a coffee house and parks. The coffee house is quiet, and the waiter is a young, friendly guy. She finds herself asking what Bozeman is like for work.

"It's okay, if you like waitressing."

"Well, I need some money."

She wonders why she tells that lie, as she has liberated a large bundle of notes from one of Seth's draws in the farmhouse and it sits in her rucksack. The thought makes her wonder how much cash was burned in the fire.

When the waiter returns, he asks. "Are you passing through?"

"Yes, I'm going to California."

She curses herself for the giveaway. What if The Snakes are here asking questions? What if they hire a PI? Her best logic tells her it's unlikely and her mind returns to the conversation, grateful for friendly company.

"Wish I was."

"Bozeman looks nice to me?"

"I know, but it's small."

"Don't they make Gibson Guitars here?"

He smiles. "A lot of people ask that. Four blocks down, turn right, and just before the interstate junction on the right."

"Really?"

"Yup. You into guitars?"

"I used to have a Gibson."

"Wish I could afford one. Not much hope on the tips here."

"You into music?"

"Yes, I play and try and make up songs."

"Me too. I guess that's why I'm heading to California?"

"Can I come?"

Lucy realises he's a nice kid and only joking. "Sure."

"Well, I wish. I'm getting married in August."

Lucy smiles at him. "Congratulations."

"Thanks. I do play in a band here, though."

Lucy sighs. "Hope we both make the charts at the same time."

"Sure."

Lucy smiles as she sees him realise that the conversation is at an end.

He repeats. "Four blocks down, turn right, and you pass Gibson on the way back to the Interstate."

*

As she leaves the coffee house and drives on down Main Street, she sees the sign indicating right to the Interstate. Just as she sees the interstate traffic in the distance, she sees a Gibson sign, and finds herself driving into an industrial estate. An autopilot seems to have taken over her mind as she drives into the Gibson car park. She finds herself walking into a foyer, and a receptionist looking at her suspiciously. "Can I help you?"

"Maybe? I have an old Gibson that needs repair."

The receptionist is efficient and explains that they only make them here. Lucy becomes embarrassed and close to tears, for some reason. She pauses, holding the counter for support, and unaware that a workman is now standing behind her. As Lucy turns away, he speaks. "I'll look at it for you, young lady."

The receptionist looks away, as if annoyed that her word is not taken as final.

The workman is older, but Lucy is glad for his intervention, as he seems kind-hearted. She smiles at the receptionist as she backs further away from the counter. She walks to the car with the workman. She feels herself redden with embarrassment as she opens the passenger door of The Dog, and the broken Gibson sits sadly on the passenger seat. The old man looks at her with compassion. "That's a pretty messed up guitar, young lady."

Lucy can't stop the tears arriving. The old man comforts her. "Hey, take it easy. There have been worse accidents?"

"My Dad gave it me."

"What happened to it?"

"Drunken boyfriend."

"Leave him."

"I did."

"I'd kill him for that."

"I d-o-o-o-o-n't fancy the state penitentiary one little bit ...", she giggles between tears. Inwardly, she admonishes herself for blabbing.

"Any judge would let you off." He tries to cheer her up.
The old guy looks at the guitar. He seems to begin to notice details, as his eyes focus. "A Nick Lucas. Don't see many of these. Not this old."

Lucy wipes her eyes.

He continues. "Thirteen frets to the body ... or what's left of it. Wow. These are rare indeed. Early 30s, I bet. Bob played one of these. His was repaired too you know."

Lucy smiles at him.

He asks, "Where do you live?"

"I'm just passing through on my way to California."

"If you can stick around for a week, I'll find a body for it. We do reissues of these now. New ones are fourteen frets to the body, so it will take me some time to sort things out for the pin bridge, but this neck is still okay."

He thinks out loud. Lucy gathers herself. Lucy is glad of his company, and for the first time in days she feels not quite so all alone. Her tears return. "I can pay."

"Hey, young lady, I never mentioned money. I CAN do this."

"Really?"

"Yes, really. Do you have somewhere to stay?"

She thinks and slowly shakes her head.

"No."

"Can you bake and drive a sewing machine?"

Lucy looks confused by the out-of-context question. "Errrrm yes ... well, I can try?"

He laughs. "Well, my wife is drowning in preparations for our granddaughter's wedding, and we could sure use some help on the cake and the bunting?"

Lucy looks at him and her tears return yet again.

"Do we have a deal?"

She gathers herself. "We sure do."

"G-G-G-Great." He smiles and hugs her. "I'm Howard Smith."

Lucy smiles. "I'm Lucy Smith."

"I guess that seals our bargain, Lucy Smith."

Howard drives and Lucy follows. He drives slowly and they head south into town again, and then west back on 191. Lucy thinks the 191 is her favourite highway ever. 'Back on 191' could be a hook?

Just before Four Corners, Howard turns right, and she follows him into a rural area. Eventually, he turns along an overgrown track between trees, along a miniature valley to a secluded homestead. Mrs Smith appears on the porch. She is all smiles. Howard gives her a hug. He introduces Lucy and they invite her into the house. Elizabeth Smith is a perfect match for Howard, and Lucy slowly begins to relax, especially as Elizabeth seems to love the idea of assistance with her wedding preparations.

"Little Molly is nervous about her grandma making her wedding cake, but somehow I want to do it." Elizabeth explains over dinner.

"Saves money too." Howard adds.

"That's always a good idea." Lucy agrees.

Lucy hungrily tucks into the stew pie that Elizabeth serves. She doesn't take any persuasion to have a second helping either.

Elizabeth looks at her as she eats. "How long since you had a good meal young lady?"

"A while."

The Smiths both look at her. Howard breaks the silence. "Will that truck get you to California, young lady?",

"I hope so. I'll sell it when I get there."

Howard seems to formulate a next question but stops himself asking it. He glances at Elizabeth.

Elizabeth ends the silence. "Tomorrow, we can go to town and get some bunting material? And then we can get to work?"

Howard and Elizabeth smile as they watch Lucy finish off her second helping of pie with relish.

As Lucy awakes next morning, the sunlight dances across her room. She hears the birds sing outside and goes downstairs to find Elizabeth making coffee. Beams of sunlight stream into the large rustic kitchen. The smell of cooking and freshly brewed coffee leads Lucy to think of her failures on the farm over the last two years. They sit and chat as Lucy tells Elizabeth about her family back in Illinois.

"How come you are out in Montana?" Elizabeth asks.

"I met a guy."

"It didn't work out?"

"Not quite."

"What did he do?"

"Not a lot, but he was a talented musician."

"You play music too?"

"Yes, I guess that's what took me to the Gibson factory."

"They been good to Howard. He loves his work."

"I can tell."

They pause. Lucy continues. "I'm really grateful for your help."

"Oh, grateful nothing. He's taken your guitar to work, and it will keep him out from under my feet. Meanwhile, young lady, we have work to do."

**

The days pass and Lucy and Elizabeth lose themselves in their projects. It turns out that Lucy has quite a talent for decorative icing. She loses herself in the wedding cake preparations. Elizabeth's workroom is set up for sewing and they devise a means for mass producing cloth bunting. They create yards and yards and yards of it. Days pass unnoticed. Lucy helps Howard with his vegetable garden in the evenings.

A week or so later Lucy sees Howard arrive home and take a guitar case out of his truck. She recognises a feeling of sadness as she realises it's her guitar, and it will mean that her stay is coming to an end. Nevertheless, she shakes with excitement as Howard opens the case on the kitchen table, and Lucy sees her old guitar 'reissued'. She recognises the neck and gasps at the quality of the workmanship of the new body. The sunburst is similar, but not quite as patinated as the original. It's tuned, and she sits and rings a G chord. It shimmers and sings. She looks at Howard. "I can never thank you enough."

"I enjoyed doing it, young Lucy. I have worked on these reissued and we are lucky that the neck joint was a perfect fit. All's I had to do was move the bridge position a little and add some bracing. Could be that that's changed the sound a little, but she sounds okay to me."

"She sure does Howard." Lucy kisses him on the cheek.

Howard blushes and smiles. "Don't you never hook up with any guitar smashing men in future."

"I won't be doing that Howard."

There's a silence before Howard adds. "I mean it."

Lucy nods.

It turns out that young Molly and Neil are coming over on the following Sunday, and Howard and Elizabeth insist that Lucy stays on to meet them. She helps Elizabeth finish wedding preps on the Saturday and then the meal for Sunday. Molly turns out to be the image of Elizabeth, and Neil turns out to be the waiter from the coffee shop in Bozeman. They all enjoy the sunny day with a beer and a meal. Sometimes, everything just sits right. Lucy again realises how she has wasted the last 2 years and in the back of her mind she curses The Snakes and herself. Why couldn't they have been like the Smiths? A theory that all Smiths are good people runs in her mind, until she reminds herself that she has recently killed someone. She is the black sheep of the Smiths. Guilt runs over her in waves during the dinner.

On the Monday morning, she is up early to say bye to Howard and Elizabeth, before Howard has to leave for work. She's bought him a new embroidered shirt that Elizabeth had mentioned when they were in town. For Elizabeth she's bought an antique necklace to go with the dress she plans to wear for the wedding. They seem genuinely happy to have received the gifts.

Howard brings out a box. "We have something for you too, Lucy."

He gives her the box and Howard and Elizabeth look on as she opens it to reveal a 5 shot snub nose Smith and Wesson revolver. Lucy looks up in shock.

Howard interrupts before she can speak. "We know there can be trouble in this world, young lady. So make sure you take care and protect yourself. Remember what I told you. No guitar smashing boyfriends."

Lucy promises she will ensure that situation does not arise ever again.

Elizabeth tells her to come back and see them one day.

Howard painstakingly gives her directions for a quiet, short cut back to Highway 90, before he must leave for work. He tells her she will enjoy the scenery. He seems almost emotional as he quickly leaves for work. Elizabeth explains that Howard never did like long goodbyes. She hugs Lucy now and pleads with her to be careful. Lucy promises she will and that she will write them when she is safely in San Francisco. Reluctantly opening the driver door of The Dog, she climbs in. As she drives slowly away, she sees Elizabeth waving until The Dog and its dusty trail disappear around a bend. Lucy steals herself to concentrate once again on driving. She takes the route that Howard has described, figuring that it will be quiet and give her time to get into the way of driving once more.

Once again there is vacant Highway laid out in front of her. Monumental American scenery in front and to each side. The highway relentless, as it leads to a massive rock butte.

Lucy sings to herself and the truck. "How we gonna climb outta here, Mr Dog?"

As she gets closer, the highway turns to a dirt road and begins to zig and zag and hairpin its way up the almost sheer face of the landform. She talks to the truck and taps its wheel. "C'mon, The Dog, we can do this together ..."

Chapter 4

Highway 99

The Dog conquers the climb. No engine splutters or misfires. The howl of 2nd gear echoing from rock faces on the way up. Gravity lurks at every hairpin. Lucy doesn't dare remove her eyes from the dirt road. "C'mon Dog." The Dog is THE Dog, and Lucy howls, as he crosses the final crest. She pulls over into a small viewpoint and stops and parks. "Good Dog." Her gaze tracks along the horizon as she looks out over the flatlands she has traversed. She sees a dust trail from a vehicle travelling at speed far below and looks nervously at it. She sighs with relief as the dirt road it travels meets the highway ... and it turns away from her.

She travels on and rejoins Highway 90. The spring sunlight and blue sky is interrupted by a rogue black cloud. The cloud ushers The Snakes back into her mind. She grips the steering wheel of The Dog and presses on the gas tensely. She decides to put miles between her and Montana. She tries to think of Howard and Elizabeth, but The Snakes slither and crawl. She looks over at Howard's gift sat on the passenger seat. Did he know she was in deep trouble? Were Howard and Elizabeth some kind of rogue angels? Lucy enters a drive trance. The scenery of the Rockies passes by as she stares at the road ahead, dreaming.

Missoula, where trails cross. What fate lines passed through here? Lucy Smith adds her own. Highway 90 bends and swirls between wooded mountainsides. Her map book marks 'Lookout Pass', and that is where she will exit Montana. She hopes the state police won't have a roadblock in place, on the lookout for a single female. Heavily armed and dangerous. That's her alright. She thinks about praying but discounts it as a worthless procedure under the circumstances. Circumstances and consequences are all beyond her control now. All she has is in her fate line. She has enough fuel. The Dog will make Idaho and she will stop there for some good Idaho fuel. "Good Dog. Keep rolling."

At Lookout Pass, still in Montana, there is a bridge over Highway 90, and Officer Floyd Rose parks his patrol car at his usual spot. From here, he can survey the approaching traffic. He has a nose for traffic violators. There's always some joker leaving Montana in a hurry. His eyes scan like a fisherman on the St Regis River. Are they biting today? He pours himself a coffee from his flask, as his eyes follow each approaching vehicle.

What Officer Floyd Rose does not realise is that other eyes are also scanning the area, and they have seen him. The eyes of the eagle. A magnificent specimen too. The eagle swoops to a deserted mountain top, where the human virus has constructed some kind of long machine that conveys the humans themselves to the top of the mountain. How crazy are the humans at times? Most times. The eagle land and curls its talons around a sharp edged rock, loosened by the human excavations. It lifts it with ease, its mighty wings grabbing the air. Once above the trees it extends wings and begins a glide downwards.

Officer Rose savours his coffee as Lucy and The Dog climb the Highway 90 incline towards Lookout Pass. As his eyes lock on to The Dog, he takes another sip of his coffee. His concentration increases and his eyes narrow. He has a sixth sense where traffic violations exist, and his alerts are beginning to sound. He drains his coffee cup, sets it down, and reaches for his gearshift. He doesn't get his gear selected though, because a large rock suddenly lands with devastating noise and destruction on his bonnet. "What the FUCK?"

Lucy Smith sees the eagle above the highway bridge as she approaches the top of the incline. She sees it drop something, and she sees Officer Floyd Rose exit his patrol car looking all around and skyward. She wonders what has happened as she passes under the bridge and begins the descent into Idaho. Half a mile later, Lucy Smith and The Dog cross their first state line. She pats the dashboard. "C'mon, The Dog."

High above now, the eagle wheels away. Too much human virus to the west. It turns east and searches for thermals. It has done as instructed.

The Highway zigs and zags down to Mullan. Lucy Smith zigzag wanderer. At Coeur D'Alene, she finds gas station and diner, and relaxes a while. Her worries alleviated, slightly, by being in a different state. "So far, so good." Her alleviation would be more emphatic, had she realised the extent of the drama at Lookout Pass.

After Post Falls, she soon passes the Washington State Line, and the sky and land seem to widen to her gaze. As the sign passes, she feels some of her tension lift. No longer a prisoner of narrow mountain passes. There are more people around here. She feels more anonymous. Lucy Smith likes anonymity. She finds a motel, and spends a tired evening looking at her map book. She decides to cut southwest to Portland, and then towards the coast the following day.

"At least I want to see the ocean before I die," she sings to herself. "Before my veins run dry."

She plays with chord sequences on ressurected Nick Lucas and thinks of her dad and Howard. 'Why aren't all men like that?'

Next day, she is up and away early. She crosses Snake River at Pasco, and somehow its name shocks her. She dares not look at the Snake River to her right. If she does, she sees Seth walking on the water, his skin grey and burnt, but blood gushing from his head and chest. She manages to banish him from her mind as she reaches Wallula and sees a sign denoting the waterway as the Columbia River. She breathes a long sigh of relief. Highway 30 follows the mighty river and, slowly, she grows to love its magnificence. It is truly irresistible. She convinces herself that it has subsumed Snake River and swept the ghost of Seth away. The highway guides her through the Cascade Mountains, and she reluctantly bids farewell to the river at Corbett.

It's late when she passes through Portland, and the city is asleep. She almost surrenders to panic attacks as buildings get

taller towards the city centre, but it is quiet and docile, and she gains confidence with the help of the magnetic compass on the Dog dashboard top. She keeps heading west, until she miraculously hits Highway 99 and follows a sign for south. "South is good." Gripping tight to the steering wheel, the Highway takes her over Ross Island Bridge, before swinging south again. She feels good. She decides to stick with Highway 99; she likes the sound of it. She remembers her dad telling her that 99 starts in Mexico and runs right on up to Alaska (she also remembers him saying "it's THE most dangerous Highway", although she does remember that that's mainly down to the frozen stretches up in Alaska). She figures she will stick with 99 as long as it heads southwest. Like a true friend, it doesn't deviate, and it doesn't let her down. The old school magnetic compass is her friend too, and it keeps saying southwest. Gradually, the city fades, and green fields appear. She sings "Highway 99 runs right up to the sky" to herself, liking the sound of that. Maybe a ghost has helped himself to a lift and he is bequeathing a song? She follows 99 until it becomes Highway 18, just past McMinnville. She laughs at her dad and his unreliable stories, but she knows 18 was good from her previous mapbook studies. She says thankyou in her mind to Highway 99 and sings to herself. "Your conscience can explode on Highway 99." Still singing the tune, she now follows Highway 18 until she hits Highway 101. 101 has been in her mind since she saw it following the Pacific coastline on her map book. She bangs The Dog's steering wheel as if she had discovered the New World. "Yes, yes, YES, we made it. We crossed the immensity." She sees herself as a female Jack Kerouac. She cruises into Lincoln City and, as she catches her first view of the Pacific Ocean on her right, she sees a Motel to the left. She pulls in and gets a room. Lucy is "Dog Tired" but can't resist a walk on the beach. It's been years since she was on a beach with her family on Lake Michigan. She remembers thinking. "If this is a lake, I wanna see the Pacific Ocean." She isn't disappointed as the fresh air tumbles into her lungs and the rollers boom onto the sand. Her hair blows behind her, and the wind seems to blow the shadows and

doubts from her mind. As she treks back over soft sand, she sees a sign saying, 'Oregon State: Tsunami Warning Advice: Make for High Ground'. She smiles at it as 'pretty obvious advice', but mostly because it confirms she is now two states from Montana. It eases her mind. She hopes the Motel management will wake her if there is an incoming Tsunami. If not, it will solve all her problems, for sure.

Chapter 5
English Bob

Lucy sleeps, with road dreams running in her mind. Her epic journey to the coast replays in its grandeur. The Rockies, The Cascades, The mighty Columbia River. Morrissey and the Smiths. She wakes and stares at the ceiling. She thinks of Howard and Elizabeth. She walks out to a nearby diner for breakfast and hears the ocean between lulls in the road traffic noise from Highway 101. She almost feels happy as she walks back. On the way back she suddenly gets nervous about her guitar and her 'belongings' which she has left in the room. As she rushes back in, her guitar is still there. She is massively relieved. She opens her rucksack and Howard's gift is still in the box on top. She sighs with relief.

She takes out Nick Lucas and experiments with chords, until she finds a nice groove. She absent-mindedly begins singing the Highway 99 song she had sung to herself the previous night, on the road out of Portland. She begins to jot it down in her notebook. Finishing the song takes most of the morning and she decides there is a good vibe to Lincoln City. One song already, why not hang out another night and see if any more songs arrive?

She checks with reception and decides it's safe to leave her stuff in the room, while she takes a walk around the town. She finds a tempting little café and takes lunch there, as usual selecting a secluded corner. On the table, a flyer for "English Bob's Open Mic Night" takes her attention. She asks the waitress where it is and is directed to a bar on the street corner.

"Is English Bob really English?"

"Well, he talks real funny ... but he's a nice guy. He plays the saxophone."

"Sounds different?"

"Oh yes, they are a strange set, but quite few people turn out on a Monday, and they are nice and friendly. You could go along tonight."

"Will English Bob let me sing?"

"As long as you let him play saxophone with you, he will let anyone play."

Lucy giggles to herself, as she had lost track of the days and hadn't even realised that today was Monday. "Thanks, I might."

Lucy orders. "English Fish and Chips, please". Once again she confirms to herself. "Maybe I will move to England if SF don't work out?"

That afternoon, she finishes her Highway 99 song, rehearses it, and decides she will try out the song and the 're-issued' Nick Lucas at the open mic. As she re-sings it, she remembers how easy it is to memorise her own lyrics. She has always found it that way, she can remember lyrics from lots of older songs from her childhood too. Her own songs are even easier to remember.

As she walks into the bar that evening, a gangly eccentric older guy sees her and immediately 'gangles' across towards her. "Hello, not seen you here before. Welcome."

His accent gives away his identity as English Bob.

"You must be Bob?"

"Errrrm, affirmative. How did you know?"

Lucy smiles. "Your reputation precedes you."

"Indeed, it does, young lady. I'm famous as a noise nuisance around here."

English Bob smiles and Lucy feels at ease in his company. "Can I play a song?"

"Of course, you can, young lady."

English Bob gives her a free drink token and recommends the IPA bitter. "I'll put you on when there's a few more people in."

English Bob hesitates. "Errrrm, can I play Sax with you?"

"Of course, you can, 'young man'."

English Bob beams a smile and gives her another beer token.

Lucy thinks to herself. "Now I'm a whore as well as a murderer."

The IPA beer tastes good to Lucy as she relaxes and looks around the bar. She feels comfortably anonymous. Would-be performers drift into the bar carrying their various musical instruments. English Bob makes each and every one of them welcome. She remembers her times on the open mic circuit in her hometown. She has muchos gratitude for guys like English Bob. If they didn't make the effort to host open-mic nights, she might never have got started in music. She mentally raises a glass to English Bob and his like. She remembers how she learnt more about performing than she ever did in music lessons at school. Firstly, if you want to perform an original song, you have to HAVE an original song. She learned to complete and learn a song this way. And then, when you get the stage at an open mic, it's your gig. You need to do something to get attention. She had tried it all. Singing loud, singing quiet, inserting swear words into lyrics. Sitting, standing, wearing weird outfits. She'd even put violence into lyrics, and now she knows she really is a violent person. Of course, she is. Guilty as charged. Events have proved it. The vision of dead Seth zombies back into her mind. It lets in the rest of The Snakes, and she finds herself trying to banish visions of them hurtling west in pursuit. She takes a few large swallows of her IPA and watches English Bob nervously looking at his watch. No matter how many times you have been here, the nervousness never disappears.

It had been at a night like this when she had first met Seth. His dark brown eyes had danced as he sang and played guitar. All those tricks you could try were not necessary for Seth. His voice just carried you to another world. It's just not possible to define what it is that gives certain people that ability. Can you learn it? She had been captivated by it. Too captivated, and the imprisonment had obviously not rehabilitated her, had it? She had fucking killed him. Her body shudders as she remembers the gunshots. The ringing in her ears. Her thoughts spiral downwards. If only Seth had not shown her how to use the gun? Not that using a gun would take much working out. Any 'shit-for-brains-piece-of-shit-fucked-up-arsehole' could manage that. The whole history of the world proves that theorem. A voice brings her back from the darkness. English Bob has sat down next to her. "I didn't get our name young lady?"

"It's Lu ... cinda."

Bob looks at her somewhat quizzically. "Well, it's nice to meet you, Lucinda."

Bob looks around the room and then at his list. He taps his pencil onto his pad, deep in thought, eventually reaching a decision. "There is Blue Andy, and then the Hot Banjos. I'll put you on then if that's ok?"

Lucy smiles and nods. She feels nervous tension begin to take over. It's a feeling she knows, but this time she welcomes it - it takes her mind off the darkness.

Blue Andy rattles through some blues tunes. He is an accomplished guitar player and far more dextrous than she could ever be. He plays an old telecaster, through a Fender Tweed amp. What a great authentic overdriven sound. Lucy makes a mental note to buy herself a telecaster when she eventually makes herself some money out of music. That could be a long old time for sure. She fantasises over old guitars. Telecasters look so unglamorous. A nice road worn one would be perfect. Quite a long scale? Her hands are not that big. She imagines herself in front of the mirror trying on various guitars. She laughs at her vanity. "Well, I'm a fierce cold-eyed killer. A bit of vanity is of marginal significance."

The Hot Banjos are a guitar, banjo, and fiddle trio. They play some intricate instrumental tunes, and Lucy feels good about following them. She feels even better as she takes the stage. It's been a while, and now she remembers the buzz. It refreshes her. The adrenalin pumps her. Bob plugs a lead into Nick Lucas and Lucy checks her favourite G-chord. She mentally thanks Howard, and her thoughts return momentarily to Howard and Elizabeth's house and garden. She is content in this bubble now. She has a song, and she has an audience. An autopilot takes over.

Lucy elects to stand rather than sit. She always prefers that. She also knows that girls have an advantage at open mics, as the bulk of the clientele are men who want to demonstrate their guitar skills, but she figures girls can open a song up easier. "TeeHee". She also knows that men are always attracted to girls with guitars. Sure enough, as Lucy begins the song, the audience begin to pay attention. A group of guys at the bar put their conversation on hold and she sees their faces half turn to face her, as if to give her a chance to gain their attention-favour. She relishes the challenge. The 'fuck you' facet of her character swells, under the influence of the IPA no doubt.

There's a definite 'sigh' from the audience as English Bob straps on his Saxophone and moves to the other Mic. Lucy smiles at him. She asks him not to play until part way through the song. She IS Bruce and he IS Clarence. To her, the omens are good.

<u>Highway 99</u>

There is a mountaintop in Sausalito
That I go to when I get low
I like to know how high I can go
Like a saint climbin' on his halo
I like the air that – that you get - up there
And there's an alien in my window
And I'm not scared but
It's definitely a close encounter – The Director's Cut
And I'm not scared – but they are – everywhere
Give me a sabre of light
I don't have much energy tonight

Just like the nights with no curtains
- in our railroad room
We always knew for certain
- we would fight off the gloom
We were the sentries – of the darkest night
And I thought I'd never consider this
– but here I am
Never thought I could (take this risk) steal this kiss
well maybe I can
I won't give in – without a fight
Night dreams are easy tonight
The answer to my selfish plight
And Highway 99 runs right up to the sky
But you will cry and you can die – on Highway 99
Armies of angels assemble – right under this moon
And holy empires crumble – and about time too

There's good applause for the song, and English Bob beams. Lucy carefully packs Nick Lucas away and thanks Bob.

"NO. Thank you, Lucinda. You're the first acoustic artist that gave me some space. Sadly, the saxophone is not as popular as it used to be. At least, not in my hands."

Lucy is struck by the sincerity of his words. Perhaps the base human instinct to be creative is what sets them apart from other species, and people like her and English Bob are the chosen ones? It's a good theory.

Bob gives her a third beer token. That seals his place in her mind. "Arise Sir Bob." She puts him nobly into her army of angels. If the darkness keeps encroaching, she is going to have some considerable allies as she goes down fighting. It's a sign.

She giggles. She has always loved beer philosophy, and so she walks over to the bar and cashes a token, grateful to have got through her first performance for what must be months, if not years. She sits and listens as more local artists get their weekly fix of playing live. Lucy finds things to enjoy in most of the songs and performers. She thinks to herself. "Lucinda – Tsk." She giggles as the IPA circulates in her blood.

As the evening progresses, English Bob seems to tire of blowing harder and harder to be heard above the louder bands that now play. She sees him surrender and carefully pack his trusty saxophone away. He comes over to chat. "Lucinda." is glad of the company.

"I've heard Route 66 and Highway 51 and Highway 61 Revisited ... but I've never heard Highway 99, Lucinda?"

"I only made it up yesterday, Bob."

"Wow, an original. I enjoyed it."

"Thanks, Bob, and thanks for your instrumental breaks." Bob smiles. "We should form a duo?"

"I'm only passing through, Bob."

"Where are you going?"

"San Francisco, to see if there's any opportunities for would-be singer songwriters."

"I'm sure there will be for you, young lady."

"I'm not so sure, Bob. Music is tough and I've been out of the big swim for quite a few years."

"Well, if it doesn't work out, come back and we can form that duo. Lincoln City is okay if you like a quiet life."

Bob's flirting is kind of cute, and Lucy is quite glad of his attentions. She needs friends, for sure. Friends who'll wield their weapons in her defence, magnified by love, when the forces of darkness come for her. Beacons of light in battlefields. She conjures a vision of Bob on a white horse wielding a mighty sword and slicing the heads off snakes around his horse, the arc of his blade flashing in the face of moonlight. Christ, she had better lay off the IPA shit?

"English Bob, we could even go back to England? What's it like over there?"

"Grim. I come from Manchester and, to be frank, I much prefer it over here."

"Isn't it a little quiet up here in Oregon?"

"Yes, but after 15 years in a steelworks and being made redundant, and finally having some money, I decided to get some fresh air."

Bob draws in a deep breath and affects a posh English accent. "Pin in a map brought me here young lady."

"Good for you, Bob. Must have taken some degree of courage?"

"Courage decides and fate collects. It's worked out okay so far. Would be even better if I could share my time with a good woman."

Bob smiles hopefully and Lucy smiles back. "Well, if I was 30 years older, Bob, I would jump at the chance."

Bob immediately looks hurt, and Lucy immediately feels shitty for the crass remark.

Bob even sounds hurt as he replies. "I hope you didn't think I was making advances, Lucinda. And, anyway, you are a married woman."

Lucy is shocked. "I'm fucking not." Immediately regretting her bad language.

Bob waves his 3rd finger and points at her left hand.

Lucy realises she still has the gold ring Seth gave her. *"Oh shit"*. She is unnerved by the moment. Panicking inside. She fakes laughter and explains. "My ex bought me that, and it didn't fit any other finger."

Bob sounds unconvinced. "Ah, okay, my apologies."

Lucy calms herself and leans across to hold his hand. "We finished rather suddenly, and I have been in a strange place ever since."

Bob is convinced by her tone this time.

"I forgot it was on my finger."

Lucy suddenly realises why Howard and Elizabeth had stopped their questions suddenly. *"Fuck, fuck, fuck."* Her thoughts bounce around in her reverberant skull.

Bob breaks the awkward silence. "Are you around tomorrow night, Lucinda?"

"I hadn't thought, Bob, why?"

"I'm going down to Lincoln Beach for their fortnightly open mic. We could do a couple of songs?"

Lucy feels unable to refuse, having been found guilty of insulting remarks and unkind suspicion. "I'd love to, Bob. Thanks."

Bob smiles, the spikiness banished forever.

Lucy knows she trusts him implicitly now. One the noblest knights of her realm. *"What an honour that is?"*

They arrange to meet up at Bob's house the following afternoon, and run through a couple of songs. Lucy finishes her IPA as other musos begin to 'doughnut' around her and Bob. They are keen to talk music, and The Snakes are banished to the extreme outer territories of her mind. She hears herself laughing. The witness Lucy Smith stands outside herself, watching. Almost happy for her counterpart.

"Live for the moment, Lucy Smith. You're an existentialist."

Chapter 6
This Ring Is a Bullet

Lucy Smith, Nick Lucas on her back, staggers across Lincoln City, guided by instinct and IPA, to the seclusion of the motel room. She inwardly curses and admonishes herself. "Shit shit shit. Ms Low-Profile? Lucinda? Lucinda? English Bob is probably searching for me under Most Wanted by now?"

She sits on the bed and giggles a little to herself. "Maybe best to silence English Bob? Hmmm ... Not sure you'll make a serial killer, Lucy Smith. Maybe best leave it at one?"

She looks at the ring on her finger and tries to remove it. The ring stubbornly refuses to slide over her finger joint. She tells herself not to panic, goes to the bathroom and applies some soap to the problem area. Eventually the ring passes over her knuckle joint, and she breathes a major relief sigh. She places it on the bedside cabinet and quickly falls into sleep.

Maybe it was the IPAs or her general predicament, but strange dreams rule the night. Eagles fly over the Rockies. So high they can see the western ocean in the setting sun. One dives downwards through mountain peaks and the valleys are crawling with snakes. Suddenly, the worker-snakes part for a much larger snake to pass, slithering at speed towards the ocean. Lucy wakes in a cold sweat.

She stares at the ring on the bedside cabinet. The ring's gravity pulls her mood downwards towards the neutron star of her problems. *"Who am I? Frodo F Baggins?"* She neutralises its gravity by ignoring it and going to motel reception where breakfast muffins served. She sits alone, trying not to think.

Returning to her room, a storm is blowing in. She makes a coffee. She surfs quickly through some TV news channels dreading to hear an item about a wave of murder and arson in Montana. Nationwide police hunt. 'APB' ... Ms Lucy Snake. She turns the TV off with a vengeance. She decides to re-pack her rucksack, putting the box containing Howard's revolver and the ring from her bedside table onto the king-size bed counterpane. She stares at them both in bewilderment. They remind her of recent dark history. She sees Howard's kind demeanour and Seth's leer, and wonders which of the seven days of creation gave rise to God creating this range of human behaviour. She shudders, muttering to herself. "Heavy metal, cold steel, gold and lead. Which is heaviest? Gold, I bet?" She thinks of her dad and how he used to try and teach her about the Periodic Table of the elements.

The rain now lashes against the small window, as if trying to force its way in. Lucy takes out Nick Lucas. She looks at the ring and the gun and notices that Howard has even put a box of shells in the gift box. Nick Lucas gives her a little chordy riff and she sings to herself. "This ring is a bullet...It's a hole...in my heart."

It's enough to kick start her and she takes out her notebook. Time blurs and a ghost visits. When it releases Lucy, she finds herself staring down at her notebook. The song is complete, and she sings it to herself, thinking out loud. "This is a keeper."

Although the song seems dark, the happy feeling of having created something overrides the darkness and, somehow, enables her push away even darker thoughts.

This Ring Is A Bullet

All the jewellery you bought me
Well I don't want it
I don't even want the money
If I ever pawn it

This ring is a bullet

This bracelet is a snake
A snake round my arm
Venom in my veins
You did me nothing but harm

**This ring is a bullet
It put a hole in my heart
Don't you argue don't you start
If I had a trigger – I would pull it
This ring is a bullet**

Gold is heavy metal

As she finishes the song her conscience adopts a cynical tone. "Wow, two finished songs in 2 days. I should kill people more often?"

She tries to think of good things. Her Mum, her dad, Howard and Elizabeth. English Bob. Everyone has a dark side.

"We all got a dark side

We try to hide

Ain't it just like the night?"

She stops herself from beginning yet another song.

By lunch time, the storm has passed, leaving grey-black streak-clouds across a distant sky. Lucy decides to put her song lyrics into action and to try and pawn the ring. The motel receptionist directs her to the relevant part of town. She soon finds a suitable 'Antique Mart' and gets offered 75 bucks for the ring. She knows it's probably a bad deal, but she thinks of her song lyric and takes the money. She explores her way back to the Motel, picks up Nick Lucas and then follows her directions over to Bob's house.

Bob has a small but well-maintained garden. It's enclosed and provides a pleasant surrounding as they share a beer and potatoes and stew that Bob has prepared. The meal reminds her of her dad's cooking. "Man cooking", as her mum used to call it. Lucy asks Bob about England. He tells her about the suburbs of Manchester where he grew up. He tells her of green valleys and rainy days. English football and cricket. Jazz music, then rock and roll and then rock music. He talks at length about The Chris Barber Band and how jazz and skiffle music was king when he was young.

"Oh, they brought American blues artists over to England, Lucinda. I remember the excitement of seeing Muddy Waters. I saw Howling Wolf too back in those days. The Chris Barber Band are so dear to me, Lucinda. Do you know that Chris Barber and Pat Halcox, his trumpet player, have played together touring for longer than any other partnership in music. The success those guys deserve was kind of taken away from them by the rise of the pop bands of the sixties, but they are still working and touring to this day. I love those guys. Always did, and I always will."

Lucy nods as she listens to Bob's reminiscences, his eyes vacant as his memory reels run and run. She sees bittersweet memories in his eyes and doesn't want to interrupt his flow.

"I worked in a steelworks at the time, and spent long long weeks pulling red hot steel bars across the factory floor. It was called a 'rolling mill', and they used to pour the molten steel into chrome plated cooled moulds. We had to grab the hot bars with tongs and pull them across to the cooling bath. They would bite you if they got chance. We used to call them 'The Snakes'."

Mention of 'The Snakes' set Lucy's mind into red alert, and she visibly jumps.

Bob pauses before continuing. "If someone on the floor lost control of their snake you had to be ready to dance. They were such long long weeks and I used to think music all the time. Wishing my time away for work to finish, and then waiting for Fridays when we could get out to local jazz gigs, or even take the train into Manchester itself."

Lucy idly remarks. "Sounds like happy days Bob?"

"NO. I used to hate every moment on the floor of the rolling mill Lucy. Hot, dangerous, and fumes everywhere. Prison would've been easier. I should've escaped sooner."

He stares vacantly into space. Lucy sees lines appear on his face. "I had a steady girlfriend, but she lost interest in music and wanted us to buy a bungalow in another town. I guess she wanted all the modern gadgets and stuff, but I just wanted to carry on going out at the weekends. Took me too long to learn my lessons and she was gone."

His eyes close momentarily. "Don't EVER work in a factory, Lucinda. It steals your soul, five days a week, if you're lucky. I've seen grown men cry. Music could be one way out, but that was a cruel business too. You need the talent, or you need to be lucky enough to find a band with talented people. I used to play in a trad band back around Manchester in the sixties," a sadness in his voice, "but the times were changing I was a fossil even then, Lucinda."

Lucy feels confident enough with Bob now and tells him, "I'm really Lucy. Not sure why I said my name was Lucinda."

Bob snaps out of his memory-dreams and looks thoughtful for a moment. "Not as if I go through the wanted posters young lady."

She feigns a laugh, but inwardly wonders if The Snake Family will actually engage the law? She hopes not, pinning the hope on her memories of Seth telling her of their hatred of law enforcement in general.

She changes the subject back to music. "Is that why you learned the saxophone, Bob?"

"Kind of. My love of music goes back to my dad and his incessant playing of what he used to call 'LP Records'." His old record player was his pride and joy. He had an LP for all the musicals."

"OMG, my dad used to play those old records too, Bob. He always told me that his uncle would play them all the time when he was a boy."

Bob smiles at his memories. "I used to love Carousel."

He breaks into song. *"If I loved you – words wouldn't come in an easy way….."*

When he stops, Lucy sings. *"When I marry Mr Snow…"*

Bob beams, surprised that someone so much younger knows the song. "You can't not mention 'When you walk through a storm ...' Can you?"

Lucy shakes her head in unequivocal agreement. "What a song."

"The King and I?" - *"Getting to know you."*

"My Fair Lady?" - "*I have often walked - down that street before.*"

"Brigadoon?".

"Is Scotland really a magical place, Bob?"

"No, it's a shithole, Lucy. Full of Jocks"

"Jocks?" She looks confused.

"It's what we call people from Scotland."

"Like we call you Limeys?"

"Yeh, similar, I guess. I've not been called that for a while though, Lucy."

"You don't like Jocks?"

"Well ... Great Britain is full of rivalries ... these things can easily get out of hand ... I think it's more that they don't like the English? People sometimes have long memories – too long."

"I like Limeys, Bob. You and Morrissey for starters."

Bob smiles again as Lucy continues. "I once made up a song about my dad and his love of musicals."

"Let's do that one at the open mic tonight then?"

Lucy smiles and nods. She thinks of her dad, dancing around their front room as he played old musical soundtrack albums on his ancient record player.

They finish their meal, and then get around rehearsing the song. The process clears Lucy's mind. Her problems banished to mental wastelands and she feels relaxed. When it is time to go, Bob gets his car from his double garage. Lucy waits on the drive as Bob reverses out in, of all possible vehicles, a legendary Ford Mustang.

"Wow, Bob, nice wheels"

"Motor vehicles and music are my weaknesses, Lucy."

"Strong weaknesses, Bob."

Nick Lucas and Bob's Saxophone are on the rear seat, and Lucy feels the thrust from the passenger seat into her back as English Bob gives a 'YeeHaaaaa' as he 'fast forwards' into the sea air.

Bob tells Lucy of his liking for American highways and vehicles. "I have a Harley Davidson Fat Boy too that I like to use in summer. You only live once, Lucy, and I started late."

The drive down the coast is relaxing for Lucy as Bob enthuses about his Mustang and his Harley and his old Yamaha YTS23 Tenor Saxophone. Lucy enjoys his enthusiasm. As she tells him about her plans for San Francisco, Bob tells her how he bought his Harley from a garage down there. She tells him that she will be selling The Dog when she gets there and asks if he has any advice.

"Oh man, Lucy, you should go and see Marv at Marv's Motors. He's part hippie, part Hell's Angel, part Muso and, although he's been around the block a bit, he will give you a fair deal ... if he likes you."

"Thanks Bob, don't let me leave without getting his details offof you. Is he trustworthy?"

Bob pauses in thought, eventually concluding. "I would say so."

"Good, because The Dog is old, and I'd prefer it if the last owner couldn't ever trace it."

Bob looks confused. "'The Dog'?"

Lucy laughs. "It's what I call my old Dodge truck. It lost a 'd' and 'e'."

Bob nods, gives Lucy a suspicious look, and then a knowing smile. "Marv is your man, Lucy. He cut me good deals with both my vehicles."

Bob takes an inland detour from Highway 101 into the hills and enjoys showing off his mustang. There's a silence as Lucy takes in the coastal scenery, passing through a nature reserve.

"Nice car, English Bob."

"Marv's Motors - Keeps America Rolling."

Lucy smiles at his enthusiasm. "I'll sure go and see Marv when I get to SF, Bob. Thanks."

Bob promises to give Marv a ring and tell him to expect her.

The open mic venue is a scenically blessed bar with picture windows looking from a cliff edge over a Pacific beach, the ocean itself shimmering in the middle distance. Lucy enjoys meeting Bob's eccentric friends; Boris the Cranium and Wangly Dangly. They all have drinks and are deep in conversation about crazy physics. Boris seems to lead the discussion and he is currently working on a theory that is supposed to unify the forces of gravity and electromagnetism. From what she can gather, Boris has developed an idea that all atoms get distorted a little, to turn them to really really small magnets. If you put two bodies near to each other, the billions of little magnets switch so that it creates a really really weak force, which is gravity. Boris smiles at Lucy as he concludes one aspect of his theory. "Bob's your uncle Lucy ... well, in your case your friend from Lincoln City ... old enough to be your uncle though".

"Not so weak if you jump off the Empire State, Boris?" Lucy gives him her glare.

Boris doesn't seem to notice. "Ah, but. Everything is relative you know."

Boris rattles on about relativity, making Lucy think of her dad. It mostly washes over her head, but she grows to love their company and their enthusiasm. She asks Boris if he could make her a time machine.

"You've got your whole life ahead of you, young lady. No need to turn back time and you certainly don't want to rush forward."

Lucy gets a little spiky about being called Young Lady. "You're the millionth person to call me 'Young Lady', Boris The Cranium."

English Bob quickly diffuses the spikiness but looks concernedly at Lucy.

Lucy senses his concern, smiles and offers a hint of explanation. "We all make mistakes that, maybe, in retrospect it would be good to go back and correct."

Boris The Cranium observes. "Hmmmm, that would contravene the laws of physics as presently understood. But, for you Young ... (he stops himself) Lucy, I shall see if I can't extend my latest theories"

Lucy laughs and thanks him. She doesn't notice English Bob looking at her thoughtfully.

Boris is talking to himself now. "Hmmmmm, what if it turns out that Einstein was wrong and the speed of light can be exceeded? Just because his relativistic formulations reduce to Newton at low speeds, just how much do we actually use Einstein in this context? We know he was wrong with his 'Cosmological Constant', so what if there was another error? After all, it's a big assumption to pull from thin air? Like Planck, where the fuck did he get that from? Just a mathematical artifice to help the jigsaw fit, Miss Lucy. That's the thing you see. The only truth we have is math. That's what they should tell kids at school, not make them do exercises. Math is our window into the world and the universe outside. Or maybe many universes? Never mind the religious texts. Prophets only tell you lies." Boris rants now.

Wangly gets some more beers in and places an IPA in front of Boris, as he is lost in thought now. They all smile.

The compere calls English Bob and Lucy to the stage. This audience seems disinterested. It's a good feeling for Lucy because it somehow fortifies her confidence once again. The "I'll show these fuckers." mentality takes hold. She looks across at English Bob and nods. They perform Lucy's Highway 99 song and follow it with their rehearsed song about the old musicals.

Lucy introduces it. "This song is dedicated to Billy Bigelow, Anna and The King and – most of all – to the writers of the true gospels – Rodgers and Hammerstein. It's called 'Wake Me Up When'."

Wake Me Up When

I was dreaming of those old records that you used to play
Like Carousel and Brigadoon and Russ Conway
Dansette discs rolling round at 33 and a third
The worst record player - but the best music I ever heard

I was a kid in bed with an empty head and I loved all those sounds
Pianos ringing and the angels singing all around

Lucy enjoys putting the song over and playing a little more energetically. She stifles a giggle, as English Bob drops in some cool moves around the stage behind her. He obviously likes the song and Lucy likes his saxophone noodling. Nick Lucas seems to coax an edgy tone from English Bob's trusty old Yamaha Tenor.

As he blows, English Bob thinks how his old Yamaha Tenor has been with him all these years. He'd sell his Mustang and his Fat Boy before he'd ever sell his YTS32.

The song even goes reasonably well with the audience. New songs are always a difficult sell but, nevertheless, the newly formed duo get sporadic applause. EB and Lucy take a bow, and return to their table.

Lucy chats to Bob afterwards, as Boris and Wangly have now moved on to discussing the finer details of Heaviside's contributions to electromagnetic theories. It all passes way over Lucy's head.

"I do realise audiences don't normally listen to me, Lucy. I have really enjoyed playing these songs with you."

"Thanks, Bob – it's mutual. I always thought sax goes well with acoustic songs."

"You're not wrong Lucy. I used to listen to a singer-songwriter called Mike Cooper way back in 60s and 70s and he worked with a tenorman called Geoff Hawkins. That's kinda when I fell in love with raw saxophone." Lucy nods along to 'English Bob Radio' as it delves into its archives, until Bob pauses, looking at her with concern. "Lucy, I'm a worrier, and I suspect you really do have things in life you'd like to go back, and correct?"

She doesn't reply, and Bob carries on. "I really wouldn't bank on Boris completing his time machine." Lucy smiles, and Bob continues. "But you can depend on me."

"I know I can, Bob. Really. I'm so glad I stopped off in Lincoln City. It's a highlight."

After all goodbyes, hugs and well-meant but unconvincing choruses of "see you again", they drive back north in a happy silence. Lucy is a little nervous that English Bob has had a few  drinks, but she dispels the thoughts on the grounds that she has broken so many laws recently, she can't criticise anyone else. English Bob would probably get a commendation for killing Lucy, even a reward. The Manchester Bounty Hunter. He doesn't bother bringing them in alive, it's too much trouble. As it turns out though, the roads are quiet, with no FBI roadblocks and EB seems in control. Eventually, he pulls the Mustang into the Lincoln City Motel car park as Lucy tells him she is going to head south to San Francisco tomorrow morning. Bob gives her detailed directions of how to get to Marv's Motors and tells her he will phone ahead to make sure they will expect her. He makes sure Lucy has his number too. Lucy kisses him on the cheek, climbs out of the passenger seat, and carefully retrieves Nick Lucas from the rear.

As Bob starts the Mustang, he leans his head out of the driver window. **"Marv's Motors – Keeps America Rolling."**

Lucy responds. **"English Bob – Keeps America Rocking."**

Chapter 7
Marv's Motors

Lucy is up early next morning, nervous about the forthcoming drive to San Francisco. She has decided to get there and lose herself in the city, as soon as possible. Nice as the Oregon coast is, she has spent long enough there and needs to say goodbye to The Dog. She heads south on Highway 101. English Bob's instructions for finding Marv's Motors sound easy enough, but it is a long time since she has driven in a city. Portland in the dead of night was scary enough.

"Follow Highway 101. South then straight over The Golden Gate. Then follow 101 through the city. Richardson Avenue, Van Ness Avenue. After crossing Market Street take the elevated 101 for 3 or 4 miles and come off east on Cesar Chavez. Under the Interstate and 5 blocks on the left. Left into Illinois Street and find Marv's Motors on the left."

She reads English Bob's directions to herself, until she has them memorised like a song lyric. Even so, she keeps the printed instructions on the seat next to her as she gets close to San Francisco. Reaching The Golden Gate Bridge, she pulls off into the visitor area to gather herself. It's a bright day and she

sees the city laid out before her to the left of the bridge. White clouds drift in across the bridge, as container ships and sight-seeing tourist boats pass under. The sun hovers over the city. She sees Alcatraz Island in the middle of the bay, and a shiver of guilt runs through her. She blocks the prison island from her mind. She sees the traffic flowing over the bridge like corpuscular blood. The lifeblood of the city. *"Please, no police. I've gotten this far."* She readies herself, turns the ignition key and The Dog starts obediently. Together they join the other traffic but somehow this monumental structure makes Lucy feel special. She wonders if all the people in all the other cars crossing the bridge feel as special as she does? The first time is always special. She wonders if The Dog feels special? *"Don't be dumb Lucy. He's a man-made thing – but he is special anyway."*

To her surprise, it all goes as planned. Crosstown Traffic. She remembers the Jimi Hendrix track. On the elevated 101 she even begins to feel confident about her driving and she blows English Bob a kiss out of her open driver's window. She decides 101 is definitely her favourite highway and she is sad to leave it as she guides The Dog onto the down-ramp. *"East on Cesar Chavez"*. She sings English Bob's direction lyrics. No direction home.

It's a slightly menacing area as she finds Illinois Street and turns left into it. She slowly cruises up the street until she sees the "Marv's Motors" sign. A few Harleys are parked outside, and she sits and observes for a while, thinking things through. She reminds herself that she does have to say goodbye to The Dog, or it might be a trail leading any pursuers to her. Eventually, she takes a deep breath for fortitude and drives slowly into the Marv's Motors yard. She picks up her trusty rucksack and Nick Lucas and steps out of The Dog. A group of menacing looking guys are stood looking at a Harley. They see her and all stare in silence. Lucy walks slowly up to them, smiling. *"I must be getting quite confident in my old age."*

The guys are textbook angels. Biker boots, Levis Originals. Some in worn leather jackets, oil stained and ripped T-shirts. Some are older, some younger. One of the older ones deems himself the spokesperson and walks across towards her. Lucy rethinks her new-found confidence under the countenance of

this guy. His movement is economical, graceful and silent. He doesn't smile but his eyes sparkle. She should be nervous but, for the moment, she isn't. "Hello, hello, young lady. What brings you to M&M?"

The nearby Angels stare, stare hard, as she pauses before replying. Strangely, it's the "young lady" that gets to her, rather than the threatening demeanour of the guys hanging around. *If one more person calls me 'young lady', I'll get my gun out and start shooting."*

She keeps her feist under control. "Is Marv around?"

"Who wants to know?"

"I'm Lucy. I think he's expecting me?"

"We don't generally do appointments around here, but I'll take you to him."

As they cross the yard, the Angel speaks. "I'm Don Estrada. Marv mentioned you might be arriving. You're a friend of English Bob?"

"I am indeed."

"This ain't no business, like Ford Motors." He then effects a strange version of an English accent. "But we do like English Bob. Air-hair-lair, how are you?"

Lucy finds herself laughing. Don Estrada is a strange manifestation; initially, his impression is that of a sleaze-time-drunk-stoner-lifer, but as they walk Lucy suddenly becomes even more aware of his gravity and power. Aren't gravity and power the same? Well, similar, she would confirm their physical equivalence, or otherwise, with her dad, or Boris The Cranium. Nevertheless, she is drawn to Don Estrada and her mind runs a debate. He has power but grace, threat but warmth, chaos but calm. Gravity for sure, but is it not repulsive as well as attractive? Fuck, she has discovered a gravitational magnet. Where the fuck are her dad and Boris when she needs them? Hasn't she had enough of boneheads like Don Estrada for a lifetime? As if to confirm that proposition, she shudders as Jake Snake slithers and bludgeons into her consciousness. She should conclude this business and slide on out of Marv's Fuckin' Motors as soon as good grace allows. However, she still can't resist a sideways glance at Don. Their eyes meet. Don's eyes still sparkle and Lucy finds herself smiling in return. What is going on here? Don is a conundrum for sure.

They pass into a workshop area. An Angel looks up from a heavy, slow-moving mechanical hacksaw machine. As Lucy looks down at the machine, she notices a shotgun is clamped into it. The barrel being shortened.

The angel looks at Don. "This motherfucker is fuckin' takin' for fuckin' ever, Don."

"Al, that language might be offensive to our customer."

Don Estrada seems to command some authority, and the Angel takes a pace backwards and stares at Lucy in bewildered silence.

Don looks at the work in progress. "That's ordnance grade steel, Al. You can't rush it."

Al nods and moves back to observing the machine aggressively.

As they walk on Don mutters, "Kids."

Don opens a half-glazed door and leads the way into some kind of office. He bangs on a door to an adjoining room and shouts, "Marv. Customer."

There is a sound of someone moving around on the other side of the door. Lucy's imagination presents various possible manifestations of Marv, for her consideration. They are mostly outdated, as the door opens, and Marv appears. If it was not for Don Estrada's considerable presence, Marv would dominate most rooms. He's older, but Lucy wouldn't bet on accurately forecasting his age. He wears leather jeans (Lucy wonders if he slept in them) and a sleeveless denim shirt, not yet buttoned up.

Lucy sees various chains and tattoos. Marv looks old(er), but tough as the quality leather of his trousers. He walks slowly over to a coffee machine and asks, "Anybody want coffee?"

Lucy gratefully accepts. She realises she is still tense from the drive across San Francisco. She mentally thanks English Bob once again for getting her this far.

Marv puts her coffee unceremoniously on the table, next to where she sits. Marv sits opposite and pulls on his biker boots. "Lucy, is it? English Bob says I can trust you."

"He says I can trust you too." Lucy smiles.

"That's the trust department sorted then."

Lucy laughs, and Marv continues. "Long time since English Bob was down here. He okay?"

"He seems fine, yeh."

"Bob has been a good customer and helped us with a few metal working problems. He's a good guy. A dumb limey, but a good guy."

"He helped me too."

"He says you need to lose your Dodge truck?"

"I do. Yes"

"Is it yours?"

"Kind of ... but I need rid now."

"No paperwork?"

"No."

"Where have you come from?"

"Montana."

"Well, it's a miracle you got here without heat on you."

"I look honest, but I'm a fierce killer, with eyes like fire."

Marv laughs, but then stops and stares at Lucy for a few seconds, as if he suddenly realises there may be some depth in her statement.

He continues. "I don't need to know your 'business', Miss Lucy. I'll give you a fair price for the truck."

Lucy is hesitant. "It needs its identity changing, because people may be looking for it?"

"We have the technology."

"I'm serious, Mr Marv. There could be nasty people looking for it."

"Do we look like we scare easy?"

"Well, no," she laughs, "but, I wouldn't want anyone getting hurt."

"Okay, Lucy, we'll take that into account in the price, and thanks for the warning."

Marv stands and shakes her hand. "What brings you to SF anyway?"

"I need a new life and I'm into music."

"There's a lot of people in that queue, Missy. It's a tough business, especially in this city."

"I know. I've been through it all elsewhere. One dead end after another."

"Most of the 'dead ends' seem to run the business, but, still, not many better buzzes than fronting a band." He pauses, as if reviewing his memories. "But hard to make a decent living?"

"I'm happy to lay low for a while, until I find my way about."

Marv looks at her. "You got somewhere to stay?"

"I figured I'd find a hotel, until I get to know my way around."

Marv looks over at Don. "Is Ronee still in that big house in Haight?"

"She sure is, Marv."

"She still with that bass-man that plays in Mike Remo's band?"

"Not sure, Marv. I had to give him a talking to after he upset her. I let him live, though."

Marv laughs. "Musicians, eh?"

Don nods, frowning.

Marv asks Lucy for the keys to The Dog, so he can look it over. As he exits, Don Estrada seems to look Lucy up and down. Lucy feels his piercing eyes scanning her.

Eventually, he speaks. "Ronee has a big house across town and a lot of her friends are musos. I know because we've done work on one their band vans. She's a real nice girl and her ex-boyfriend plays the bass."

Lucy senses a serious tone in Don as he continues. "He's harmless enough. For a musician anyway." Don seems to be half talking to himself now. "They call him 'Thunderman'. He's a good player, but never makes much money. Music is a hard business. Late hours, tours, distractions."

Lucy wonders who Ronee is, and why Don is thinking out loud about her. As Marv returns, he and Don walk over to the corner of the office and look out into the yard, where The Dog is parked. Lucy can't hear their discussions. Eventually, Marv walks over to a safe and opens it.

"$1400 cash, Lucy? The truck, this deal, and this conversation never happened?"

Lucy stands and they shake hands.

She repeats her warning. "Mr Marv, the people who may be looking for the truck are pretty evil people."

Marv smiles. "You know where you stand with evil people, Miss Lucy. It's the in-betweeners that can be scary."

Lucy can't help herself. "I guess we're all in-betweeners?"

Marv elongates the moment as his eyes scan Lucy as she is gripped by his handshake.. "May ... be Missy. Maybe."

As part of the deal, Don offers to drive Lucy over to Haight Ashbury, and introduce her to Ronee, who might have a room to let in her house. Lucy clears all her belongings from The Dog and says a fond farewell and thank you, patting him on the bonnet.

On the drive over town, Don explains how Marv used to front a band in 'bygone years' but found he could make more money looking after people's transportation needs. He had a speciality in touring buses for the many bands out of Haight around that time. He tells her that he is part of 'what's left of part of The Oakland Chapter', and how Marv's place is their base this side of the Bay. He tells her about Ronee and her ex, seeming to forget his previous ramblings,

"A bass playing dude. Goes under the name of Thunderman. I think he's a good guy. He better be, because anyone hurting Ronee is liable to disappear."

Lucy doesn't doubt the validity of this statement from the tone in his voice. She senses Don is fond of Ronee.

Don keeps talking. "He plays in some band called 'The Lowdown Dirtkickers'. Marv sold them a van a few years back. Marv and their front man, Mike Remo, go way back."

Lucy makes mental notes as best she can of all the names and connections. She is already excited by San Francisco and this introduction to the city. This is a bonus. She wonders how much English Bob has told them about her. She giggles to herself thinking. "Ronee, whoever she is, has a Guardian Angel."

"My advice to you, young lady, don't get involved with no musicians." Don pauses and adds, "But then, I would never take my advice either."

They smile and laugh.

As they arrive at a house in a nice quiet residential street in Haight, Don gets out and knocks the door. A woman of similar age to Lucy answers and gives him a hug. It seems incongruous to Lucy that a young and smart dressed girl is hugging a full-on 'angel'.

Lucy gets introduced, and immediately gets along with Ronee. It turns out that the previous girl renting a room in the house had skipped and not paid the last 3 months rent. Lucy is more than glad to take the spare room in the house at a very reasonable rent. The house is in need of considerable repair, but Lucy immediately begins to feel at home. She moves her belongings into her room (which doesn't take long), and then gets busy helping Ronee assemble a flat-pack table for the kitchen. Lucy enjoys the practical task and slows down Ronee's impetuous nature. They both stand back and admire the results when the table is complete. Lucy offers to walk around to the Chinese store around the corner and cook an inaugural meal for the table. She loses herself in thoughts of what to prepare.

As she lies in bed that night, Lucy has a glimpse of some kind of contentment; so much so, that she becomes nervous of it all being fucked up by unresolved circumstance. She thanks her lucky stars for the breaks she's had. She now realises how easy it would have been for her to be stopped by Highway Patrol, and then she'd have been dead in the water. She trembles at the thought, realising she has been running on adrenalin and not thinking straight for days, or was it weeks? The Snakes slither into her mind and she shivers. She banishes them and decides she has a chance here, and that she will lay low and just survive, for as long as it takes. She has no idea how long that will be? She lies in bed and listens to the distant sounds of the city.

Ronee has just landed a new job as a legal clerk and is off to work early the next day. True to her word, though, she has left a list of bars and cafes that hire and pay fairly. Lucy walks into Haight and soon finds herself in casual work: no records and cash in hand.

Lucy doesn't see too much of Ronee, as she falls into a routine of bar work, but whenever they are in the house together, she and Ronee get along well. One Tuesday evening though, they find themselves at the house together and Ronee is insistent that they go down to Deirdre's Bar for a beer. Lucy is not keen to spend her first free evening from bar work in yet another bar but her first taste of IPA in a while soon persuades her it was the right decision. Deirdre herself seems to know Ronee and asks after Don. Ronee gets the beers and Lucy selects a quiet corner table.

Ronee is inquisitive. "How the hell did you get to know of Don and Marv?"

"A friend in Oregon recommended them."

Ronee laughs. "Recommended The Gruesome Twosome?"

"Well, I was told Marv would take a truck off my hands for cash."

"Marv would take your hand off for cash."

"They seem okay to me?"

"Well, as itinerants go, they are okay ... I suppose."

"You don't sound convinced?"

"My Mum once attacked Don with an axe."

"Woh?"

Ronee stares into space. "That was just before she moved to LA with her boyfriend though."

"How come you didn't go?"

"I didn't like her boyfriend."

"How come she didn't end up in jail?"

"Don wouldn't press charges. He always says it would be embarrassing for an angel to resort to the law. Beneath him."

"He seems fond of you?"

Ronee pauses before replying. "Well, he rents me the house."

Lucy decides not to pry and instead, recounts a heavily censored version of how she travelled down in The Dog from Montana.

"What did you do in Montana?"

"I lived with my boyfriend."

"You split?"

"We did, yes. He turned into a complete shitwit."

"What did he do?"

"He was a musician. That's how we met."

"I used to go with a bass player. He is okay really but spends a long time going nowhere. He's happy, as long as he has a drink in his hand and somewhere to sleep."

Lucy is reminded of English Bob's story of work in a steel plant, and how it was really a jail sentence. "Lot to be said for that, Ronee. No-one has control over you. If you're gonna work, may as well work for yourself and do something you enjoy."

"I guess."

Ronee returns from the bar with two more beers. "So, you left him and used his truck as a getaway vehicle?"

Lucy smiles. "I guess." She pauses before continuing. "I'd decided to leave anyways, and I think he'd realised."

Ronee notices as Lucy nervously clasps her glass, knuckles white.

The beer fuels Lucy's mouth. "His family were scary. Really scary. I mean fucking scary. I figured Seth was even scared of them too. Well, he told me that when we first met. Seth was a crazy good musician, and his father ran a band. A good band too if you like real lowdown threatening blues. I went to a couple of gigs, soon after Seth and I ended up in Montana. We'd tried to build a following as a duo in Chicago, but it didn't work out. Out of the blue, Seth told me he owned a farm ... or at least his father had put one in his name."

Lucy rambles. "Oh shit, their gigs were scary. Lowlifes know how to party. I'm pretty sure his father dealt drugs. Seth did introduce me one time, but his father and brothers just ignored me. I don't even know if Seth told them much about me. Keerrrrrissst, Ronee, his dad was so so scary. His brothers too."

She takes a mouthful of her beer and giggles. "Their surname was Snake, and the band was called The Snake Brothers, or sometimes Snakemen."

Lucy adopts a hiss as she speaks of them.

Ronee listens intently. Lucy sees she has Ronee spellbound. "Funny thing is they actually look like snakes."

Ronee splutters her beer, laughing. "Fuck off. You were with a snake? Did he have a snake in his trousers?"

Lucy laughs too. "It's true ... but Seth was a good-looking snake."

"Was?" Ronee asks, feigning seriousness.

Lucy realises her slip and quickly adds. "Well ... I mean he was a lot better looking before he started back in the family band full time. They drank a lot. He used to come back from gigs in vicious moods and always looked older somehow."

Ronee looks puzzled, possibly not quite believing the story, as Lucy carries on providing information, more to cover her conversation tracks than anything else. "There is a sister too, and she plays bass in the band, but she doesn't look like the men. She is slinky, but in a different kind of way. I could never get Seth to talk about her really."

Ronee interrupts. "Won't he be after you to get his truck back?"

"Noooooo ... I don't think he'll be too bothered."

"LuLu, you are so naïve. They always want their trucks back."

Lucy suddenly looks worried, and Ronee notices. A tear descends from her left eye. Ronee reaches over the table and puts her hand on Lucy's.

Lucy looks at Ronee, tearful now. "They might come for me."

Ronee tries to backtrack. "Hey, don't worry, it's only a truck and it would be a long way to come. Would they know where to find you anyway?"

Lucy trembles. "No ... but we were married."

"She-ite Lucy – you never told me that. You were married? Did you D-I-V-O-R-C-E?"

"No."

"So, you are still married?"

"No...well...yes." Lucy is panicking.

Ronee calms her down slowly. Eventually, Lucy explains how they tried to get married in Vegas once, but Seth had no official papers, so they couldn't, but a couple of weeks later he said he had arranged it all in Reno. It was very rushed, but Seth had been keen to do it that way. She never wanted to cause her family the expense of a wedding or anything, and it seemed romantic at the time. She looks so lost as Ronee listens. Ronee holds her hands tight.

"Look, LuLu, if you were married, then sooner or later you will need to get it annulled. That's not like divorce, because it means you got married under false circumstances. Like maybe he never told you he had a criminal record? It could even be that you weren't ever properly married? Sounds to me like that could be the case."

Lucy frantically pulls her thoughts together. "I can't ever let them know where I am."

Ronee calms her down slowly. "Hey, leave it with me LuLu. Let me check if you are actually married? If not, you are in the clear. If you are, then we'll have to work out an annulment somehow. There will be a way."

Lucy trembles as she repeats, "They must never know where I am."

Ronee realises how desperate Lucy is and comforts her. "Leave it with me, LuLu. First, we box off the problem, and then we find the best way to solve it."

Lucy nods in agreement, her mind spiralling downwards.

**

A couple of weeks pass slowly for Lucy. She changes her hair colour and style. Ronee compliments her but understands the real reason. One evening, before leaving for the work, Lucy prepares a meal for her and Ronee.

Ronee sets her briefcase down, sits at the table, and asks, "Hey, LuLu, your ex was called Seth Snake ... right?"

Lucy looks up in concern. "Yes."

"And you said you were married in Reno?"

"Yes."

"So, I checked the marriage registers in Nevada and Montana."

"Yes?"

"And there is no mention of any Seth Snake or Lucy Snake, nee Smith."

"So, that means I was never married?"

"That's right, The Mascara Snake."

Lucy laughs at the Captain Beefheart reference, but inwardly a load lifts from her mind.

Ronee continues. "I also checked records in Montana, and there are no records of any Seth Snake. So, even if you had been officially married, it would be a void marriage. That would be an easy process."

"You're the top lawyer in the whole universe, Ronee."

Ronee smiles and stands with hands on hips. "I rest my case," and then adds for good measure, "It would be my contention that the lowdown sonofabitch piece of shit just wanted you to think you were married."

Lucy nods and lets out a long sigh. "Fuuuuuuurrrrrrrrckkkkkk. How dumb am I?"

"So, Miss LuLu Smith, I think it's about time you got yourself out and about a bit more and got back into the singing. I've heard you singing at home and it's good."

"Maybe I should."

"No maybe about it. I'll get in touch with my old boyfriend, Thunderman. He can give us the buzz on the best places to play."

Lucy thinks carefully. Although she has studiously kept a low presence for what must be 6 months now, she has begun to get used to life in SF and decides that she does need to circulate a little more. "Thanks, Ronee, I'd appreciate that. I appreciate it all. I owe you big time."

Lucy is in sleepless-night-city. Part of her feels happier, much happier. Part of her feels bad for not having told Ronee the full story, but then, how could she? Ronee is right, she IS/WAS totally naïve, and she should've realised the marriage was fake. Seth was a FakeSnake. They are all FakeSnakes. She wonders how that changes things. She thinks back. Jake Snake never spoke to her, and neither did the rest of the family. They never visited the farm for the two years she was there with Seth. She should've just left, instead of waiting to explain it was over. How naïve was she? On a scale of naivety from 1 to 10 she was FUCKING naïve. She figures that, with any luck, The Snakes won't know anything about her, apart from what Seth told them. What could he tell them? She told him she came from a town overlooking Lake Michigan. She told him her dad had a qualification in Physics. He knew her surname, Smith. So, what the fuck? Wasn't it the most common name in the world? Her biggest fear was a photograph. If the Snakes involved the police, they could put out the proverbial 'APB'. She hoped that The Snakes were as bad as she suspected, and they would never go to 'the law', but, on the other hand, they would be looking for her. She reasoned that Mrs Snake would be distraught. Course she would, she'd lost a son. Shot twice and burnt to a crisp. Oh fuck. How bad was she? As she finally drifted off into a snake infested swamp-sleep, surrounded by rank mist and the sound of gators sliding from muddy riverbanks into dirty water, her last logical thought was that, with any luck, the state police or FBI wouldn't be involved. The disappearance of Seth Snake would not be reported. The Snakes would be looking as far as they could cast their web (wasn't that spiders?) but they wouldn't ever find her. Maybe she'd ask Ronee about the mechanics of changing your name? What about The Dog, though? Could they ever trace it? She's taken every precaution. She figured Marv to unload it anonymously. She's been running, running, running; running on adrenalin, and taking respite in short bursts wherever and whenever. She had nightmare thoughts of The Snakes slithering out of Montana, interrogating Howard and Elizabeth, slithering through Seattle shit filled sewers and, under dead of night, torturing English Bob, before sliding noiselessly into the Bay at Sausalito heading for San Francisco. She wakes in a cold cold cold sweat.

It was good news, followed by a bad night. She opens the curtains to a nondescript grey day, and for some reason she feels better. Much better. Perhaps she has a chance after all? For the first time in weeks, she takes Nick Lucas from his case and wonders where her song notebook is. She has to delve deep into her rucksack for it, where it is still packed under the box containing Howard's gun. She is still shocked by the weight of the package. She puts the package on the bed next to her and, as she does so, she thinks of Howard and Elizabeth. Then, she looks at her song notebook, and the idea to make up a song about the gun appears. She opens the package and stares at the weapon. She shivers. She wonders if she could use it on Jake Snake if he walked in now. She's done it before, she could do it again. She looks at Nick Lucas and thinks, "The things I do for you." She shivers and wishes Ronee was home. The gun becomes hers and Nick Lucas' friend, and as she begins to string chords together and scribble in the book a ghost enters the room. A lot of ghosts carry gun stories.

She has no idea how much time has passed, but now she stares down at a set of words with very few corrections. She plays it through a few times.

Waiting

There'll be a time when you need me
When burglars invade
There'll be a time you want me
When you're consumed with rage
And you'll need more of me
When you got a war to wage
You all love my simplicity
The whole world is my stage

Until then I'm just waiting
That's what I do
It's not frustrating
Patience is my virtue
You know where I am
You know what I do
No evil in me – is it with you
My aim is true
My aim is up to you

You've loved me for centuries
No need to be scared
I'm company for sentries
Stop who goes there?
You need more than muscle
When your arms are bare
With me in your pocket
You are safe everywhere

Give me ammunition
It's your decision
I offer protection
From all insurrection
Life is safer - for both of us
Pull the trigger feel the buzz
My aim is true
My aim is up to you

If you desire – I can be vicious

I never make mistakes
And I do as I'm told
If you don't like someone
I can stop them getting old

Weeks pass to find Ronee and Lucy walking down Columbus Avenue and entering an open mic bar. Ronee introduces "Thunderman" to Lucy. Thunderman is friendly, energetic, enthusiastic, childish, jovial but immediately concerned with rekindling things with Ronee. Guys on their 'best behaviour' are usually pretty obvious. Lucy likes Thunderman, though, and she giggles to herself as she imagines Don Estrada giving him a 'talking to'. Lucy's mischievous self suggests mentioning Don, and seeing how Thunderman reacts, but Thunderman buys them both a beer, and Lucy resorts to sitting nervously, waiting for a chance to play.

The compere guy in charge pays no attention, until Ronee asks TMan to go across and fix it with him. On Thunderman's intervention, the compere looks over to Lucy and nods. Lucy nervously takes the stage and quickly takes out Nick Lucas. She's all clumsy fingers and klutzy thumbs as she tries to get settled. The compere seems impatient, and the sound man is less than attentive. The compere asks her name and, not wanting to use her real name, she goes with Ronee's nickname for her. He asks where she's from, and she replies. "Illinois."

"Ladies and gents, a big welcome to LuLu from Illinois." There's an unenthusiastic round of applause.

She plays her Highway 99 song, figuring that it went down okay in Lincoln City, with English Bob on saxophone. However, she is nervous, and this audience is bigger and a lot tougher. The sound is not right.

She checks the tuning of Nick Lucas, and struggles with nervousness, finding herself talking a little too much as she struggles with tuning, and tries to think of what to play next. She listens to herself with dismay as she finds herself burbling about her saxophone player not being here.

She is suddenly aware of a 'presence' on stage next to her. She thinks she is being ushered from the stage, but the presence introduces himself as Mike Remo and unpacks a saxophone.

"I'll play some saxophone for you?" He smiles.

Lucy remembers her song 'Gravity' and tells Mike the key. Mike smiles and encouragingly pats her shoulder.

"I like your voice, LuLu. "

Mike takes the mic for a second. "What do you call 500 soundmen at the bottom of the ocean?"

The audience fall silent. Mike is quite obviously a well-known 'presence' in the whole club.

No-one offers any answers, so Mike answers his own question. "A good start."

The sound man looks up from a girl he is talking to. Mike stares over at him. "I'm sure the sound is good here, though."

The sound man looks down at his mixing desk, suddenly in full concentration.

Lucy starts the song, and she hears the adjustments kick in. Nick Lucas sounds way better, and her voice projects. Mike Remo smiles over at her, and it gives her a confidence.

<u>Gravity</u>

There must be some kind mathematical beauty
A brutal empire can't crush
Some kind of unification theory
Space and time is twisted enough
All the planets spin around
We are prisoners of the ground
Gravity drags us all down

We got tablets of stone
And we got rulers sittin on thrones
But the Queen dropped her crown
It's broken on the ground
Gravity drags us all down

Birds might fly
High in the sky
But everything falls
Nobody knows why

I don't need St Teresa's heart in a glass
I got a lover's heart to trespass

Mike doesn't add anything until the end of the song (unlike many saxophone players), and he's happy to just look cool. He's mastered cool. Lucy even begins to wonder if he is actually going to play at all, until he tags on a really nice break at the end of the song. Mike obviously commands a high degree of respect around here, as the audience fall silent, and this time there is applause. Good applause.

Lucy packs Nick away and thanks Mike for his help. He smiles back. "No, thank you that's a beauty little song. Let's collect our free beers for playing?"

Lucy smiles. "Of course." Soon, they are at the bar, each with an IPA in hand. Lucy remembers Mike's name from her chat with Don Estrada the Angel.

"Are you a friend of Marv?"

Mike looks over to her with surprise. "Marv's Motors: Keeps America Rolling?"

"That's the one."

"There's only one Marv. Everyone knows Marv, especially the police. Me and him go way back."

Ronee comes over and joins them. She jumps up and down in excitement. "Hey, LuLu, that was really good – even with some neckend saxophone player trying to ruin it for you."

She nods to Mike, smiling cheekily. "The 'Only One' Mike Remo. Mister Skulk-Rock. Still sucking on the Saxophone, eh?"

Mike Remo opens his arms to Ronee. "Always Ronee. How is my old friend, Don Boy Estrada?"

"He's good, Mike."

"Still threatening to kill me."

"Well, you're still alive, aren't you?" Ronee stares blankly at Mike Remo.

Mike stares blankly back for a blank moment before transmuting it to a full smile. "He's a badass for sure Ronee, but me and Thunderman could take him, though."

Ronee laughs. "Sure you could, Remo. You and The Thunderman couldn't take a taxi to Tenderloin. The toughest musos in town." Ronee shakes her head. A cheeky grin painted ear to ear. Mike Remo laughs, but Thunderman is most certainly not laughing. Lucy remembers Don telling her how he had given Thunderman a 'talking to'.

Chapter 8
Party Like A Demon

Weeks pass like San Francisco clouds. Lucy slips into a routine, of sorts. She now has two casual bar jobs and just manages to pay the rent Ronee charges and put a bit to the side. She grows to love Ronee, like the sister she never had, even though they don't see so much of each other. Ronee's job is going well, and she seems to love the work, whereas Lucy is usually working afternoons or evenings, and nights now. Whenever they can, they share cooking duties. As the winter slowly passes, Lucy finds time to get out to a few more open mic nights and, as spring brings fluffy white clouds to the city, she even gets offered gigs at a few folky bars. Ronee has an 'on/off' time with Thunderman. Lucy likes him, even though Ronee is wary of musicians.

"Hey, Lulu, you should get out to more gigs?"

Lucy smiles at Ronee. "I still need to keep a low profile for a while Ron. If I make The Late Show, The Snakes might see it."

"Do they have TV in Montana?"

"Unfortunately, yes."

"Well, Mike Remo's band is playing in Castro this weekend. Thunderman wants me to go. I don't fancy hanging without a friend while he's onstage?"

Lucy finds herself liking the idea but reminds herself that she really ought to lay low. In the back of her mind, she always has The Snakes, and she knows she can't get lower than The Snakes, no matter how low. Always present, always a worry. The Fucking Snakes.

Lucy snaps out of her day-nightmares, as Ronee continues. "Mike Remo is a good contact and he seemed to like you and your songs?"

Lucy smiles at Ronee, knowing how much she owes her. "Okay, let's go. I need a night out, for sure."

Something in Lucy's mind still tells her to "keep low", but her lonely life of recent weeks needs alleviation. Anyways, she always enjoys Ronee's company.

"Sounds great, Ronee."

It's after dark when they set out. Lucy feels suitably inconspicuous as they walk through Haight towards Castro. As they approach the venue, Lucy becomes aware of a tension. She can't work out why.

On entering the venue, the guy on the door seems to know Ronee, and he smiles. "Hello, young Ver-row-nica. It's been too long.".

His leer would be funny if it wasn't so scary, manifested from somewhere inside a thatch of beard, hair, and oil. Unwashed since 1974, in Lucy's estimations. What bit of face Lucy can see appears to be criss-crossed with scars.

Ver-row-nica smiles back. "Howdy Razorface. How is your Mum these days?"

"She's good. She got a new sugar-pappy."

Ronee smiles, and he lets them in free.

As they enter the venue proper, Ronee explains. "An old friend of Don's"

Lucy smiles, and asks, "Wanna beer, Ver-row-nica?"

Lucy sucks her beer bottle, becoming more and more tense, as the crowd seem to be wired; not dissimilar to the people who generally attended Snake Brothers gigs. Maybe that was it? It burrows into her mind. Can snakes burrow? She feels nervous electricity run along her spine and into her hair. She mentally tries to shrink herself, and moves to the side of the room, standing by a pillar. Ronee looks concerned and gets them both a couple of beers.

"You okay, Lulu?"

Lucy nods nervously, looking around her. She thinks out loud. "This reminds me of SnakeGigs"

"Nah, these are The Dirtkickers. They are nice guys really. They got this concept of 'Skulk Rock', but it's just a front.

Personalities they like to hide behind. Anyway, you met Mike Remo and Thunderman already. They are nice guys."

Lucy looks downwards, slightly tense, but Ronee clinks her beer bottle against Lucy's and smiles. "The band sometimes attract the old 'angels' crowd and consequently try and  appear mean and lowdown, like their name, but they're harmless. Let's have a beer and forget the world outside."

Lucy nods and tries to smile.

Mike Remo and The Lowdown Dirtkickers take the stage. It takes them a while to get the audience onside, but eventually the atmosphere becomes more exuberant, and a better humour seems to pervade the venue. Mike Remo works the audience.

 Mike can handle any kind of hecklers, it would seem. Lucy looks around. Suspicious characters abound, and some stare at her and Ronee. As a few menacing guys move closer, Lucy is on the point of walking out, until Don Estrada seems to appear from nowhere. He hugs Ronee and smiles at Lucy, shaking her hand. The menacing guys now retreat. They are lightweight in comparison to the presence of Don.

The audience suddenly erupt as Mike Remo announces one particular song. "Party hard and party long, you're not round for very long, we're all bad people, worship at the crooked steeple, party like a fuckin demon."

Party Like A Demon

As the song progresses it seems to encourage worse and worse behaviour from the audience. At first, it's funny, but then turns darker; people always pushing at boundaries, and the boundaries seem to give way easily here. Bad behaviour and unlikeable characters begin to rule the night.

Lucy looks more and more ill at ease. She whispers to Ronee and begins to edge her way towards the exit. As she moves through the crowd, she looks back at the band and seems to catch the guitar player's eye. He looks kind of out of place, a little like she feels. As she makes it to the exit, she hears the song end and the audience hooting. She thinks, "Fucking stoners."

Outside, she finds a railing and leans on it, catching the twinkle of the spring stars. She thinks of her father and his amateur cosmology. Maybe Boris The Cranium is right and gravity is electromagnetic in nature. She thinks her dad would get on well with Boris. She wonders how English Bob is these days. Anything to take her mind off snake-behaviour.

A strange accent shocks her out of her thoughts.

"Hello. Starry night?"

She turns to see the guitar player from the band leaning on the railing too, with a bottle of beer. His opening line dazes her, as she inwardly panics thinking he might be from Montana. She gathers and looks him over, trying to look unapproachable, but he continues. "Are you a friend of Mike Remo's?"

"I hope so. He helped me out with a song once, so I am a friend of his, for sure."

"That's it. You sang with him in a bar downtown before Christmas. I knew I remembered you."

Lucy thinks, "Fuck, fuck, fuck, so much for keeping a low profile."

"I'm James. You are good. Been working much?"

"Too much."

"Speak to Mike, he knows where all the good gigs are."

"Oh, not in music. I have some bar jobs"

"That's a waste."

"Where are you from?"

"Manchester, England."

She looks him over again. "You know Morrissey?"

"I wish."

"Me too." She finds herself smiling, until she remembers the last song.

"Are all your numbers like that?"

"No, but that one always goes well. The Devil's Music, you know."

"He can keep it."

James tries to laugh. "Hey, you should hear some of our other songs?"

Lucy looks scornful. "I've had a bellyful of songs like that. My ex used to play in a band that majored in it."

"A San Francisco Band?"

"No, was up in ... errrrrm ... Idaho."

"Wow, you're a long way from home?"

"This is home now, was hoping it would be an improvement."

"I'm sure it will be. So, your ex is definitely your ex?"

"Oh yes. I finally managed to convince him of that."

Lucy begins to move away. James places a nervous hand on her shoulder, but she brushes it away. "Come see us again, we have nicer songs that I made up."

As she turns the corner of the building, she looks back. James is still looking at her and smiling. She finds herself smiling back, before walking off at speed.

She mutters to herself. "Party like a fucking demon." Then, an afterthought. "Nice accent, though. Another Limey. I wonder if he knows English Bob."

Chapter 9

The Saloon

James sits alongside Thunderman in The Dirtkicker's van, as they sit in the early evening traffic on Columbus Avenue.

James drums on the dashboard. "Three sets tonight, TMan?"

"It will be."

"We never make so much money, though."

"I know, but Mike likes to do this gig. Him and the manageress go way back."

"She lets us charge five bucks entry. All the dumb limey tourists love it. They wanna hear 'The Blues' man."

"Hey, nothing wrong with us Limeys TMan. I told you." James feigns aggression and then sarcasm. "And we give them Skulk Rock."

"Indeed we do, Jimmy English. We need to educate them. Dumb Limeys."

"Skulk Rock is the way forward, TMan. Just that the world don't quite know it quite yet."

"But they will."

"That's right, The Mascara Snake."

"Fast and Boolbous"

"Boolbous, also tapered?"

"Yeh, but you gotta wait until I say ... also a tin teardrop."

They collapse into laughter.

TMan asks, "You're in a fine mood Jimmy E, not in love again, are you?"

James laughs and does not answer as he continues drumming on the dash, his thoughts elsewhere. TMan stares at him momentarily, smiling to himself.

They arrive at the venue and unload the equipment. There is a house PA and drum kit that TheGnome is happy to use, and he presently arrives with his cymbals and Mike Remo. Mike sorts business with the manageress, as the 3 Dirtkickers check the setup and sound.

Twenty minutes later brings up Beer o'clock, and The Dirtkickers sit and chat as they address their hydration levels,

and wait for the venue to fill up. James looks anxiously at the people entering by the door at the far end of the bar.

Thunderman notices and asks, "Expecting someone, Jimmy English? "

TMan looks at TheGnome and they smile. "Wouldn't be the Susanville Supermodel by any chance?"

"Those 'Supermodels' can't get enough of Jimmy English. What you reckon, Gnomio?"

"He's been waiting every gig since Susanville."

James studiously ignores them.

Then, they sing. "She's a power dresser – A Harley won't impress her."

TheGnome slaps his thigh and carries on. "Legs so long and heels so high - You need a pilot's licence to look her in the eye …"

They roll about laughing, as James glares at them as he feels blood surge in his cheeks. They're still laughing as Mike Remo sits next to them.

TMan splutters through laughter, "Jimmy English is still lovesick, Mike."

"Not the woman who put the Susan in Susanville, is it? That was months ago?"

James reddens even more as Mike sings. "I'm ready for you – but there's no you – I feel so low when you don't show – so so so sad and blue."

He yodels the last line, and TMan and TheGnome roll about laughing.

James looks at them and splutters, "Fuck off you shitheaded pieces of shit."

The 3 of them turn silent … staring at him … before laughing, even more voluminously.

Mike Remo calls over to the bar. "Four beers please, Marg. We got a lervsick geetar player."

They all smile. Happiness is a bar and a gig.

As their beers are finished, they take the stage. The first set goes well, with the crowd composed of some regulars and some tourists. Marg never rips off the tourists and the Europeans find the beer prices attractive. At the end of the first set, the band sit in a corner; some people leave, others stay on. One English guy is complimentary and pleased to find out Jimmy English is from Manchester. The conversation makes James think of home.

They sit around for another 30 minutes, before Mike Remo decides to start the 2nd set. As they play, a new clientele wander in. This time they get a few dancers, one of whom is extremely attractive. James watches her entice a succession of shy and not so shy men onto the dance floor. Mike Remo walks over to James during a drum and bass breakdown and asserts, "We should have her at every gig. Dancers are always welcome." He adds, "Don't go falling in love again, Jimmy English," with an evil grin and a wagging finger.

As the 2nd set ends, The Saloon is now filled to capacity. The gig is going real well and it's a relaxed Dirtkickers that take the stage for the final set. The attractive dancer works her magic and there is plenty of gyration on the dance floor. As the set progresses, James again finds himself scanning the audience. He scans for Felicia. He can't help it. Every gig since Susanville is the same. The 'advice' of Mike Remo, Thunderman and, TheGnome bounces around in his head, and he tries to forget her. That sadness apart, the set goes really well as they get to the last of 3 encores.

Mike Remo announces it. "Thanks for skulk rockin' in San Francisco. Here's a song about living for the moment so, please, get another beer and enjoy this moment. See y'all next time."

<u>Nothing Outside Of Today</u>

All time is trapped tonight
And we got it all
Put real life outside
Under the stars in the sky

They ain't ever gonna fade away
They ain't ever gonna fall
There's nothing outside of today
Nothing at all

This life is nothing to me
That life is like a movie
They all want to sue me
But I got nothing to fear.
The moment that you try
Is the moment you start to die
Don't ask me why
It's God's idea

Stars never fade away
They never fall
There's nothing outside of today
Nothing at all
Is there a fate
Time just delays
And we're too late
To change our ways

Throw my star into the night sky
Teach my thoughts to fly
The limitations of this life
Are in the body not the mind

Stars never fade away
They never fall
There's nothing outside of today
Nothing at all

James thinks to himself, "Wow, this is one of our best gigs."

He loves his guitar sound and the electricity returning from the audience. The extrovert dancer moves to a position in front of him, and smiles as he rips his guitar break. Why has he let his expectations of Felicia turning up to a gig spoil his enjoyment of the last few SF gigs? The rest of The Dirtkickers are right. He needs to forget her. He smiles at the dancer.

As the audience sways with the music, he notices a ripple of faces turn, like a tidal current through the crowd. Slowly, the 'disturbance' moves forward past the bar area. Finally, the crowd seems to part, and Felicia appears. James feels a shock of electricity. Her presence alters the equilibrium of the whole room. A strange phenomenon to behold, as a zone seems to establish around her. Men look, but look away, in case she turns them to stone. The atmosphere changes as the extrovert dancer no longer rules the room.

As the song ends, Mike Remo thanks the audience and informs them of the next gig. James immediately leaves the stage and goes to Felicia.

"Hiya, you made it."

"Only just, it would appear."

"Well, I'm glad you made it. Can I get you a drink?"

"A cold beer would be great."

James gets the beers and sits with Felicia. He is nervous. "Great to seat you. I mean see you."

Felicia laughs confidently. "I do so love your accent. What brings a Scotchman to San Francisco?"

"Hey, I'm English."

"Isn't it the same?"

"Fuck no. They are strange."

Felicia looks puzzled.

"I'll explain on our 3rd date?" (James grows in confidence).

Felicia laughs. "It's a deal. For our 2nd date you can take me to a party? It's up in The Heights"

"Okay. When is it?"

She laughs. "It's now. As in tonight."

Mike Remo looks over at James as he packs away his saxophone. He smiles. He takes time out and walks over. He waves his finger at Felicia.

"Susanville. I never forget a face." He looks at James. "Jimmy English, we'll take your rig back to HQ and see you Sunday?"

James smiles at him. As Mike walks away, Felicia sparkles. "Looks like you're a free agent? 2nd date it is then?"

She tosses her head back as she smiles. The shockwave it creates ripples his thoughts. It seems to slow down time. Whiplash waves slowly traverse the length of her dark hair, scattering light across her cheeks. A wayward strand crosses her forehead, until her slender finger slips under it and herds it back into line.

"I'm not usually that easy. But, against my better judgement and, if you insist?"

She stares at him for two million years, but he never gets bored. Never even blinks. She smiles, her eyes dance and sparkle, and he begins to map the fall and curl of her hair like Captain Cook discovering a new continent.

Eventually, she speaks. "Okay, let's go."

Most things, other than Felicia, drain from his mind, although he does excuse himself to go over and pack his guitar into its case. He smiles at TMan and TheGnome, and gives them the Skulk Rock Salute, and then the finger, smiling. He wanders through the bar with Felicia, feeling the jealousy waves from men (they want to be with her) and women (they want to be like her) alike.

Chapter 10
Felicia

Felicia has a Porsche. You got to be kidding? No, man. And it's parked nearby. James feels a rush of excitement as he slides into the passenger seat. 'When the leather runs smooth on the passenger seat'. Soon they are hurtling north on Columbus, before Felicia hangs a sharp left and guns the Porsche up a hill west. He glances at her heels and her expert feet on the pedals. The muscles and tendons flex and manipulate. He's happy to be manipulated. That's for sure. The city lights blur as they fly past. Strangely, he feels at ease with Felicia, and no pressure to talk for its own sake. He looks as her hair floats in the night air, revealing her neck. He notices she wears no jewellery tonight. He looks at the night sky where stars are appearing from behind clouds. He purposefully blinks, fully expecting to wake up soon; perhaps, back in Manchester, with the smell of frying bacon drifting up the stairs. He is mightily relieved when he opens his eyes to see them fly past the lower end of Lombard Street.

"Where are we going?"

"Private club in The Heights. They have a band I like, and, with any luck, we can get a beer and find a quiet spot to listen in peace."

James smiles.

"I think you might like the band," she adds.

James senses Felicia really means it. He looks at her in silence as she drives, confident in her decision making. They pull into a driveway and Felicia links his arm, as she guides him up the street.

"Sometimes, people just wind me up, Jimmy, and I remembered your band were playing tonight."

"Glad you did, Felicia."

James is somehow pleased with himself for saying her name. Even more so, as she smiles. He looks down the street as they walk, and sees the moon over The Bay. He sees Alcatraz shimmer in moonlight.

"You escaped for a while?"

She looks at him. "I did."

Two security men on the door seem to know Felicia, and open an inconspicuous door for her. James feels their eyes burn into him. He feels like he's been picked up on a Star Trek Tricorder and he's not sure they like his life form. He doesn't care, as long as Felicia does. He follows her down some stairs into a wide-open basement, and thence to a room where live music is playing. As they enter, she directs James to a quiet table at the rear, and goes to the bar. She returns with two large beers. The band are a 3 piece.

Felicia seems quite excited as she tells James about them. "They're English too."

"What are they called?"

"Distant Meteors."

James pauses for thought. "Wow, good name."

Felicia giggles. "Yes, I saw them here once before. You reminded me of them."

James enjoys the music, and he enjoys watching Felicia enjoy the music. He watches her ankle flex as her foot taps. He begins to wonder if he has a 'thing' for ankles? Then, he watches her wrist flex as she drums her slender fingers on the table. He begins to wonder if he has a 'thing' for wrists? His brain cells seem to soar. They follow his gaze along her slender arms. She looks at him and smiles. For some crazy reason, he thinks of home. He can't work out why. Maybe he feels settled all of a sudden? He looks at the curl of her hair around her ear. He tries to slow down time, but he knows it is speeding up, like it always does when you are happy. A distant dark star somehow radiates a message to him. He somehow knows these moments can't and won't last, like life itself. He banishes the thoughts, as his eyes follow the line of her eyebrow and down the slight curve of her nose. Strangely in keeping with his thoughts, the singer of the band introduces the "last number for tonight".

"Thanks for listening, ladies and gentlemen. This one is called 'Time'."

Time

This is the crazy song
Because all of your love is gone
This is like a world gone wrong
This is the world where I belong
This is the world where I belong

And I'm stuck in the Starlight City
I want to fight but nobody will hit me
My girlfriend just told me
This life is so lonely
If I love you only

Time can't change me
I change time

And I'm runnin' like a Baskerville hound
Time is travelling all the way down
I'm still as fast as ultrasound
Catching up with the world spinning round
Catching up with the world just spinning around

Time can't change me
Cos I change time
Time can't change me
I change time all the time

Cold twilight all along this street
I've got shadows that begin at my feet
But I've still got my speed

As the song finishes, there is scant applause from the audience and James feels slightly self-conscious, as he finds himself applauding loudly and whistling (a loud-whistling talent he'd always been blessed with). Felicia looks at him and smiles, un-embarrassed by his appreciative response. "I'm glad you like the band, Jimmy English."

"I really did."

"People in this club are not so into music, Jimmy. I sometimes feel sorry for the bands."

"Is that why you liked us?"

"Nooo, Jimmy. When I first saw you, I saw different audience reactions than here. That time, up in Susanville, the audience loved you."

"Skulk Rock is going to take over the world. The time is nigh."

"I hope so."

James detects a sincerity in Felicia's statement. He is shocked by her real interest in Skulk Rock. It's a bonus. He knows now that he is in love for sure. He nervously holds her hand. No negative electricity flows into him. It's a positive sign. They smile, and James goes for more beers. He waits an age at the bar for an airhead barmaid to fix some complicated cocktails for a bonedome shithead in a suit. His inner self screams. "Fucking useless bitch. You wouldn't last five fucking minutes in The Duke of York." He can't find it in his heart to disagree with his inner self either. The consensus sets in stone as she charges him $25 for two beers. "Fucking useless bitch." As he returns to the table, he nearly drops $25 worth of beer, as he sees Felicia deep in conversation with three more jaw dropping women. His jaw drops accordingly. Felicia looks almost apologetic as she introduces Amanda, Yolande, and Miranda. He realigns his jaw and smiles at each of them as they are introduced. The girls are friendly, but inevitably chat to Felicia about things they have in common. James tries his best but finds himself free-falling out of the conversation. Felicia exchanges a look with him. James contemplates suicide, before excusing himself to walk over and have a word with the three guys in the band, who are busy packing away. It turns out they are from Newcastle, England, and on a mini-tour of the Pacific North West. It refreshes James to chat with English guys again and, as he walks back to Felicia's table, he is once again thinking of his parents.

As he approaches the table, his mood is rock bottomed out to see his seat next to Felicia taken up by a well-dressed, but obviously inebriated guy. The girls seem to dote on his every word as he moves ever closer to Felicia. Two other men stand in front of the table and form some kind of physical and social barrier to him reclaiming his seat. He fails to attract Felicia's eye, and retreats to the bar for another beer. Suddenly, his gleaming spaceship that swept past stars is grounded by a gravity it can't handle. He flicks through the manuals for a way to handle this situation, but it is a circumstance he has never encountered before. He goes to the weapons' manual and begins to read the section on multiple targets. Should he set phasers to stun or kill? He leans on the bar, suddenly an out-of-place figure amongst well dressed and confident revellers. This time, he hopes the 'useless bitch' behind the bar keeps him waiting even longer. As his mental tricorder scans his targets, Amanda peels off from the table and comes over to the bar. She stands next to James, and sympathetically explains, "An unexpected guest." She smiles at James.

"I worked that much out." He tries to smile.

"Felicia's fiancée. He was supposed to be out of town this weekend."

James can't hide his sudden depression.

Amanda sees his disappointment and carries on. "I'm sure 'Flea' didn't expect him, and I'm sure she's grateful you were discreet." She touches the back of his hand on the bar and adds. "I'm sure she'll be in touch."

"Who is he?"

"Oh, that's Rich. We call him 'Rich Guy' he's very very loaded." Amanda looks vaguely ashamed as she explains and appends. "But he's okay, really." She smiles at James in an understanding manner and repeats, "I'm sure Flea will be in touch." As she walks back to her table, James' radar scans her ass and his conscience 'tsks' him admonishingly.

James draws a deep breath and curses under it. He curses again and again. He exits the club and draws even deeper on the fresh night air. He walks around a corner and, once again, way sooner than he ever wanted, sees the shimmering bay under moonlight.

He is lost but knows which general direction to walk in as he sings to himself. "When you're lost in the fucking night – In Pacific Fucking Heights." A ghost walks with him.

Pacific Heights

When you're lost in the night
In Pacific Heights
And nothing turns out right

And everything you do
Turns to the blues
And your brain just blew a fuse

When the crazy neighbourhood command
Can't understand
Why you're waiting for a new escape plan
So only the brave die slowly
So lost and so lonely
Live a life so lowly
If only, if only, if only, if only

My phasor set to kill
Death can be such a bitter pill
Tell me your last wish if you will?

In orbit round a dim star
Upholding intergalactic law
With silver spurs and a tin star

If I could fly in the sky I know I'd fall over
But if you buy me a pint then I'll buy you another
And another, and another, and another

So only the brave die slowly
So lost and so lonely

Live a life so lowly
If only, if only, if only, if only

Chapter 11

Stealing Stars

Lucy walks through San Francisco streets between bar jobs. For the first time in a long time, she feels restless. She is Ms Low-Profile for too many months now. The Snake-Mares have faded, just a little, and she wonders how to map the future. "What future?" she says to herself. Seth's ghost walks into her

mind and she tells it to, "Fuck Right Off."

It's a quiet night in the bar, as she watches a never-ending baseball game, on call to deliver beer to the regulars of the bar. She hears a Harley Davidson cruise past as the bar door opens and Ronee enters, followed by Don Estrada, Marv (of Marv's Motors), and Mike Remo. They take a quiet table at the rear.

Ronee comes over to the bar. "Hey, LuLu, Mike Remo is putting together an all-dayer and he needs some performers, so I brought them down here." Ronee looks pleased with herself.

"I dunno, Ronee," Lucy hesitates.

"C'mon, LuLu, you need to break out and make some more of your talent?"

Lucy is struck by the sincere intent in Ronee's tone. Something, a large something, inside her, is grateful for Ronee's affection for her music. Maybe it's fate's subtle reins, but a decision balance inside her mind wins the day and, internally, she decides to check the idea out. She wanders back to the table with Ronee.

Ronee sits down as Lucy asks, "What can I get you guys?"

Mike Remo smiles, Don smiles at Ronee, and Marv looks as if his mind is busy trying to recollect how come he recognises Lucy. They order beer and burgers.

Ronee smiles. "Hey, Mike, give LuLu a slot at the all-dayer. She's got some great little songs."

Mike smiles at Lucy. "Yes, I remember." He pauses thoughtfully. "Are you up for it?"

Lucy's internal voices raise a frantic debate as she hears her external voice calmly respond. "Yeh, for sure."

She shocks herself with the confident tone her voice strikes, as she thinks, "WTF am I doing?"

Mike seems pleased and Lucy loves his calmness. She is confident in his ordinances.

Mike explains, "It's over in Sausalito and it would be good to add in a few Stevie Nicks type songs? That would appeal to the audience we're likely to draw over there?"

Lucy nods, liking the idea. Lucy had actually gone over to Sausalito one day and searched for Sound City, where Stevie had recorded with Fleetwood Mac. She loved rock and roll history and was drawn to the idea of walking in the footsteps of the greats.

Ronee enthuses, "It'll be a good day out."

Lucy nods and thanks Mike. She notices Marv looking at her and wonders if he has unloaded The Dog yet. There is a short silence before she spins and returns to the bar. Lucy's mind races as she draws the beers. The SnakeDoubts return. What if Mike Remo publicises the gig somehow? What if her picture gets onto the mainstream?

Inwardly, she speaks to herself. "They didn't know much about me, though? It never made national news. I could be anywhere in the world by now."

Whatever logic she applies to her situation can't completely remove the 'SnakeThreat'. She resigns to it and takes the beers over.

As she puts them on the table, Marv suddenly remembers her. "The girl with The Dog. Man, I knew I knew you from somewhere."

Lucy finds herself smiling. There is something likeable about Marv, although she can't work out what on the earth it might be. He seems like an absent-minded Iggy Pop.

Lucy risks an inquiry. "That's me. Did you get rid of it?"

"Not yet. We thought we'd keep it under wraps for a while, increase its antique value." Marv's face is in a wry smile.

Lucy finds herself smiling back. She tries to reinforce the message that it was never hers and had come from an out-of-town guy.

Marv laughs. "You building a truck theft empire, Missy? I run a clean business."

The whole table looks at Marv in disbelief.

Don pats his shoulder. "Sure you do, Marv."

They raise their glasses. "Here's to business."

Marv smiles. "Don't worry, Missy. It's a lost dog."

Lucy feels strangely re-assured. She reminds herself that she has a lot to thank Marv and Don for. She giggles once again, as she thinks of them as her 'Guardian Angels'. Marv looks after her trucks, Don looks after her accommodation, and Mike is her music manager. She is well set now. What can possibly go wrong?

**

Mike Remo's all-day session sits heavy in Lucy's mind, until the day arrives and, suddenly, she seems strangely calm. She welcomes the challenge. She thinks to herself, "Wouldn't it be Sod's Law to find fame when I really don't want it."

Her dad has a physics theory to explain 'Sod's Law'. The theory says it is a mathematical inevitability that is a corollary of a theorem of Chaos Theory, an 'Entropy Wormhole'. She thinks of her dad as she packs Nick Lucas into his case. She ought to introduce him to Boris The Cranium.

She and Ronee enjoy the trip across town to Fisherman's Wharf, and then by ferry to Sausalito. The fresh sea air seems to easily fill her lungs, ready to sing.

Arriving at a busy venue, a variety of revellers are already filling the space and there is a nice atmosphere. Mike Remo gives Lucy and Ronee beer tokens, and Ronee gets the beers whilst Lucy sits at a stage-side table. She scans the crowd for anyone she might recognise. The only one she does recognise is James, as he sits on the opposite side of the table. He looks at her and looks away as she smiles. She is embarrassed to remember their last conversation at the gig in Castro. She admonishes herself for her spikiness on that occasion. She tries to think of a way to start a conversation with James, as Mike Remo calls him to the stage.

"Good evening, Skulk Rockers ..."

Audience cheers.

"There will be three sets tonight, one from us, and then one from the lovely Lucy Smith, and one from both."

"We are going to start with a song by our friend from over in little old England, Mr Jimmy English. There he is on the guitar. It's called 'Sick For The Sixties', and we all are. In fact, we are currently building a time machine, and Jimmy English is gonna pilot us back to England. You might find us supporting The Beatles or walking down Carnaby Street in Cuban heels and flared trousers, and when we transport back here, we will be established pop stars. It's definitely a good plan."

Lucy remembers Boris the Cranium once more today and wonders how he is getting on with the time machine he promised her. Meantime, on the stage, Mike Remo looks over at James as he starts the song on guitar.

<u>Sick For The Sixties</u>

When the future belonged to the left
Well now there is nothing left

I never ever thought I'd ever get this far
In my old jelly mould car
Morris minor mirror memories show us what we left behind
Before we wasted all that time

And the old generation
Are still longing for their dance band days
Steam train railway station
Taking us all away

We're sick for the sixties
Do you think they miss me?
Build a time machine to take me back
And I won't ever miss the CD
I won't miss reality TV

I'm going to build model aircraft fighters
Well why were the winters much whiter?
In this dream mirror where I look
Was life ever that good?

So blame it on the transistor
Or blame it on ambition
Greed is a whore and you can't resist her
Blame it all on Bob Dylan

We're sick for the sixties
Do you think they miss me?
Build a time machine to take me back
And I won't ever miss the CD
I won't miss reality TV

I'm going to go to university
I'll get a grant and I'll do it for free
And I might save the dead Kennedys
Be in a band with Dave Dee, Dozy and Beaky
And then I might fly up to the moon
But most of all I don't want to grow up too soon

The relaxed crowd, the venue and sound are good: some tourists, some locals, all in the mood to listen, drink and groove. The music goes down well. Lucy begins to like The Lowdown Dirtkickers. She was hasty at the last gig. She reminds herself what a bad judge of character she obviously is. Goes with being a criminal, presumably.

Lucy is suddenly nervous as she sees a photographer moving through the crowd, taking pics. As the photographer moves towards the table where she and Ronee sit, Lucy retreats outside. There is a large waterfront balcony, and Lucy looks out over the bay. She sees Oakland in the distance and the lights of a large container ship slowly moving towards the docks.

Gazing up at a bright low-slung moon, she whispers, "Are you following me?"

Her vision seems to zoom in on the moon as it hovers. She sees, or imagines she sees, eyeballs staring back at her. She wonders if her father is looking at the same moon through his telescope, back home in Illinois.

Lucy is still staring at the moon as Ronee's voice interrupts her thoughts. "Mike says they're ready for you, LuLu."

As she walks back, in the noise of the audience chatter is increased, and she realises that the audience has swelled even more during the Dirtkicker set. An army of nervousness masses on her horizon yet, somehow, a calm resolve descends over her mental defences, as she reminds herself what an experienced musician friend once told her: "When you get to the stage it's your gig, your gig, and no-one else's. No room for uncertainty." She deploys her legions accordingly. Bit of 'swagger', bit of 'wiggle', and carry Nick Lucas under your arm, casually, like you are used to stages across the state.

"You're a star, Lucy Smith."

Mike Remo escorts her to the stage and sets the microphone for her. She elects to stand. Mike tells her he will oversee the sound as she tunes her guitar. Now, she hears her own voice over the PA system. Lucy plays a short set on her own. It goes well, and she knows it. Mike is a wizard at getting the 'sound' right. The audience are also receptive and enthusiastic. Her confidence soars. It's a good feeling. Lucy knows she has the audience, as the Dirtkickers join her and busk along with some more of her songs. Mike Remo is happy for her to be centre stage when it comes to encores. Lucy introduces the final song. "This song is called Stealing Stars."

Stealing Stars

The night breeze is a welcome guest
It carries the scent of your breath
The only freedom for a slave tonight is death
And I am Spartacus – nailed to a cross
All that's left of us – is the time that we lost

Do you believe in ghosts like you are never alone?
Do you hear footsteps following you?
On your way home?
And do moments like these - always end too soon?
And life turns lonely and you're howling at the moon

I been in your mind
I know what you been dreaming of
Take whatever I can find - I don't need to be in love
I got stolen stars I left behind – that was my only crime
Memories that I rewind - now I gotta do the time
I see clouds floating by - and rain from the fallen sky
I'm so glad I learned to fly but I never meant to get this high

Years disappear into memories

Not long into the song and audience noise subsides. Lucy realises the extent of her control. Her voice swoops over the audience. 'Nick Lucas' feels alive in her hands, and 'sings' along as she plays an acoustic link. She even sees Howard and Elizabeth in her mind's eye. She feels the audience's scrutiny and she senses everything is right, somehow. The Dirtkickers get the song straight away. Lucy loves the groove. By the key change break in the song, the audience are silent. She looks around at the band, as if to thank them. Her eyes meet those of James. She smiles.

As the gig ends, the applause is good, and eventually attenuates as remnants of sound escape the venue and drift out across the bay. The moon looks down until a single dark cloud stains the sky, and drifts across to conceal its bright beauty.

Lucy sits back at the table. She mentally checks that she has carefully packed Nick Lucas away and runs a visual check that the case is still where she left it. Organisers are busy chatting to Mike Remo, as Thunderman walks outside with Ronee. The MetroGnome begins to dismantle his drum-kit. The stage is being cleared.

A 'jolly' audience member walks over and smiles at her. "Really enjoyed your set. Thank you."

She thanks him for listening and is suddenly aware of James sitting down next to her with two beers.

"Thought you might like a beer."

She smiles. "Most certainly I would. You guys carried a good show tonight."

"We rock. It's Dirtkicker Skulk Rock." He smiles and juts out his chest.

She laughs. "Are you top of the Skulk Rock charts?"

"We most definitely are tonight."

"Who is number two in the Skulk Rock charts?"

"There isn't a number two, such is our dominance of the genre. But you went really well. Lit by the moon, I noticed."

He points up to the roof-lights, as the moon is now becoming visible through trailing wisps of black cloud. It seems to sit over the venue. Lucy feels a cold sweat. She nervously looks down at her hands on her knees.

James continues. "You play Moon Rock?" He nervously laughs, still trying to move the conversation through the gears. James also remembers his last conversation with Lucy and is not keen on the concept of another 'rejection'.

She smiles. "I do. The Moon seems to follow me. It watches everything I do."

"We never get those moons in Manchester, England."

"You're from Manchester?"

"Yes, didn't the accent give me away?"

"Well," she giggles. "I worked out you are not from round here."

"Is it that obvious? Even after more than five years?"

"I met another guy from Manchester up in Oregon. He is called Bob. Do you know him?"

James smiles. "Errrrrrm is that Bob the Throb, the bass player?"

Lucy smiles back. "Errrrrrm, no. This guy plays sax."

This seems to stir some kind of memory with James. He momentarily retreats, interrogating the memory banks for a moment. "Funny you should mention it, but there was a guy a couple of streets away from us who played saxophone. I used to listen to it some evenings when the wind was in the right direction. A lot of the neighbourhood weren't too keen, but I loved it."

They both laugh. Lucy takes a long sip of her beer. "You must know Morrissey, though?"

"Well, of course. We were big mates growing up."

James beams, as he recites, *'We may be hidden by rags*
But we have something they'll never have.'

Lucy's smile opens up. "I do love your accent."

James is emboldened, and ambitiously drifts into his John Cooper Clarke voice. An impression he is always particularly proud of.

"Rebuild the Berlin Wall
Capitalists - I hate 'em all
We need something to keep 'em out
They make you work and give you nowt
Minimum wage
Just like a slave
"You've got to speculate - to accumulate"
They've got a negative interest rate
How did we ever reach this state?
It's capitalists I bloody hate."

Maybe this was a bridge too far though. It used to work with the girls back home in Manchester (in his dreams), but this time, Lucy stares at him in bewilderment, as if he is speaking a strange dialect from a strange planet, at the outermost edge of a distant galaxy. Inwardly she is smiling at his dumb limey accent, but she lets it hang. She enjoys seeing him struggling to think of something to say to keep afloat in this conversation. She confesses to herself that she is one evil bitch.

They both break into laughter at the same moment. As they look up, Ronee and Thunderman are stood there looking down at them. Mike Remo and TheGnome join the table, as they all cool down after the gig. Lucy has known band life in the past, but never like this. There is fun and relaxation in the air. They talk of Skulk Rock, and how it will be the next wave. Mike Remo is somehow a source of energy, and a sun they all orbit around. Lucy begins to feel happy in the sphere of The Dirtkickers. She talks music with James. She looks across at Ronee and sees her holding TMan's hand. The organisers send jugs of beer over. The snake-shadows in Lucy's mind retreat to the outer reaches of her thought galaxy.

They all travel back in the Dirtkicker Van, Lucy and James between drum cases and amps, Ronee and Thunderman between PA cabs. TheGnome and Mike are upfront. The van sways in the crosswind of The Golden Gate. At least Lucy hopes it is that and not TheGnome's erratic driving? A few corners and hills pass, and the van stops. The rear doors are opened by TheGnome doing his strange dance. Lucy giggles. TheGnome sings. "Here we are at the lowdown lair of The Bassman."

TMan and Ronee stand. He passes his bass case down to TheGnome and helps Ronee down. Ronee turns to Lucy, smiling. They all smile.

Before closing the rear doors, TheGnome smiles. "Next stop, the lair of The Limey."

The van sways and climbs on hills, before lurching to a standstill. This time, Mike Remo opens the rear doors. Lucy finds herself holding James' hand as he helps her down. Mike reaches into the van and passes Lucy her guitar case. He looks at her. "We can run you over to Haight, if you like?"

She smiles. "It's okay. Thanks, Mike. And thanks for the gig. Thnxalot."

She walks over and kisses his cheek, as Mike stares at James over her shoulder.

As the van pulls away up the hill, Lucy and James climb the stairs to his 'penthouse flat'. A small twinkle star appears from behind the moon.

Chapter 12
Little Joan

James' flat is one large room with a kitchen area in one corner and a bed in the other. Lucy puts Nick Lucas, in his guitar case, against a wall. She sits at a table and stares through the skylight window. James walks over to explain how he has always loved the view out over the bay, but he is also stopped in his tracks by the sight of the moon looking like he has never seen it before.

He stares too. "Firk me."

Lucy smiles nervously. "It's a Blood Moon."

"What's a blood moon?"

"Some kind of eclipse. My Dad told me about it once, a few years back. They don't happen often."

The moon just hangs looking so close. James' mind returns to his school physics. Gravity always captivated him.

"We're all prisoners of gravity."

Looking at this moon, he finds it hard to comprehend orbits. It just hangs; there must be another explanation. He asks Lucy if she'd like a cup of tea. She nods absentmindedly. As he waits for the kettle, he stares at the moon too. Both in silence now. He adds the boiling water to the loose tea in his trusty teapot and breaks the silence.

"It must be some kind of sign?"

She doesn't respond, as he places a cup of tea next to her hand on the table.

She breaks into a Morrissey song: *'Mother I can feel the earth falling over my head.'*

James picks up on her change of mood and tries to resurrect their earlier Morrissey conversation. "Loved his version of Moon River?"

Lucy stares and begins to speak, her tone different now. "Where I was staying in Montana, the moons were so so bright. The moonlings see everything on the earth."

James laughs. "Moonlings?"

Lucy forces a laugh too. "They can't be subpoenaed."

He thinks, "What beer was she drinking?" Then, he asks, "What could they tell?"

There's no response. The Blood Moon dominates.

"What did you do in Montana, Lucy?"

"I was a farmer."

"A farmer?"

"More accurately, a farmer's wife."

"You're married?"

"I thought I was."

"What happened?"

"He died."

"Oh wow, sorry."

"Don't be."

James looks puzzled. There's a pause. A long pause. Eventually, he asks, "What happened?"

She takes a sip of tea. "Ask the moonlings."

"Do you have their number?"

He inwardly smiles, as he finally gets another half-smile from her. "Nobody does, luckily for me."

James looks puzzled. "Ah-haaaa, so they could incriminate you?"

Lucy looks out of the window, as a tear runs down her cheek, followed by more tears.

James is horror struck. He holds her. "Oh no, have I been insensitive? I'm so sorry."

"Don't be."

"I am."

"Don't be."

"How could I be so insensitive?" Then, he thinks to himself, *"I sound like Hugh 'Fucking' Grant here?"*

"You're a guy."

"Look, I'm sorry."

"Don't be."

"Why not?"

"I killed the fucker."

James drops his drink. She stares at the moon, not even noticing.

In the time it takes him to towel up the mess and pour himself another cup, she still stares. "No one else knows that."

James is speechless. He stares with her. The Blood Moon hangs, radiating truth serum waves. James has dropped off the edge of a flat sane world, and now he tumbles through a troubled aether. He can't make sense of anything as he falls. His mental guidance systems are not prepared for this situation. Not at all.

Lucy turns from the moon, her face stained red from the reflected light. She is in floods of tears now. Her mind whirlpools with blind panic thoughts for having 'blurted'. A voice inside asks her, "Why?" She tries to control herself. Part of her feels easier for having confessed to someone. Why did it have to be a weedy English dude, who can't even speak proper English? Why hadn't she fully confessed to Ronee? Ronee is her best-ever friend and has done so much for her. She realises she must tell Ronee. She will. Later. Maybe. Maybe is a big word that should be dictionary defined a 'probably not'. Well, maybe it's because of the moon. The same moon that was watching her on that evil night in Montana. Oh no – it's a gravitational effect; she is a lunatic. The moon that witnessed her uncontrollable-self. Her violence. Her arson. That moon is controlling her. No, no, no 0 that can't be possible. Where the fuck is Boris when you need him? Alternative theory. Maybe it's because she likes James' songs? He's a kindred spirit. A fellow traveller. Ghosts must visit him too? The good gig she has shared with him, and the beer, has made her reckless. She has ignored her own rules. The same thing that happened up in Lincoln City with English Bob, when she 'blabbed'. That was down to beer and music. There must've been a heavy moon that night too. She should learn her lessons.

James tumbles on in confusion. He tries to grab hold of anything solid in all this. This whole thing can't be true? It's bullshit. Well, if it is she must be a good actor? A method actor.

Christ, she is better than Robert DeFuckingNero. She looks so lost. So forlorn. So vulnerable. So attractive. He should run. Run. He doesn't though, he hugs her, he feels her shaking. He questions his actions. What is he doing here? He should be running round to the police station. He loves her songs though? Ghosts must visit her too? Who knows the circumstances here? Certainly not him. Certainly not some desk sergeant or bent detective or arrogant posh-speaking lawyer or pain-in-the-arse judge or even a jury. That's all bollocks. He can only base his own judgement on what he sees before him. She is hot and he likes her – a lot. He even takes note of that line for a song.

James gets some sort of control and calm by invoking the standard response to difficult situations. He asks a stupid question. "Are you on the run?"

Lucy looks up and stares at him. "What the fuck do you think?"

James stifles a giggle – not very well. "Want to tell me about it?"

Lucy gathers herself, she tries to figure a way of backtracking, but can't stop her mouth hesitantly beginning the story. "Seth ... my husband ... was brilliant at first. I met him singing in a bar. I was on a trip west. He was a talented musician, could play anything. He was the youngest of a musical family. Trouble was ... the family."

"How so?"

"You name it. Anything bad in Montana and they were into it." Lucy knows she is exaggerating. "Seth convinced me he was trying to get out of the family, but over the months, after our marriage, he was drawn back in. Slowly, nice Seth turned into Seth Snake."

"Seth Snake?"

"Yes, that was their family name. There was Mrs Snake, King Snake, and two brothers and a sister."

"King Snake?"

"That was his dad. A real skin-crawling evil sonofabitch. I only met him a couple of times. I wouldn't ever go back to their farm after that."

"So you lived on another farm?"

"Yeh. Seth had a farm, they all had farms. King Snake bought them all farms. Apparently, land is cheap in certain parts of Montana, and it is some kind of way of laundering money. Some kind of deal with Native Americans too. They had financial stakes in casinos. There's some sort of law that allows Native Americans to run casinos. Don't ask me."

"Casinos? Sounds like it could have been good."

"Well, the farm was a struggle and neither of us knew much about it, but at first it was fun. Seth and I used to get out singing and did some song writing together. The farming was like a hobby. Something else we could share. But, fun drains away slowly like it always does and more and more he was drawn back into the family band. They were good too and did wild wild gigs. I stopped going to their gigs. All too wild for me. Like your gig over in Castro but worse. Seth started coming back drunk and saying the money was in rock and roll covers, and he did make money. A lot of money."

James sighs. "He could've been right there."

"Sadly, but there could be a jackpot in song writing. If you do covers, you are a Karaoke singer. Do your own stuff and you are in the big game."

"I agree with that Lucy."

Lucy manages a smile. "You're just a yes-man, James Smith." She pauses, and glances once more at the moon, as if it's now a priest taking confession. "Anyways, Seth didn't agree, and it all just got gradually worse. We fought and I got hurt one time."

She shows James a long scar on her upper arm.

"He did that?"

"Yes, the whole rotten family carry knives. And worse."

"Why did you stay?"

"That's a tricky question. I guess I'm not the first to ignore something glaringly obvious? I was planning to leave, but I think he realised. Anyway, he hurt me bad that time and then, the final time, he came back from a gig and he smashed my guitar on purpose."

"That does demand the death penalty."

"Well, that's what he got."

"Shit-Fuck, Lucy."

"Will teach him to leave guns round the house."

"But how come you are in SF now?"

"I came in his truck."

"But what about the police?"

"I very much doubt that The Snakes would call the police, but they will be looking for me." She looks around nervously once again.

"It's a long way from Montana?" James tries to find a positive.

"Tell me about it. Possibly not far enough, though."

"How did you get here?"

"Just told you. I drove in his truck."

"Can't they trace it?"

"Well, no-one outside of the family knew he had it. It was an acquisition of his that he'd spent years working on. On and off. Anyways, it got me here okay."

"But where is it now?"

"I sold it to a garage guy over in Dogpatch. The guy promised me he had a confidential client and would never advertise it anywhere."

James looks thoughtful. "Did you trust him?"

"He seemed trustworthy?" Lucy looks nervous again, thinking. *Did I just describe Marv as 'trustworthy'?*

James has another attempt at positivity. "You should be okay, then?"

Lucy gets tearful. "It was a big moon that night too. Just sitting there, watching. It's always following me, like a night shadow, like a black cloud, like a death eagle."

James hugs her.

Outside, the Blood Moon still hangs, it's companion star  somehow brighter and bigger. They both watch this astronomical event. Speechless. There's more to this universe than dumb humans can conceive.

**

Lucy's eyes open wide in shock, as a painfully loud bird on the ledge outside the window makes a threatening sound. She throws back the curtain to reveal a large raven staring at her. She reels backwards as sunlight streams in through the loft window. The raven departs at its own leisure. She staggers against Nick Lucas in his case leaning against a wall. She turns to see James, now awake in the small bed behind her.

He laughs. "The seagulls can be annoying here."

"It was a fuckin' big raven."

"Coffee or tea?"

"Tea? What the fuck is this tea shit? Have I really spent the night with a goddam limey? It's a fucking nightmare."

James is marooned in embarrassment for a moment before she turns and smiles. "Coffee, please."

They both laugh. James makes coffee, and the bright spring morning and coffee aroma makes Lucy feel almost happy. She thinks of Ronee, she thinks of Howard and Elizabeth, she thinks of English Bob, and she thinks of her mum and her dad. What did they ever do to deserve her?

The seagull caws and its shadow moves across a sunlit wall as it moves in front of the loft light window. James brings over a coffee and sits at the table, smiling over at her. "Hey, Lucy, is your guitar a Nick Lucas?"

She smiles. "Yes, it is."

"Thirteen frets to the body?" He smiles, half expecting his guitar obsession to be a character flaw in her eyes.

"I knooowwwww." She extends the syllables to make him feel small.

He gains in confidence. "Bob had one."

"I know. I stole it one night, after he invited me over to Woodstock."

James feigns amazement. "Wow. Really?"

"Really."

He pauses, smiling at her. "That means you're in deep trouble, because I want to be a close personal friend of Bob's, and when I squeal on you it could be my big opportunity?"

"You want his number? You wouldn't even get past the dial phase of the conversation." She points gun fingers at him. As she does, she thinks of Howard's parting gift and wonders if James realises his mortal danger. She worries herself, by worrying how serious she might be. Her mum always said she was a 'worry-wart'.

James asks, "Can I have a go?"

She smiles and nods. James carefully unpacks Nick Lucas. His eyes take in details of the guitar as they scan the body and neck. He tentatively voices a chord and is not disappointed by the complex harmonies that reward him. Lucy sips her coffee. "Sing me a song about England."

"Have you ever been to England?"

"No, but I might go soon?"

"How so?"

"On the run. Will you marry me, so I can get citizenship?"

"Sure."

She giggles, and James adds, "But not sure you could handle Manchester after San Francisco?"

"You can teach me the language."

James thinks, and, once more, engages his John Cooper Clarke 'voice'. "Maybe we should try the Balearic Islands?".

"Where the fuck are the Balearic Islands?".

James, once again, lapses into verse.

'Peter the Porter
Said that we ought to
Really enjoy Menorca
Theres lots of Cafes
And coastal paths
Perfect for a walker
Hazel's advice
Was - it's very nice
In Menorca
Secluded bays
In a tropical Haze
Perfect for a snorkeller

Sadly, his "Maximum Manchester" accent defeats her once again. She ignores his doggerel and just stares at him, mustering her full sarcasm. "And, we'll have a little house in a Manchester suburb, and be able to open the back door to a nice country garden with flowers in bloom, and an apple tree laden with apples, and a swing, with a little daughter, called Joan, sat on it."

Joan is his mother's name and James is reminded of a conversation he had with his mother back in Manchester, the day before his own guitar was a victim of mindless vandalism. The memory stuns him to silence.

Lucy notices his sudden catatonia. "Don't worry, Jimmy English. I'm not hinting we should get married. I don't need another husband to kill quite yet."

James slowly surfaces from his memories. "Why Joan?"

"What?"

"Why Joan?"

"I dunno. Just the first name that came to mind."

"My Mum is called Joan."

Lucy stares at him and sees a sadness surface in his eyes. Her mood softens.

"So is mine."

Nick Lucas breaks the silence, as James fingers a chord and begins a song.

Cowboy Drunk

I'm wishing I was back in Manchester
Having a drink with my ancestor
There was not that much to do
But we could always have a few

Now here I am so far out of my comfort zone
I never did want to wind up quite this all alone
Well maybe I should contact home
But I ain't got no mobile telephone

I'm a cowboy drunk
I'm a lone wolf
I lean to the left, I piss to the right
Well hey little baby I can drink all night
But people call me a C ...
Crazy guy
They don't ever say why
My heart's so heavy - my head's so light

And here I am in a bar listening to music
And all the people all dancing to it
Well not me me cos I'm just on the piss
And I don't even know what day it is

I'm a cowboy drunk
Yeah I'm a lone wolf
I lean to the left and piss to the right
Well hey little baby I drink all night
And people call me a C ...
Crazy guy
I don't ever know why
My heart is heavy - my head is light

I'm a cowboy drunk
Yeah I'm a pisshead punk
I gravitate to the left - urinate to the right
I'm a cider samurai
And everybody says he's a C ...
Crazy guy
They don't ever say why
My heart is heavy - my head is light
My head is light

James runs a soothing hand along Nick Lucas' patinated neck. *"How could anyone hurt a guitar like this?"* Lucy smiles at him, as he puts Nick Lucas carefully back in his case. James fastens the case and looks at her before speaking. "Hey, Lucy, I enjoyed last night."

She pauses. "You're probably just saying that, in case I kill you?"

"I think I'm safe, as long as the cup of coffee is okay."

They laugh. Nervously. Tentatively. Awkwardly.

Lucy sits next to him. She thinks of last night's gig and all that followed. "I enjoyed last night too." She finds herself gripping his hand quite tightly. "How long has it been since I had a night like that? Forgotten what it's like. She's as reckless and irresponsible as her dad once told her she was."

Their common solitude is disturbed, as they are startled by the sound from the window ledge as the seagull takes flight and glides out towards The Bay. James walks over to the window and watches it glide into the distance. His gaze meanders from The Island, across to Oakland. He finds himself wondering about Manchester. He feels a spasm of guilt as he thinks of his mother and how long it's been since he wrote or rang.

Lucy breaks the silence. "Shit flat, but great view." She joins him at the window.

James replies, "There's Sausalito, where we were last night. Fleetwood Mac recorded Rumours over there."

She gazes out.

James ventures, "We could do that Lucy? You be Stevie."

She laughs. "And you'll be Lindsey?"

"I'd love to try."

"I kinda already had one scary experience writing songs with a psycho."

"Lindsey is not a psycho."

"I meant you. Neither was Seth, until I got to know him."

James looks downcast.

Lucy looks at him with penetrating eyes. "Anyway, Thunderman told me you had a girlfriend?"

"Thunderman is full of shit."

"All men are."

"I doubt that."

"You doubt it? What, that all men are full of shit or that you have a GF?"

"Both."

"Oh, yeh?" Lucy's tone changes.

James smiles. "Oh, I doubt all men are full of shit. I think I knew a guy back in Manchester who wasn't. And, I doubt I have a girlfriend, although I hoped I did."

He continues. "They tease me about Felicia. She appears and disappears"

Lucy begins to gather her things. James' mouth is on autopilot. "I like Felicia, but I can't give her what she needs. She needs money."

Lucy laughs. "Thunderman said she was a 'superbabe from planet of the babes', or words to that effect."

"Thunderman says a lot. He's never short on bullshit. She's a free spirit."

Lucy smiles suspiciously. She begins to regret her situation.

James tries to change the subject. "How did you meet Ronee anyway?"

"Don Estrada took me over to get a room in her house."

"Don Estrada? He's a real character."

"He seems to look after Ronee?"

"Okay, well the guys in the band are a bit scared of him."

"How so? He seems quite caring under his 'Angel' guise."

"What makes you say that?"

"He told me he had to give Thunderman a 'talking to' for messing Ronee about."

James laughs. "I remember that. TMan was running scared for a long while. Never seen him so pale and quiet."

"He's taking that risk again then?"

"Seems so. It's a big risk too if what he told me is true."

"What's that?"

"He told me Don used to be a hitman back in the day."

Lucy mocks. "Sure."

"So, you are saying TMan is a bullshitter? Maybe you are the bullshitter, LuLu?"

Lucy is stung by the remark and realises she has gone too far. "Sorry sorry sorry. Didn't mean to question a skulk rock originator."

James smiles. "Too right. Could get Don to deal with you. They reckon he is 'trained'."

They both smile.

James continues in a jovial tone. "TMan reckons Don used to advertise for business in the hippie press. He worked under the name of 'Paul Bearer'."

"Fuck off. Now you are bullshitting me."

"Ask Mike Remo. He will know."

Lucy pauses. "I think probably best not to follow that line of enquiry too far."

James nods in agreement.

As he muses, Lucy's mood changes rapidly. She gathers her things and prepares to leave. As she reaches the door, Nick Lucas in hand, she stops. Stops and thinks and turns and speaks, slowly, and the words fall to the floor with slow running gravity. "Hey, Jimmy English. me, you, and moonlings never speak of certain things"

"No, Lucy."

"I do mean never. Not even under the worst torture imaginable involving hot spiky metal objects and bodily orifices?"

"Not even then."

"Good, cos you know what happens?" She smiles

"I wouldn't want that because I want to see you again?"

She opens the door and steps out, before walking back, smiling. "I'd like that."

She blows him a kiss and is gone. Her thought idling. *"Little Joan? Who would want me for a mother?"*

**

An Alcatraz ferry bounces across the bay under vague white clouds, heading east. James gazes silently from the window. He wonders about all Lucy told him. It crosses his mind that she is some kind of fantasist. His mind begins to whirl. He tries to imagine her as a 'farmer'? He thinks of her songs and her edgy but beautiful delivery. He makes coffee and watches the day wake up. Life isn't so bad. He resolves to contact his mother today, as he searches for some biscuits. He thinks about his life in San Francisco. It's been seven years, and he feels settled. He has (kind of) achieved a life's ambition to be a musician/songwriter, yet where has it got him? His only family around here is the band. He is happy in the flat but realises that he has little security. If Jimmy Ho, his landlord, finally gets to buy the adjoining property to develop, he will need somewhere else to live. Staying in the city could be a problem with rising costs. Mike Remo would sort something out. His thoughts turn to his home in a little town called Romiley, near Manchester, England. He remembers the leafy woods and green fields of his childhood. He remembers how they were gradually taken over by housing estates. As a child, it was good because they played for hours in the part-complete buildings. Collecting balls of putty and developing a cheaper form of paintballing with his friends. Shootouts in part-built houses. How they could spend hours trying to start dumper trucks left idle in the evenings. Adventure playgrounds indeed. During the daytimes, James remembers watching the hod carriers skip along bendy planks, ferrying bricks to bricklayers on the scaffolding; wiry men, with a constant cigarette hanging from their lower lips. How he thought it would be one of the best jobs for him to get, because he loved mindless tasks that were repetitive and didn't require detailed problem solving. He had always been obsessive about things and was always content to do what others might find repetitive. He thinks about his father and regrets not speaking to him for so long. He remembers how his father loved the game of tennis and tried to get James interested in it. He had enjoyed the game, before music took over his life. He giggles to himself as he thinks that this trait may have better suited him to tennis than to music. For a long while he was obsessed with the 'serve'. He must get more on the ball. Cheap points aces. Perhaps he could come up with the ultimate unreturnable serve. That would mean you could not possibly get beaten. The game would become a mockery and he would be the man who ruined it. Yes. A true iconoclast. However, a chance listen to an old Bob Dylan single on his friend's old record player had seized his mind and diverted his tennis evil intention. Bob's voice had seemed so beautiful to him, and he could never ever understand why people said he was not a good singer. There were whole lifetimes in Bob's voice: a cast of thousands, and even more characters in his songs. 'Like A Rolling Stone' had sent James back to folk songs and the guitar, and then forward into rock and roll. Even though everyone in his youth had dismissed his musical abilities as a 'craze', he had always loved it. Everyone either told him, or implied, that he had no talent. Especially his music teacher at school. Mr Fucking Meadows. Mr F Meadows was a shitsucker and James would show him. He loved making up songs too, but he had massive uncertainties about his abilities as a musician. He could improvise and make up original songs, but he considered himself useless as a professional musician, playing what he had to in a covers band. Even with all his practising, he considered himself 'ordinary' as a guitar player, but his punk background had given him a suit of armour, and he loved to think 'covers are for karaoke singers; when you do your own material, you are in the big game.' Here he was, a big game hunter looking for that elusive prize. One hit song could make him a living, and he would keep on knocking them out until he got there. He had been so lucky to fall in with The Dirtkickers at a chance crossing of paths on SF's open mic circuit. Mike Remo gave him this chance and he would rather die than disappoint Mike Remo.

James skips as he wanders around his flat. He thinks of Lucy and then, once again, thinks of all she has told him. Her 'story' whirls in his head. Could it all be true? Could part of it be true? Could any of it be true? The bitch was winding him up? He picks up a guitar and plays, trying to rest his thoughts for a while. He can't concentrate. He gazes at the view. A strange plume of smoke in the north winds its way into the sky. It looks strangely like a snake coiled, and, raising its head, peering into the distance.

"Oh shit, it's The Snakes," he giggles to himself. It's a false giggle, though, and his mind soon turns to serious thoughts. Then, he pauses in thought. He looks at the weather and decides to take a walk down to an internet café he knows in Chinatown. There is a skip in his step as he meanders across town. He loves San Francisco.

In the café, with his coffee, he goes to a termonal and types in 'Snake Brothers'. The search returns nothing at first. He adds 'Montana' and 'Band', and some video clips appear. He even becomes nervous as he presses play.

A shaky camera shows a drummer adjusting a kit, before he clicks into a song. The groove is straight, but strangely scary, with an overdriven Saxophone on top. As the vocal begins, James physically recoils from the screen. A "presence" appears full screen, and his countenance is immediate. This weird demon seems to exude malevolence in large doses, as it stalks the area in front of the band and delivers the lyric. It looms even larger during a weird guitar break in the song. The front man's Les Paul seems dwarfed by his physical manifestation, and he seems to send his malevolence forth through the camera, as if seeking prey.

Illinois

And no mistake
No hiding place can ever remain
Outside of my gaze

Going to Illinois I got a bullet to deploy
Law breaking woman broke my heart
She's hanging around on the wrong side of town
She's hiding in the dark
First we find her
And then we remind her
That this is just the start

We're going to find you again one day
And no mistake
No hiding place can ever remain
Outside of my gaze
There's no getting away

You're in the dark matter
I can feel your pull
And this is never over
'Til my dream skull is full
Your space is empty
And my time is curved
Your fates have sent me
My orbit swerved

Calling down a curse pick you up in my hearse
The traffic's getting worse
We've been driving round this lowdown town
Now it's nearly sundown
I've got my eyes on
An event horizon
And it's coming my way

I'm going to find you again one day
No mistake
No hiding place can ever remain
Outside of my gaze
We're surfing in on a gravity wave
Get out of the way
'Cos nothing on Earth can get in our way
We're coming today

Going to Illinois I got a bullet to deploy
Law breaking woman broke my heart

James mutters to himself. "So, you are 'King Snake'?"

The whole band exudes evil menace. Each band member, other than King Snake, seems almost blurred, as if some evil aura won't allow them to be captured on film. King Snake seems to fade in and out of focus, as if tempting the viewer into some altered universe.

The lyric begins to burrow into his mind. They are searching for a woman. Could it be Lucy? The lyric implies that their intentions are not likely to be beneficial to that woman either. He looks for a date on the video, and sees it's five months old, and posted after Lucy arrived in San Francisco. James exclaims, in an English accent, "Sonofabitch," as he wonders if the woman they seek is, indeed, Lucy? He slumps in his chair, his energy sapped, as if he had gazed too long into a Palantir. James would have been lying if he had said he wasn't nervous. He gets a cold feeling that forces are gathering on the horizon. His horizon. Like the Duke of Wellington and Von Blucher trapping Napolean in a 'pincer'. Was it a pincer at Waterloo? He should've paid more attention to history lessons at school. Why does his mind wander so much? He drags it back but it's fevered. The café becomes a goldfish bowl, and his eyes swim around and around. His energy drained, his blood cold, he feels as if he has fought his way back to shore, after an evil tide has tried to suck him out into a desolate ocean. He's felt like this a few times recently but puts it down to drinking his coffee too hot, too quickly.

He winds the video back again, and this time the female bass player takes his eye. She doesn't look like the others. Her dark hair hangs loose and curtains her face. She is slim and tall, striking in a short cut snakeskin jacket over a ragged T-shirt. A tight black leather skirt, black tights, and heels accentuates her slim athleticism. This is a different breed of snake indeed. King Snake is a muscular cross between a cobra and a rattler, for sure, the fruits of a strange entanglement in the depths of hell. The bass player, however, is an athletic snake, who could slither at considerable speed, if necessary. You wouldn't feel her bite until the paralysis began to take over your body and shut down your life force. Even so, James feels a force of gravitational attraction from her, whereas the intense gravity from the rest of The Snakes is repulsive in nature. Could gravity ever be

repulsive? He thinks not. His head still swims, as his time on
the terminal expires.

He staggers back up the hill from Chinatown, his head still
swimming. Breathless, he sends his mind out on a mission to
find happy thoughts, and all it can return is Lucy's idea of a
suburban garden in England. Flowers, and apple tree, and a
gorgeous little girl sat on a swing. Little Joan.

Chapter 13
The Snakes

The same blood moon, reflecting its blood-stained light to Lucy and James in San Francisco California, hovers above a Montana highway, as a large black van rolls through the night. Inside, in the front seats, are Jake 'King' Snake driving, and Edward 'Sly' Snake in the passenger seat. Simon 'Si' Snake sits

in the rear, with 'AJ' Snake, who is dozing with her raven dark hair hanging down and obscuring her face. The van slows and stops in the middle of the seemingly empty highway. Empty except for the silhouette of a deer, visible on the crest of a rise ahead. The driver's window silently glides down, and King Snake's muscular tattooed arm appears, holding some sort of firearm. The gun makes a dry clacking sound, as if a woodpecker is nearby. AJ wakes with a jolt. Bullets fizz on the road around the deer, and it staggers, before falling to the ground. The van draws forward and King, Sly, and Si exit, and load the deer carcass onto a rack attached around the front of the bonnet.

Si Snake enthuses, "YeeHaaa, Pa, you can't miss with those woodpecker guns." His compliments disappear unnoticed, as Jake doesn't respond at all. They climb back into the van.

The van rolls away again, before swinging off the highway into a large farmstead. The occupants all walk silently into a rambling farmhouse. The premises are large and tidy, with a strange mixture of modern and traditional furniture. A contrasting variety of vintage musical instruments and weaponry are sitting around. King Snake is menacingly silent. As they each slide away towards different parts of the house, King snarls, "Tomorrow, I want a progress report." His tone is calm, his voice embodied with a strange accent, with a slight hiss to it. His eyes follow AJ, looking her up and down, as she silently walks away along a corridor. King slowly walks after her, but turns into another room, where a slim, older woman sits at the dressing table, slowly brushing her hair. He hisses as he slowly closes the door.

As a lowdown morning sunlight streams into the large central room, Sly, Si, and AJ now sit at computer screens that look strangely out of place. King stalks impatiently around, eventually picking up a hefty modern handgun. He pauses for thought, idly pointing the gun at AJ Snake.

"How come we don't know nuthin about the bitch?" He pulls the trigger, and the empty gun clicks. AJ Snake flinches.

Si Snake laughs at her discomfort, and answers for her. "You know Seth used his fake id to get married in Reno, Pa."

"That's the problem with fake marriages boy. No records. That line of 'invesssstigation' is shitbox."

"We ought to ask the po-lice for more help, Pa?"

"And risssk them taking an interesssst in us? How dumb are you? Are you the dumbessst of my boys? That's pretty dumb."

King Snake continues. "I pay the goddam sheriff enough every year, but sssomehow I don't think he could ignore a murder. I told him to try and trace the truck and the bitch, but with such a common name he has found Jack-Shit-All. No sign of the truck, either."

Edward "Sly" Snake, speaking from behind a PC computer in the corner, ventures, "We're workin on it, Pa."

King doesn't look impressed. "Sssly Fuckin Sssnake. And I was thinking of putting you in charge of family ssshit, so I could concssentrate on acquiring more land from Fort Peck. A wizard on computers? Don't messsss with my mind. I thought you could track anyone these days."

"We need something to go on, Pa."

Mrs Snake enters the room. She is slim and tall with solid black and collar length hair. Incongruous in skirt and elegant heels.

King looks at her. "And what the fuck do you know, my sssexy Sssioux? You spoke to her more than once?"

Mrs Snake stares him back. "I know she made Seth happy for a while, Jake. And my people are Assiniboine."

"He's not happy now, isss he? He is fuckin' dead. Burnt to a burger, in a house worth a rucksack full of cash."

Mrs Snake looks sadly down. "We've been over this a million times, Jake. She mentioned Illinois and the cold winters. I think her name was Smith."

Sly Snake shouts over. "There's eighty seven thousand Smiths in Illinois Ool-jee." He accentuates the syllables of her Indian name. "I've tried a million searches, and if I add music, all I get is some weaselly english band, called The Smiths?"

Mrs Snake asks, "What about the police?"

"They are a weaselly English band too." Sly is pleased with his quick wit but no-one is in the mood for joviality. Quite the contrary.

King slowly walks over to Mrs Snake, and a silence envelops the room. He grabs her by the throat. The Snake family look on in silence. AJ looks concerned, but Si and Sly look on with interest. Mrs Snake turns red in the face, before he releases her. She coughs and gasps, staggering on her heels, before regaining her composure. They all return to their computer screens.

Sly suddenly exclaims, "California."

King mimics. "California...CaliWhatafuckinbout it?"

Sly Snake shouts, "San Francisco, California."

King looks over. "Lossss Angelessss, Ssssan Diego, Oakland, Ssssacramento. Is this a geography classssss?"

"No, Pa. There's a truck like Seth's truck on eBay. Location says San Francisco."

King walks over and gazes at the screen. Sly shows him the various pics. "Re-sprayed, but that could be it."

King Snake exudes an extended hiss-breath. "Got her. The bitch is gonna die sssslowly when I find her."

"You reckon that is the truck, Pa?"

"I reckon sssso boy. I'd recognise that old truck anywhere. Was my first truck, SlyBoy. I used to run up to Canady in the 'old dog', when I started in the businesssss. Can you get any pictures from the front?"

Sly clicks through the various pictures.

"Ssssee." King Snake points at the screen, as a picture clearly shows 'DO G' on the hood. "The D and E were frozen off one winter. Found them lying on the frozen ground one morning. Truck still started, though."

"We gonna go to California then, Pops?"

"We sure are, boy." King Snake is already deep in thought.

"I always wanted to see California, Pops."

King seems to formulate a course of action. "Okay, Well, we might just be able to take the snake to California. I'll have to square it with BossX but, as it happens, Mrs Snake and I have a meeting with the old prick at the casino this afternoon." He lets his alveolar sibilant affectation slip as his mind concentrates but it returns as he giggles and appends, "It'ssss about time those Sssssanf Francsssssisssssssko Cssssity-Billies learned about real music."

Si asks, "Can we film her end, Pa?"

King looks over, his cobra hood neck seeming to expand, red and veined. His snake-self is back with a true vengeance and he hisses. "For once a senssssssible ssssugestion."

King walks to a polished mahogany cabinet and opens it. Inside, a variety of ornamental knives are displayed. King picks a favourite knife, and his hiss intensifies. "A ssssssurgical blade for a sssssslow fade."

"Mad, bad, on our way to the bay." Sly enthuses.

Ajei Snake walks from the room, tossing her head back in some kind of impatience as the male Snakes eyeball the PC computer. Ooljee Snake bows her head in a sadness. Weighed down. Her black hair piles up on the shoulders of her silk blouse before falling forwards and covering her face on each side. Morning light dances in her hair as it sways. She straightens her pencil skirt and walks slowly from the main room. She glides along the long hardwood hallway and into a sparsely furnished, but carpeted room, with a piano and a variety of guitars and other musical equipment. She picks up an old Harmony Stratotone 'Jupiter' electric guitar, which looks totally out of place over her 'secretarial' black skirt and blouse. She leans over on her heels plugs into a battered old Fender Tweed amplifier and waits for the valves to come to operating temperature. Her slender fingers excite the strings, and a spiky, resonant, harmonically rich, texture of air waves is generated. She idly picks out some melodic chords, before the door opens again, and King Snake's shadow violates the room.

"You look good today Ooljee. Just how I need you. Perfect for our meeting with BossX. At least we got something to report this time. We got to leave for Wolf Point Casino in an hour."

Mrs Snake mutes the guitar. A tear runs down her heavily made-up face. She slowly resigns her mind. She steadies the Harmony Stratotone hanging from her shoulders and walks over to where she has left its reinforced cardboard carry case on a table. She opens the case and retrieves a leather pouch. She loosens the leather drawstring and dips her finger into the powder contained. She inserts the finger into her mouth and then circulates it around her gums. The concentrated expression on her face slowly changes. The tension lines in her face relax, but her face paradoxically ages. She tightens the drawstring of the pouch and carefully places it back into the guitar case. She sinks onto a chair and slowly extracts a gold chain from her bosom. At the end of the chain is a semi-opaque stone. She stares into it, whispering in a native dialect. She replaces the stone inside her dress and begins to bark out chords from the guitar. A wiry sound of tension.

Prison Ground

I spit on the graveyard wall
When I'm walking to town
That's where your spirit crawls
Under the prison ground

Frost sparkles all around
Like diamonds in the dark
Does it get to six feet down?
And does it warm your cold heart?

Stars were deep in darkness
That you painted on the skies
You were the one that drowned us
In the pisswater of your lies

So bury me with another name
In a cloak and with a knife
I'm scared that I might meet you again
In the afterlife

I wore your necklace
I wore it with no pride
And the devil he never left us
He was at your side

You poisoned my body
You said I was yours to lend
You said I was your property
When you lent me to your friends
The shivers of your dark demands
Are still shaking in my hands
I'm know you will understand
I need another man

So bury me with another name
In a cloak and with a knife
I'm scared that I might meet you again
In the afterlife

Again, I'll never be your whore
Again, I'll never be your wife
I don't ever want to see you again
Not even in the afterlife
Not even in the afterlife
Not even in the afterlife

As she plays the song, a dream sequence runs in her mind. Cold stone ruins, graveyard walls and tombstones. In the distance, she sees a native American, sitting on a horse. His headdress and feathered spear are easily recognisable in silhouette against the setting sun. Mrs Snake stares at him. As her dream zooms over the high plains and swoops down to the Indian's face, it is clearly revealed as an eagle's face.

Thought visions now race through days when the sun burns desert rocks and nights, when a cold clear moon fires light down onto sparkling frost.

She shudders as her thoughts blur and refocus on a beach with an overturned vehicle. She sees bodies laid out on the beach, and the incoming tide washing over them. Slowly, they turn to snakes and slither away into an ocean.

Mrs Snake looks at the clock ticking around and steals herself to do as King Snake has instrucred..

"Ooljee Ooljee." She speaks her own name, as if to call herself to a place of safety. She looks into the mirror and adjusts her makeup. She looks at herself in a full-length mirror, checks her skirt and blouse. She smiles at her slim figure and shapely legs in the black heels. As she turns, AJ Snake is watching her from the doorway. Mrs Snake tries to smile at her daughter. Ooljee embraces her daughter as they pass.

AJ whispers in a low whisper, "I hate him, Ma."

"Ajei, my daughter. He owns us. We were sold into this and, believe me, it is better than the alternative was."

Ooljee closes her eyes in despair at her own inadequate and desperate explanation, and whispers to her daughter, "The spirits will save us daughter."

"They scare me, Ma." Ajei is near to tears. "They killed a dear for no reason."

"Never let it show, Ajei. The white man parasite senses fear and takes advantage."

"They enjoy killing?"

"They have brought life and death."

"My skin crawls across my back at their greed."

"This earth will allow so much, but then it will shed them like fleas. The white man has no vision. They don't respect the earth, and they don't respect the earth they leave for their children."

"Are they are going to travel to San Francisco?"

"Most probably. They have lost one of their own and Jake's evil spirit has grown into his whole being. Something that partly belongs to BossX is missing those people seek to retrieval, as well as revenge. "

"I sense him looking at me, Ma."

"That would be his death, Ajei. He knows that. He was not born evil. With him, it took practice."

"We need to escape."

Ooljee tries to reassure. "The moons tell me things will change, daughter." She pauses. "Soon. I feel the great spirit watching."

Ajei looks impatiently at her mother. "The Great Spirit had better stop fucking around mother because I'm fucking sick of this bullshit."

Ooljee smiles as she waves a finger and shakes her head. "You have spent too much time in the parasite white man's world, daughter."

They both laugh quietly until they hear King shouting, and Mrs Snake hugs her daughter one more time, before slowly walking away down the passageway towards the ranch doors. Ajei wipes away a tear and picks up her mother's guitar.

Chapter 14
Business

Highway 13. The 'Unlucky Highway'. Jake Snake's best truck's pistons effortlessly propel it south. Ooljee stares from the front passenger seat at her ancestral lands on either side. Wide open plains where buffalo used to roam. At Cattleman's Cut they turn right and westwards and cruise into Wolf Point. Ooljee remembers history where her people were corralled and starved. She shudders. She didn't make the world.

Jakes turns into Casino Land. Ooljee sighs. The white men brought them rifles, whisky and stole their best land and buffalo. Now her people bring the whiteman gambling, whisky and everything associated and replace their dreams with nightmares. Revenge. Of sorts. Not enough. She didn't make the world.

Jake pulls into reserved parking next to a large black GMC Blazer. "Looks like BossX is here already." Ooljee knows Jake is nervous. She knows.

Jimmy Newshoots watches, from his office at the casino entrance, as Jake walks in with Ooljee. Ooljee glides on her heels. One of the many skills of the whiteman's women. He sighs and looks down at his accounts.

The men around the boardroom table are silent, looking straight ahead, as Jake and Ooljee are led to vacant seats by a secretary. BossX sits at the head of the table with his tall gaunt bodyguard directly behind him at the edge of the room.

Jake nods to the bodyguard. "Hi Skinny." Skinny nods back.

BossX speaks. "Jake. Welcome. How are you both coping?"

Jake responds. "It's been difficult Boss."

"We know Jake ... but ... St Helena and our associates are still concerned about our missing product and missing cash Jake. We need to know there is progress Jake."

"Good to know Jake. What is the progress?"

"Well, we are pretty sure the bitch has scuttled away to San Francisco."

"How so Jake?"

"We have traced the truck she took."

"Traced? We thought you had tried all that?

"Yeh, but my son found it for sale on the ebay."

"You sure it's the same truck? Our contacts in the police have been unable to trace it anywhere."

"We are sure yes. Plates have been changed, but that was probably down to Seth." Jake pauses in emotion.

"So, what are you going to do Jake?"

"We are going to go to San Francisco and cut her."

"And what else Jake?"

Jake pauses, working out the correct response. "We are going to find out if she knows where the product and any cash is?"

"Yes indeed Jake. In fact, you are going to bring her back to St Helena. We have some experts in extracting information."

Jake thinks carefully. "Yes, ok Boss."

BossX pauses. He looks around his silent partners before speaking. "Jake, can we trust you to take the product you have to San Francisco and sell it there, whilst you locate the girl and the truck?"

"Sure Boss."

"Bring back a profit, the girl and the truck?"

Jake smiles and looks at the delegates around the table. "We can easy handle that. Same business model as around here. I'll get our agent to organise some gigs for the band and we can soon find a 'customer base'." Confidence.

BossX turns and takes whispered discussion with his associates sat either side. He then looks hard at Jake and Ooljee. "Jake and Ooljee. Business has been good around here. Look what we have built." He opens his arms to indicate the casino. "That has been thanks to a good relationship with your people Ooljee. I would hate to jeopardise those arrangements." He looks hard at Ooljee.

Ooljee feels a shiver upwards along her spine. She manages a nod of agreement. She knows that BossX knows that she hates him.

BossX keeps his gaze on Ooljee. "How is my friend The Chief?"

"Chief is good BossX. He does not move far from the Reservation these days. Except with the spirits. He sends his regards to you."

BossX nods slowly in acceptance of her statement. "That is good to know Ooljee. Time comes for us all. I would stay in St Helena if business allowed. Please give him our best wishes."

"That is settled then Jake. You and your 'band' will travel to San Francisco. You will find the girl ... and the truck ... and bring them both back here. Are we still hopeful there may be product hidden in the truck? Something that didn't perish in the fire?"

Jake responds quickly. "Yes," he then adds, "we still consider that a possibility."

"That's good Jake. We will arrange for a safe house for your accommodation while you are in the city. I trust your 'agent' will arrange for your 'concerts'?"

"You can trust us."

"I know I can Jake ... and Ooljee."

The ride home is quiet. The sun beginning to set on their left.

Jake is first to speak. "Sssseee that Ooljee. Told you the band would be going to Ssan Francssisssssco. I got BosssssX round my little finger."

"Sure you have Jake. Does Ajei have to go with the band?"

"Do you know any better bass players who know our set Ooljee?"

Ooljee silently sighs and closes her eyes.

****

A full golden eagle swoops from a streaked grey sky and lands in a singular tall tree, somewhere on the Montana Plains. It stares down at two native Indian figures in full tribal wear.

The younger figure is Ooljee, and the elder figure wears a full Indian headdress. They speak in a strange dialect, as if to the eagle. Presently, two smaller birds appear in the distance and approach the tree with a wavering flight against the breeze. The two ravens land on a branch near the eagle. As the ravens land, the elder figure below moistens a finger in his mouth, and then dips it into a leather pouch. He then puts the finger, now coated in a red-brown powder, into his mouth again. The three birds are still, as his incantations increase. Ooljee bows her head, with arms outstretched. The elder rises to a long-sustained wail, with a vibrato that soars on the wind.

The ravens launch into the breeze and land one on each of Ooljee's outstretched arms. She remains still as the eagle launches, and drops to the ground, some fifteen feet in front of her. The elder now speaks again in the dialect, but his voice is elevated in pitch. The eagle walks from side to side, as if considering a proposition. Ooljee sings too, her voice heavy with emotion. The two ravens stare at the sides of her face. As the elder and Ooljee fall silent, the eagle lets out a call, and the ravens take to the air. The eagle stares at the elder and Ooljee in turn, and then takes to the air itself. They watch as it circles higher and higher, looking for a thermal current. Suddenly, it succeeds and rises quickly, becoming a dot in the grey sky. They watch as it swings westwards and disappears towards the horizon.

"The new humans are a problem, daughter."

"That is old news, father. The worry now is Ajei and they are taking her with them to the whiteman city. There is danger.

BossX is bound to send people in California to watch The Snake's progress in finding the white girl ... and the truck"

"We have sent the followers to watch over her and to help with the white girl."

"I think only of Ajei. I've seen 'The Snake' looking at her."

"The spirits tell me that The Snakes will pass."

"Will it be soon enough, father? And, what about BossX and his 'associates'?"

"The damage the new humans do will one day end. The earth will rid the plains and mountains of them. Their wicked machines that burn the air and choke their own children will kill them all. Their cities will crumble. Some of them have love in them, but the force of greed rises too high within most. They have it within them to foresee their own end, but still they do nothing. Their thinking is lost. They worship fake gods. Evil machines have grown them to too many. We can only do what we can do, Ooljee, my daughter."

"The Snake is now a totally wicked being, father. I am weary of his presence."

"Our people have made mistakes too, daughter, and your need to be with The Snake is the greatest sadness of my heart. We have 'business' with BossX and that will temper his responses. Casinos are more important to him than his other interests and we have control there."

Ooljee looks out to the west and the setting sun with weary eyes. "I survive, Father, but I cannot survive if Ajei comes to harm."

He reaches out and places his hands gently on his daughter's shoulders. "You are the finest daughter a man could ever imagine and Ajei is the finest granddaughter. Let us hope my visions are not mistaken."

The eagle rises until the white man scar roads become invisible to its vision. With its wings now extended and seldom moving, it glides westwards and southwards. It looks for dark green patches of tall forest or grey shadows of crags. In the morning, it flies at first light and takes a plains' rabbit. Sustained, it again climbs and heads south and west. It sees more scars below. It can't gain the height to lose them from its sight. It hates the signs of the plague of new humans. The thought of reaching the city has no appeal, but agreement has been made. It has agreed to watch over Ajei.

In days, it reaches the foothills of the Rocky Mountain and sees the scars marking human ways through. It stays high on a crag overlooking a main scar passing through the mountains. On day two, it sees its quarry. It launches and swoops over the vehicle. It passes over the vehicle unseen a few times, easily using the thermal currents between the mountains to match the vehicles reduced speed on the winding and inclined scar. It sees Ajei sat in the rear. It decides to mark the vehicle so it can eventually be located in the city.

It picks a spot where the scar runs between crags and swings around, and finally swoops down in front of the vehicle. As it does so, it sees one of the parasites emerging from the side of the van. All the better. It unloads directly onto the vehicle and the parasite, before sweeping up and into a stall turn over the road. It sees the vehicle travelling on, now marked and traceable. The Ravens will find it easily in the city.

The eagle now uses valuable energy to gain height and is soon riding thermals above the mountains once again. It heads south and west. It remembers the vast ocean that is out there and the bay city it has flown over once before. The city will be difficult, but there are high mountains made by the human parasites themselves, and it should be possible to survive on top. The ravens will be of assistance too.

Chapter 15
The Smiths

An enthusiastic bar impresario introduces Lucy to the stage. It's a reasonably well attended gig, and she gets a good reception from the assembled audience in the bar. As she takes the stage, she sees a clear full moon outside the window.

"Good evening. It seems that every time I play here there is a big fat moon outside. It follows me." She giggles as she tunes her guitar.

**

The same moon also looks over a mountain highway as The Snake-Van, travelling west, crosses the border from Oregon into California.

"Isn't San Francisco full of computer geeks like Sly, Pa?" Si Snake smiles.

"The whole of California is, boy."

"We got many gigs booked?"

"A few. Will give us chance to earn some money while we find the bitch."

"Good thinkin, Pa."

"Someone has to think for you fuckers."

Sly and Si sing in sweet harmony. "Bitch has got it comin, she's goin down. This ain't no love-in, Snakes are com-in to town."

Above them, an eagle wheels across the darkening night sky. Its silhouette blurs across the moon, the same moon that Lucy describes to her audience at that very moment. The eagle invokes a strange call as it begins a dive. AJ Snake hears the sound. She's heard it a few times during rare periods in the Snake-Van, when they don't chatter like demons to each other. As Sly drums on the dash and King and Si are singing, they are suddenly silenced by a diving eagle swooping low over the road in front, heading directly for the windscreen, until ascending at the last moment. The event silences the three men.

Si asks, "Shall I get the woodpecker gun, Pa?"

"Sure thing, boy."

Si gets the machine gun and takes a drink from the bottle they have on the go, before hanging out of the window with the gun and scanning the evening sky for the eagle. As he turns, a shadow flits across him and he draws his head and shoulders back into the van, covered in excrement. The other two Snakes laugh, until the smell turns their laughter to swearing. AJ Snake is the only one that hears a bird call in the distance. The van swerves, momentarily out of control as it passes a sign requesting "Please Drive Carefully in the Sunshine State".

**

Well-meant applause from a previous song dies away, as Lucy announces, "Here's a cheerful song. This is about looking death right in the eye and seeing who has the stronger will. We all got it comin', but we all got to fight before time comes to tow us all away. We don't worry about that around here? Do we?"

<u>Around Here</u>

There's a sadness around you today
You got the Black Dog on your trail
We gotta keep him at bay
Around here

Cos we need good memories to keep

I get bad dreams if I'm asleep
And it's hard to stay awake
Around here

High ideals hide dirty work
Ugliness in beauty lurks
There's a heart of darkness
Around here

Darkness at the heart of the empire
Politicians just walking the wire
Church has a crooked spire
Around here

He's got a ruthless criminal mind
Hidden behind those eyes that shine
He's a fierce killer with a heart of ice

I was talking to Doctor Death
We were discussing my last breath
He said "you got a few years yet"
Around here
But we still own your bones
You are gonna die but - all alone
You're too well known
Around here

You got a grim fate in China
When a doomed ocean liner
Out of control and heading your way
You're on a beach in Ty-Phai

This high moon drives me crazy
These timetables delay me
Nobody ever even pays me
Around here

We're on the run - we're always high
We're night shadow on the sky
We've got a darkness in our eyes

Lucy Smith is gaining confidence looking out into the audience. She looks down to the mosh and sees a figure push to the front and recognises James. She smiles.

As she enters the quiet phase of the song and confronts 'Dr Death', she stray-gazes through the window and sees a dark cloud cover the full moon. A concentrated frown dominates her face. She never loses the groove though.

After the gig, Lucy is packing up and chatting to some inebriated guys from the audience. They are complimentary.

She deals well with their attentions and produces some copies of her CD, even managing to sell a few copies. James catches her eye as he takes a couple of beers to a corner booth. When her 'fans' move away, Lucy brings over Nick Lucas, neatly packed in his case, and sits with James.

"Headliner with CD sales now?"

She laughs. "People can't get enough of me. Only got to sell another seventy-five CDs, and I'll be in profit."

"Or wait until a top producer or manager is in the audience? Just a matter of time LuLu."

She smiles at him. "Surprised you are here without a bodyguard? I'm a dangerous woman, you know."

"If anything untoward happens to me, like bullet wounds or blunt instrument trauma, there's a letter with all details lodged with my lawyer."

Lucy looks at him suspiciously. She holds the look, even until he thinks she is serious. Then, she lets her expression change to a smile. "I sometimes use a knife too. No need for bumps or bangs." She mimics an Italian accent.

He moves to a posh English. "Oh, I say. Let's be civilised here?"

She grasps his hand, as there is a lull in the conversation.

He suddenly remembers. "Hey, I researched The Snake Brothers on the internet."

Her grip tightens, so much so that James snatches his hand away.

Lucy is suddenly enraged. "What the fuck?".

Some drinkers in the bar look around. James raises his hands in surrender, until the moment passes.

"Calm down, Lucy, I only looked."

"What if they detect a hit from SF? They are unknown outside Montana."

"They've got 15,000 hits already. That can't all be Montana Mountain Men."

"They're connected. I'm pretty sure Jake Snake is involved in some kind of drugs business and, who knows what else?.

Don't even think about them. E-R-A-S-E them from your pathetically small English mind."

James thinks again before speaking. He realises how shocked and nervous she has suddenly become. "Hey, LuLu, I was thinking about this, and they are more likely to find you by tracing the truck you sold."

She looks worried. "I know, but the guy who bought it told me he would only sell it privately, and he had a buyer."

"Who was that? Can you trust him?"

"Marv of Marv's Motors."

James laughs. "Of course. Dumb me. I should've realised when you told me you knew Don Estrada. Marv's Motors. Keeps America Rollin? Over in Dogpatch?"

"Yes." She looks quizzical.

"Marv don't know what day it is most days, Lucy."

"You know him?"

"Everyone knows Marv. We bought the band van off him. He's fixed it a few times since. He's an old friend of Mike Remo's. They used to have a band together. Marv was quite a frontman, by all accounts."

"Now you got me worried."

James smiles. "It's cool. Marv is sound as a pound, if a little forgetful."

She mimics. "Sound as a pound. What kind of limey shit is that?"

James ignores her jibe and sits and thinks. "Why don't I swing by and see if he sold it or what?"

She thinks and nods. "I'd appreciate that."

James smiles. "Glad to be of assistance."

"It'll make you an accessory after the fact."

"Hey, I'll risk it. Does it mean we're in a relationship?"

"Yes, one built on violence and murder, you dumb limey."

"We could add love and friendship."

"That just means you want to fuck me again? I know how the male mind operates."

James is without words. He looks at her, trying to decide if she is serious or winding him up. He sees the 'I've just finished a good gig' look in her eyes, and smiles.

Lucy looks at him sarcastically. "And, what about your supermodel girlfriend?"

James looks thoughtful. "Felicia. I explained that."

"Not really."

"Felicia and me are just not compatible. I can't provide what she needs."

"You weren't that disappointing." She smiles.

He manages a laugh as she stares at him. "Well, all that needs to be accompanied by money, comfort, clothes, homes, cars, jewels."

"Materialistic bitch whore."

"Hey, I am fond of her." James looks away, clearly annoyed. Very annoyed. "Very fond of her."

Lucy realises he is phased and she has pushed too far. She too looks into the distance and eventually breaks the silence (in fake British accent). "Only joking, old boy."

"I'm afraid Felicia has a boyfriend, a rich one."

Lucy looks thoughtful. "Why don't you kill him.?"

She smiles, but James looks down. Eventually, he speaks in a confessional tone. "I've killed enough people, Lucy."

"Errrrm, no, James. I'm the fierce cold eyed killer bitch. if you remember?"

"Well, I got form too."

"How so?"

James casts his mind back and chooses words carefully. "Just before I left Manchester, I had a big argument with my dad."

"It happens."

"But this time he tried to take my guitar off me."

"Always a questionable procedure in a dispute," Lucy agrees.

"I swore at him, after he put my guitar in the trash."

Lucy goes quiet. James continues. "I just left home. Moved to London for a few months to earn enough to move out here. Before I left, I did hear he was in hospital."

Lucy asks, nervously. "Was he okay?"

James carries on, lost in memory. "I never got back home."

"So, who exactly did you kill?"

"Him. He died, six months later."

Lucy looks thoughtful, then asks, "What did he die of?"

"He had a breathing problem. My Mum told me it was to do with his work in a factory. Something about blue asbestos in electrical installations."

"Sounds like an album title."

James ignores her cheap comment. "That's why he was so concerned about me getting a good job. He didn't want me to work in a factory like him, but he also didn't seem to think Skulk Rock was a good career path."

"You didn't exactly kill him, though."

"I guess not." James doesn't look convinced.

"You just want to be a most wanted criminal like me. You got no chance, Jimmy English. I'm a badass whore from the Missouri Breaks. What dickhead said 'killing someone is easy, it's getting rid of the body that is the tricky part'? I just leave rotting carcasses all across this continent for someone else to clear up. You're just a dumb limey with a conscience."

James ignores her once again, continuing with his thoughts. "The sad thing is that my dad really loved his music. He was always playing music from the old musicals."

This additional information gains Lucy's full attention and she musters some sympathy. She sings.

"There's a bright golden haze on the meadow. There's a bright golden haze on the meadow. The corn is as high as an elephant's eye ..."

James has started to cry, and tries to sing, through the tears. *"And it looks like it's climbing clear up to the sky ..."*

She holds his hand across the table. As she waits for his attention to return, she remembers English Bob.

James regains his composure and goes on. "He loved Rodgers and Hammerstein. Especially Carousel."

Lucy sings. *"When I marry Mr Snow…"*

He looks at her. Smiling now. "You know all the musicals too?"

"My Dad liked them too."

"Dads, eh? We have a common bond then, Lucy?" He tries to laugh.

"Yes, indeed. We should start a band. We could be called The Smiths."

James laughs. "Our favourite band. It would be most fitting."

Lucy smiles and adds (casually), "Maybe the Two Smiths."

They both stare ahead, and James goes on.

"I decree that life is simply taking and not giving

England is mine and it owes me a living."

They sit and stare. Eventually, Lucy sings.

'In the room downstairs – We sat and stared.'

James looks at her and laughs. "Anyone who thinks it is 'depressing' music is a shithead."

Lucy smiles. "It's a well-known fact."

"Well, it's well known amongst Skulk Rockers."

"Oh, I'm a skulk rocker now, am I?"

"I'm afraid so. You passed into the kingdom of Skulk Rock at the gig the other week."

"Who decides that?"

"I do."

"There isn't even a Skulk Rock committee?"

"There are various sub-committees, but I have been invested with the power to induct any willing female applicants as and when appropriate."

"I'm sure there have been many female applicants too?" Her eyes narrow and pierce his armour. "You want another beer?"

"Why not?"

Chapter 16
Fourteen Hundred Dollars

James takes a crosstown bus down to the Dogpatch district and walks into Marv's Motors. Marv sees him coming across the yard. "Hey-yo, Jimmy English. You're a walkin' man. What's with the Dirtkicker-mobile, now that you're walkin? This is America, nobody walks. You gotta put gas in it, you know."

Marv laughs at his own joke.

"Nice one Marv. No, it's something else."

Marv echoes. "No, it's something else," in an attempted English accent. "Would I blend in walking down Piccadilly, Jimmy English?"

"You sure would, Marv. You'd look like you were fresh out of Eton and on your way to a city bank to start work. You'd need a bowler hat, though, but it would be a good look with the leather and oil-stained denim."

Marv sticks out his chest and smiles in defiance of the whole world. "Marv the money man. Make money with Marv."

"You're surely in the wrong business, Marv."

"The world of wheels is where I am, Jimmy Boy. I'm a wheeler-dealer. So, what's your problem?"

"No real problem, Marv, but a friend of mine, Lucy, told me you bought a truck off her?"

"A nice little girl from the north and an old Dodge?"

"Yeh, that's the one."

"What's with you and women, Jimmy? Are you one of those heterosexuals?"

"I guess I am, Marv."

Marv wags his finger in admonishment. "Well, the first buyer I had lost interest, cos the gearbox had a warped mind of its own. So, I had to change the fuckin' gearbox out."

"You still got the truck?"

"Yes and no. I had to advertise it on the 'Fishing Net', and I had a guy from out of state who wants it."

"Marv, didn't she ask you specifically not to advertise it?"

"I know, but a few months had passed, man, and I thought it wouldn't matter no more. I have re-sprayed it and sorted engine and chassis numbers out. I got a cash flow situation here, Jimmy E."

"Marv the money man, eh?"

"Just a market swing, Jimmy. Marv will resurface."

"Where's the buyer from?"

"He wouldn't say. Didn't like the sound of him, to be honest. Sounded like a fuckin' swamp dweller. Crawled out of a drain somewhere. A piece of shit prick end from a sewer pipe, if ever I heard one. Not that I like to pre-judge."

"Did he leave a name?"

"He just said King."

James shivers. "Uh-oh, Marv. There're some real bad dudes after little Lucy, and that could well be them."

"Don't worry, I won't tell him nuthin'."

"Hold on, Marv. I'm talking really bad dudes here."

"Seen 'em all, Jimmy Boy. Fuck with Marv and you fuck off or fuckin die. Thanks for the warnin', though."

James thinks. "Hey Marv, let me buy the truck. I'll pay your askin' price, and then you tell the bad dudes you sold it to a buyer from out of town somewhere and add in how you had acquired it off a guy from Sacramento. That will throw them off the trail. Make them think it's not the truck they thought it was."

Marv laughs. "You want to be a Dog owner, Jimmy?"

James looks at him quizzically but doesn't bother with any follow up questions to delay his intended business. Marv walks him out to the rear yard, where there is a group of Angels sat playing cards and having a beer. Marv nods in their direction. "Never too early for a beer at Marv's Motors."

They find the truck in a secluded corner of the yard. James notices the missing second "D" and the "E", so it really does say 'Do g' on the bonnet.

"So, it really is a Dog?"

"Sure thing, Jimmy. American engineering. None of your British VW shit."

"VW is German, Marv."

"Fine by me, Jimmy English. $1400 to you. She's a big old heavy gas guzzling Dog, though."

"$1400. Fuck me, Marv that'll clean me out."

"Rock bottom price, James English. That's what I paid for it, and you're getting the replacement gearbox into the bargain."

James thinks.

Marv continues. "I would say that that constitutes a C-A-N-T."

He beams at James, who looks bewildered. "A Can't Afford Not To. C.A.N.T."

Marv slaps his thighs as he laughs. The infectious laughter reaches James too, as he thinks, "What the fuck has he been on today?"

A chanting builds up behind him, and the gathered angels are grunting. "Can't afford not to, can't afford not to, can't afford not to ..."

"Is that your latest sales catchphrase, Marv? I'll look out for it on TV."

The Angels slowly move under the awning, to where some musical instruments are strewn about.

<u>$1400</u>

I got 14 hundred and 14 dollars and 14 cents
It's my life savings but I don't know where it went
So I got weapons – and I got an evil intent
They told me to leave town but I'm still resident

**I just gotta keep running
I got lawmen on my mind**

I like the cemetery - on Halloween
I like chemistry - I got a mind full of dreams
I got a Kawasaki - that runs on K-1 Kerosene
I got a bitch – she runs on morphine

I just gotta keep running
I won't ever do their time

I look after myself - I don't need to carry a pistol
To use on people who talk and never listen
I take their money – I'm on a mission
And nobody knows my name
cos I was never christened

You can hear my songs on 50,000 Watt Radio Stations
You can hear my riffs in Buddhist incantations
But a man's gotta know his limitations
And you gotta beware of cheap shit imitations

I just gotta keep running
I won't ever do no time
I just gotta keep runnin
I keep one bullet behind
I keep one bullet behind
I keep one bullet behind

The song begins and James is tapping along to the rhythm. This is a groove tune, for sure. Marv moves to a vocal mic. The whole 'band' rocks out. Each member has Angel charisma. Angel women appear and start dancing. It reminds James of the movie 'Grease', but with more menace. A lot more. During the instrumental break, a particularly evil looking Angel appears and twirls a sawn-off shotgun, like a drum majorette. James watches in open jaw amazement. He remembers Stevie Nicks doing similar, although that was a baton rather than a shotgun. What the hell. They finish their song and return to cards and drinking, as if the interlude never happened.

James smiles as Marv walks back to him. "Okay, Marvo, you got a deal."

Marv smiles. "Marv's Motors - Keeps America Rollin. I just love the 'You got a deal' phrase. It's music to my ears, Jimmy E. Hey, Jimmy E, you should do that song. Me and Michael Remo used to do that one in a band one time, back in the day. Want my fuckin' royalties, though. Marv is a money mad man."

They walk into the office and Marv fishes the keys from a drawer and throws them across.

"You know I'm good for the money, Marv."

"I know that, Jimmy English. And I also know where I can find you if I need to. You got two weeks."

As James starts the truck, he leans out of the window. "Marv, real bad dudes, you be prepared."

"Always prepared at Marv's Motors, and I can always call for re-enforcements, if necessary." Marv nods in the direction of the assembled Angels, as he shakes hands with James through the truck window.

****

James risks the crosstown drive without papers, figuring that it's only a short distance to the Dirtkicker's lock up facility and practise area in Castro. Nevertheless, he takes a back street route to minimise the risk of being pulled over. It's a hot day and the Dog vibrates heavily on the San Francisco inclines. He curses as he misses a gear on the strange gearbox, and suddenly feels dizzy and breathless and has to pull over. Resting, he watches a mother and young daughter walk slowly up the hill. He puts it all down to nervous tension of negotiating with Marv and the heat. He swims back to the surface as his breathing returns to normal and the dizzyness slowly fades. He sits for a few moments motionless in thought, until his dream-patterns are interrupted by a pair of ravens landing on the bonnet of The Dog. Their feathers are luxurious, like black rainbows, and they seem to stare at him through the windscreen. He shudders, watching them, transfixed. One launches to the air, and he hears it land on the cab roof, its feet audible as it moves about above him. They call to each other. What language is this? He remembers a guy in the Deirdre's Bar one night, telling him how ravens are the most intelligent birds on the planet; how they can work in teams to corner quarry or trick them into

death by misadventure on highways. The bonnet raven seems
to stare at him, holding him in a gaze until it casually shits a
large load onto the Dog bonnet.

"Fuck." He starts the engine, and he sees the two ravens fly
up to an overlooking rooftop. He curses them once more, puts
The Dog into first gear, and judders away up the incline.

**

As The Dog disappears over the top of the incline, the
ravens caw to each other. They survey the street before
descending to an open trash can. Raven-one keeps surveillance
until raven-two emerges with a roast chicken, thrown to the
trash, half-eaten. The two birds peck away, until a new human
approaches up the incline. They caw and launch. They spiral
slowly upwards, charting a
course for the area of new
human mountains. The tallest
building stretches skywards
into a misty white cloud. The
ravens can't quite achieve that
height and settle on a new
human mountain that ends just
below cloud level. They caw
loudly at intervals.

**

A young child at play, on a floor close to the top of the
Fremont Apartment Building, is fascinated by the misty clouds
that form around her building today. The clouds come and go
in the breeze. She waits to get glimpses of the facetted
Transamerica Building. This time though, as a crook in the
clouds reveals the tall spire, she sees a large bird perched on the
very top. She calls her nanny, but the nanny is busy with a
vacuum cleaner in another room. She drops her doll, as the
large bird spreads its wings to become a much larger red-
golden bird, glimmering in the sunlight penetrating the cloud

- 161-

cover. She watches it launch and glide and circle above the cloud, before disappearing through the mist. As the nanny enters the room, the child turns to face her in surprised excitement, pointing at the clouds below.

The eagle dives through cloud cover and emerges close by the flat top new human mountain, where the ravens await. The eagle dwarfs the smaller birds as it makes a running landing behind the building parapet. It walks to a corner area and tosses a carcass and fruit over to the ravens. The ravens caw, as if imparting information to the eagle.

**

As James pulls into the parking yard of The Dirtkickers' lockup, Mike Remo emerges from the practise room door. "What the fuck is that, Jimmy?"

"Long story, Mike."

On Mike's insistence, James relates some of Lucy's backstory. He leaves out the details of the murder.

Mike looks at him suspiciously. "So, just why are these dudes looking for little Lucy?"

"I guess it's that they want their truck back, Mike."

Mike looks unconvinced but leaves it there. He looks at James for a few extended moments.

"You look like a man with problems, Jimmy. You okay?"

"Can't put one foot in front of the other today, Mikey. Guess it's my bio-rhythms, as they say."

"Nothing wrong with your limey rhythm." Mike slaps him on the shoulder.

As they walk into the practise room, Mike fixes James a strong coffee. He sits at a desk in the corner and fishes in the top drawer. He turns to Jimmy with a business card. "I do pay medical insurance for this band, Jimmy. Go see this guy and get a check over."

Mike hands James a card with a Richmond address on it. James looks puzzled, but he knows when not to question what Mike Remo says.

Mike adds, "'The Doctor' is an old friend and he can be trusted, Jimmy. Ring for an appointment and tell him I sent you."

"Thanks, Mike, I will. Are we rehearsing today?"

"We sure are, my man. TMan and TheGnome are on their way. Let's finish that 'Crazy God' song of yours."

James sits back and finishes his coffee as they wait. Mike phones around booking some gigs. James tunes up his old Harmony Stratotone Guitar that he acquired in an out-of-town pawnshop. He still can't believe the tone of this guitar. Made in '63, with hollow body and a 24-inch scale bolt-on neck. He often

wonders what gives it its sound. Got to be a combination of the Dearmond Goldfoil 'GoldenS' pickup and the hollow body and the short scale. It's a magical formula unbeknownst to Fender and Gibson. Only Skulk Rockers know this. Every time he plugs it in, he is rocked by the tones it generates. He plugs it into the old Fender Tweed amp and his low bio-rhythms become a distant memory. Mike looks over as James runs the song down and takes out his old Conn alto sax.

"I love the sound of Skulk Rock in the afternoon, Jimmy English."

Presently, TMan and TheGnome arrive, buzzing as usual. James mics the Tweed amp and adjusts the practice room PA, as TMan pulls an almost acoustic tone from his Precision. Mike picks up his saxophone. "Lay this one back. Jimmy can sing it."

Crazy God

Give me fresh enemies – I need a new war zone
I know I'm a dreamer – and I'm the only one
I take my orders – from evil spirits
Life is not for the fainthearted – and I got to live it

Gravity waves – pull us around
I got a close relationship with the ground
I'm working for the agency – Versace and Versace
But don't designer label me – I'm an independent entity
It's a bit arty farty - for me –
Not my kinda party – don't start me

**Crazy crazy ....I'm crazy alright
And there's a Crazy God
Sitting in his heaven tonight
I told you – again and again
and again and again and again
God loves crazy people
He makes so many of them**

Some situations necessitate – anti-gravity
And I'm learning to levitate – an entire city
I think it will fascinate – the military
So I'd really appreciate – your confidentiality

Gravity waves – at my command
I rule the sea and I rule the land

I see fires – in my new glasses
And I see wires – lowdown informers
I got no secrets – I don't want no-one to know
And I got no places – I don't want no-one to go

**I'm crazy crazy ....I'm crazy alright
And there's a Crazy God in his heaven tonight
I told you – again and again
and again and again and again
God loves crazy people
He makes so many of them**

As the song finishes, they look at each other. Mike breaks the silence. "It's a keeper." He gives James a smile.

The Dirtkickers rehearse a few more songs, before Mike tells them. "That's enough, boys. The bar awaits."

James announces, "I think I'll miss the bar this time, men. Need some sleep."

Thunderman looks over before his mouth gets into gear. "Can't take the pace, Jimmy English?"

James tries to smile.

TMan continues. "Been keeping two girlfriends happy again?"

James' smile wanes. TMan has the energy of a demon, for sure, and could party all night, every night.

Mike Remo stops the banter. "You get some rest, Jimmy English, and make sure you get any pharmaceuticals 'The Doctor' prescribes."

TMan looks concernedly at Mike, as James puts on his overcoat and waves over a weak smile. The door slams in the breeze.

"Not like Little Jimmy English to miss the bar, Mike?"

"He don't feel too good TMan. Don't look too good, either."

"He'll be okay for the gig on Friday. He's a tough little limey."

"He sure will. I sent him to see 'The Doctor'."

An ominous discord sound slowly builds as James has left his guitar plugged in, and it slowly slides down the speaker cabinet, where he'd left it leaning with the amp still on. The Dirtkickers look at it in silence, as the fallen guitar sound decays to a hum. They stare in silence, until Mike walks over, picks up the guitar, and switches off the amp.

TheGnome breaks the silence. "Doctor Charlie. Oh yes, sir. The Rock and Roll Doctor will put him right. 'If you wanna feel real nice – Just ask the rock and roll doctor's advice'."

Mike Remo switches off the lights as the three Dirtkickers leave the lockup. James' amplifier light slowly fades into the silent darkness.

Chapter 17

Doctor Charlie

It's a grey but warm San Francisco day, as James takes a crosstown bus over to the medical practice to which Mike had sent him. 'The Doctor', or Dr Hubert Charles, is a big personality, a big heart and big stature guy, with whom you would have no wish to disagree. He has known Mike for a long time. The walls of his waiting room are hung with many interesting photos of jazz combos, and it turns out that The Doctor had played drums in various jazz combos, way back in the late 50s and early 60s. On one visit, The Doctor shows James an old black and white picture of a crowded club, with a mosh in front of the stage, a woman singer, with a saxophone slung around her slim neck and himself at a drum kit behind her. He laughs as he tells James that it is 'Doctor Charlie's High Rollers', and the singer is none other than Mike Remo's mother Stella.

"Those were different times, young man. We played a hard-edged drive-jazz–bop-blues. I had a snare sound like a cannon or like a whiplash. I could control a whole room with my snare and kick. Stella Remo could blow too, man. She could front any band, handle any situation. No eventuality could phase Stella. She was rock steady. Although my name was on the band, she ran it. I loved her too. Everyone did. You would not mess with Stella, either. She always took a gun to gigs, just in case. Saved my butt on more than one occasion."

The Doctor takes some time out to drift back. His eyelids slowly close. "Fuckin' rock and fuckin' roll killed things for us. Then, the 60s killed us again."

James finds himself hanging on every word of The Doctor's stories. "Then they killed us with Vietnam. I guess they figured a big black guy like me could handle a heavy machine gun. I once shot a tree down, thinkin there was an NVA sonbitch behind it. That gun could fuckin' rock, man."

"When I came back, I was mean. Didn't care nothin'. The music was gone, I couldn't find a band, and I was on too much flake. They used to call me The Black Snowman, The Black Rush, or The Dustache. I wasn't gonna play the psychedelic rock shit and I was just low down. I had snakes inside of my mind."

James thinks of telling The Doctor about The Snakes in his own mind. He is sure Doc Charlie could prescribe the necessary. Probably a head shot for each. No messing about.

"It was Stella Remo that got me straight. She asked me to sit in during one of her gigs, and I was floating way too high. The gig went a little wild, like the old days, but Stella wasn't pleased. The bitch broke my nose with my own pistol, when I shot the ceiling with my pistol to finish a solo, one time."

The Doc shows James his bent nose, as if James hadn't already noticed. The Doc smiles as he reminisces. "She moved into my apartment, with young Mike as well, and got me straight."

"She stayed while I resumed my training, and I really did become a doctor."

The Doc is lost in memories. "Until the stars took her." The Doc shuts his eyes for a few moments.

"Mike used to come round for a jam after. I love him like a son, but so did his real father. Long story."

It is obvious that The Doc initially thought James might have a drug related problem, this being 'typical of musicians'. James has been massively impressed by the detail of his examinations at The Docs, and is generally feeling 'better already', as his Mum always used to say.

James has even found himself looking forward to his medical appointments, as the Doctor's stories of the old jazz days are so interesting to him. On one particular appointment, The Doc himself had seemed 'down'. One of the world's weights seemed to have been cast upon him. James found himself trying to cheer The Doc up. James had been responding well to his medication, and his breathing was getting easier. The Doc's reminiscences took him back to Nam again.

"So many of the good guys had to go. We even killed our own. If you think 'Toot' is bad, you should know there are worse chemicals. Men who push those chemicals need to be cast down. Fuck those fuckers all the way down. Goddam fuckin' dioxin. Evil curse, Jimmy."

The Doc had been asking James about his working life in England before coming to the states. James had told him of the various casual jobs he'd taken in London to earn his passage to the states: warehouse jobs, office refurbs in the City of London. His last job had been a clean-up in an old power station that was converting to an art gallery. It had been a good earner, and it enabled him to save enough for his ticket to America. The Doctor seems interested in the details, and James is happy to reminisce himself. The crew he'd worked with had looked after him on the casual work without insurances. He'd felt at home with this band of brothers. He'd even got to live out one of his boyhood ambitions, to be a hod carrier. He found himself telling the doc of how they used to go for a beer after work in London, and how the covering of dust made them look like grey ghosts next to the dark suited bowler hat brigade at the bar. James laughs at the memory of the city workers retreating, as they all crowded to the bar, surrounded by the dust cloud that followed them. The Doc was deep in thought as James left the surgery.

James thinks of his old construction gang mates, as he takes a crosstown bus to the Embarcadero. His excitement is high because he is going to meet Felicia again. She appeared and disappeared, but during the latest manifestations they had met more regularly. Her attraction was irresistible. Totally irresistible. The 5th force of nature. An orbit that could not be broken out of. Not by him anyway. Einstein's theory would have to be modified sooner or later. Some strange new mathematics was going to be necessary. He had felt guilty, as he also saw Lucy more and more these days. He felt like a minor planet in some strange orbit around binary stars. The mysterious force of attraction could not be screened. This was strange gravity indeed. He wanders slowly along, stopping to gaze out across the waters, as grey clouds begin to give way to spring sunshine. A large container ship crosses the bay and he breaths deeply, filling his lungs with the sea air. For the first time in what must be weeks, he even feels hungry.

He walks into a Boudin's and upstairs to the restaurant. He scans the clientele for Felicia. The excitement of seeing her never diminishes. He thinks to himself, "Is she really as perfect as he remembers?" He suddenly sees her stand to beckon him, and he realises she truly is. How had he not spotted her straight away? Once seen, she is the focus of the whole room. James imagines the envy of the men and women around as he sits down with her. She greets him with a hug and the free electrons in his body race around, as though they don't know where to go to balance the electro-magnetic-gravity field she generates. One that warps all of space time.

"Hey, Jimmy English."

"Hiya, Flea." (In his best Manchester accent) "How yer doin?"

"I'm good."

She smiles, her teeth not perfect, but better than perfect somehow. He longs to run his tongue over them. He breathes deeply, savouring the sweetness of her breath. There is no part of Felicia that doesn't pump his heart into overdrive. He longs to touch her, and puts a hand on hers over the table, before she breaks the silence.

"It's been a while."

"Yes. Four weeks, three days, and six hours. Where have you been?"

"Life's pressures, Jimmy." She giggles. "How is the Skunk Rock Scene?"

"Errrrrrm, that would be Skulk Rock, Flea."

She laughs, and James has to focus to remain conscious. The room spins. A lifetime comes and goes in his mind. The whole restaurant seems to look at her in that one expanded moment. James slowly swims back to the surface and finds himself gasping for breath.

"Hey, you wouldn't marry me, would you?"

She pauses, looks, and smiles. The moment extends and extends. A seal barks in the distance.

He carries on. "Just for a week? A day? A night? An hour? And then I'll set you free again by jumping from the Transam building and knowing it has all been worth it."

She looks at him in a time-stop moment, before casting her gaze downwards. "That's the perfect proposal, Jimmy E, but, funnily enough, there's something I wanted to tell you." Her eyes hold him in hypnosis as she speaks. "I'm getting married next month."

The words bounce around his skull like a squash ball thudding against heavy concrete. Dioxin descends onto the rainforest of his mind, as it frantically searches for a new swearword that he can repeat over and over again in the dungeon into which he has just been cast. Was she joking? No, she wouldn't. She must be serious. He tries to wind back time. A leap year passes before he can speak.

"To Rich?"

"Yes, I'm gonna be Mrs Rich Guy."

He stares at her expressionless, as if he has just looked through a telescope brought by Santa Claus, only to see a luminous green kryptonite comet heading straight for his doomed planet.

"Congratulations."

They look at each other.

James breaks the silence. "This is like a scene from Four Funerals and A Wedding. All the funerals are mine."

Felicia laughs. "More like Brief Encounter. Anyway, Hugh Grant doesn't know Skulk Rock from Acid Rock."

"But he has more money than Rich."

Felicia looks hurt. "That's unkind, Jimmy English."

James apologises, and Felicia soon smiles again.

"I wouldn't bet on that, Jimmy boy. Rich is blessed in the wealth department. He's well into the fuckin' rich category."

"I'm glad for you. I never heard you swear. Swear again, please?"

"Thanks, Jimmy." She holds his hand across the table, meaningfully.

She continues. "What a pity there's more money in real estate than in Skulk Rock."

"I've noticed that."

Felicia looks concerned. "Hey, Jimmy E, you feel cold, and you look pale?"

"I'm okay, just a chill."

"I got a chill, in Susanville. That first time we met, Jimmy."

James smiles. "Gave me the shivers until this day, Flea." He feels a tear run down his cheek.

He thinks, and adds, "Do you need a Skulk Rock Band for the reception?"

She laughs. "Not sure Rich would countenance that, and he's paying for it all. Obviously. His family are a bit nervous of me."

They look at each other.

Felicia asks, "We can still be 'friends'? Once in a while?"

James' replies, "I would, but I think that I'm in love. However, I can't say for sure. That kinda thing is complicated stuff. All I know is I never felt like this before."

Felicia pauses, and then smiles. "You even talk in song lyrics Jimmy E. Who is she?"

"She's a singer friend. She's a real killer, Flea."

Felicia smiles, thinking it's a joke. "I'm sure she is, if she can steal my skulk rocker?"

James feels a hammer drill in his heart, a burning in his brain, and a sinking of his soul. He flails and gasps for some air in his thoughts. There's a gravity that keeps dragging him underwater. Where the fuck is Archimedes when you need him? He changes the subject.

"Hey, come see us play tomorrow night? It's McMurphy's Irish Bar down in Fillmore, somewhere."

Felicia thinks. "Well, I'm in town with a few girlfriends. So, we'll see? Are you playing anywhere else in the near future?"

"Sure we are. Ho's bar in Chinatown is always good."

**

Unbeknownst and above them, grey clouds melt away as the sun in the south illuminates a low-slung daytime moon to the north. The two ravens land on the Boudin roof, and an eagle crosses the disc of the moon, clearly visible in front of a blue-sky background. Not a soul in San Francisco notices anything, other than a little girl on the pier, her mother proudly looking at her in a new yellow dress. She stares to the sky pointing.

**

James jumps on an F-Line (rolling east on The Embarcadero and then north on Market Street), on his way to Dirtkicker HQ to meet the guys before their gig that evening. He thinks of Felicia, he thinks of Lucy and, for some mysterious reason, he doesn't feel down. He feels glad to have been close to Felicia. Strangely, for all her considerable beauty, it is her personality he now misses most. Nothing upsets her, and she always seems calm yet jovial, light-hearted yet attentive, cool yet red-hot, here yet not-here.

'Does the body rule the mind? Or does the mind rule the body?'

He doesn't know.

"Felicia, Felicia – So glad I got to meet yer - I'll take a bullet for yer."

He thinks of Lucy.

Thunderman is waiting, sat on his bass rig, repetitively pumping out a dance riff. "You look downtrodden, Jimmy E."

"Weight of the world, TMan."

"Where you been?"

"Heaven and back. I saw Felicia."

"I told you she was Too Much For You?" TMan laughs at his own reference to a Dirtkicker song.

"Man, she is out of this world. That's for sure."

"I told you sex with alien beings is not generally beneficial."

"Tell her fiancée."

"Oooooooooooh, fiancée? Is he on your trail? Do I take it she's ditching you?"

Thunderman is alerted to James' serious tone.

"Well, she's getting married. To some arsehole property developer."

"No, no, no, Jimmy. It's bankers that are arseholes. Property developers are scrot-bags."

"He's a rich scrot-bag anyway."

"He can afford her tennis coach?"

"Probably."

TheGnome arrives, and listens to the conversation as he sets up a trial snare drum.

Thunderman makes a suggestion. "Hey, in view of Jimmy E's bad news, let's try the 'whores and dwarves' song."

The MetroGnome don't need no second invitation and kicks out a shuffle drum lick, and Thunderman drops in before Jimmy English takes up the Guitar and Vocals.

In Bruges

Well she taught me how to party
With whores and dwarves in Bruges
One kiss was all it took to start me
Now I got something for her that's huge

And I think that I'm in love
But I can't say for sure
That kind of thing is complicated stuff
But all I know is I never felt like this before

My Daddy never told me
Goodbye is the cruelest sound
Women like that are always deadly
Take your heart and nail it to the ground

Well now the sky is upside down

And my life is back to front
And my head is spinning round and round
She's the only thing that I want

But my Daddy never told me
Goodbye is the cruelest sound
Women like that are always deadly
Take your heart and nail it to the ground

Take your brain and wash it
Take your soul - crush it
Take your mouth - kiss on it
Take your heart and piss on it

Well it looks like my nightmare worst fear
That bitch would one day disappear
Now it's kinda like a dream come true
It's the only nightmare I knew

But my Daddy never told me
Goodbye is the cruelest sound
Women like that are always deadly
Take your heart and nail it to the ground

Take your brain - wash it
Take your soul and crush it
Take your mouth - kiss on it
And take your heart and piss on it

As Jimmy E sings, Mike Remo arrives and opens his worn leather-bound attaché case, where he keeps his harmonicas. He links into harmonica breaks. The song rocks.

Mike Remo exclaims, "Okay, that's in the set for tomorrow night."

TheGnome stands behind the drum kit and does his strange dance. "I lerv it man. Whores and Dwarves, my kinda party."

He carries on dancing, as the rest of The Dirtkickers stare at him. "We should call it Whores and Dwarves."

"Hey, Jimmy E, are all the parties in England like that? We should do an England tour, Mike."

"Maybe one day, eh? Is Limey Land ready for us?"

"Well, sonbitches, I'm ready to party."

TheGnome carries on dancing.

James feigns indignation. "Hey, it's a breakup song, not a party song."

"Breaks me up, man. Kissing and pissing, whores and dwarves. You're the goddam second Shakespeare."

TMan giggles. "This world ain't ready for Skulk Rock. We are agents of destruction."

James laughs. "Iconoclasts."

Mike Remo confirms. "We surely are, let's get down the bar."

**

Deirdre brings over the drinks. She smiles. "Mike Remo and The Shitkickers. You guys are early tonight."

They all look intently at Deirdre. Mike proposes the toast. "Deirdre, the world's greatest bar manager. You are cosmic, and may you always bring our beers over in this universe and the next. There are other bars, but not for us."

She looks at the four of them, and smiles, before moving off through the bar. Eight eyes follow her.

"Gotta love that Deirdre."

"Most people have."

James looks at the other three Dirtkickers, and they each look downwards. "Well, I haven't?" James laughs out loud.

TMan giggles as he desperately strives to change the focus of the conversation. "How about a hand of beautiful woman poker?"

James looks confused. "What the ... is 'beautiful woman poker'?"

TMan explains. "C'mon, Jimmy. It's a simple concept. Even for a limey. This is how it works. You gotta name a famous woman from films or music or whatever. A woman who you don't know yet, but who you would sashay up to at a party. That's if you weren't too busy with the whores and dwarves".

He stands and mimics a slow smooch-dance. James stares in amazement.

TMan resumes his explanations. "Then, the next guy has to 'raise', by naming an even more beautiful woman? If nobody 'calls' you, then the next guy has to 'raise' again, with an even more beautiful woman."

"So, what happens if you get called?"

"Well, then it is thrown open to a vote or to an independent adjudicator for a decision, of course."

James thinks, and then states, "This is sexist shit."

It goes quiet as they all stare at him in silence, until he laughs. "But I like it."

TMan sits bolt upright, ready to start. He adopts the pose of Rodin's Thinker. Eventually, "Maureen O'Sullivan."

James looks confused. "Who is Maureen O'Sullivan?"

They all look at him in surprise. Mike explains. "Tarzan's posh wife, Jimmy Boy. Don't you have no culture over there in England?"

They stare at him seriously, as if sad for his lack of education.

Now TheGnome adopts the thinker pose. "Errrrrrrrrrm, Faye Dunaway."

TMan asks, "The young Faye Dunaway, from Bonnie and Clyde, or the Chinatown Faye Dunaway?"

TheGnome is confident. "Either."

No-one calls. They all look at Mike Remo.

"... Kim Basinger."

TheGnome shuffles in his seat. "Ooooooooooh, I dunno, Mikey Boy? Can't generally accept that. I'm thinking of calling here?"

Mike bluffs him out. "Call if you like, pal? You gotta weigh up sexiness? C'mon, TheGnome. Call it?"

TheGnome sits back in his chair, wrestling with indecision, and they all look at James. James feels the pressure. He feels a bead of sweat on his forehead. A couple of guys leaning on the bar are listening now. James' mind works overtime until eventually he blurts, "Gabriella Sabatini."

TheGnome, still simmering, immediately shouts. "Call."

Tension is high now, very high.

Mike Remo speaks. "Okay, gentlemen. The call is Kim Basinger or Gabriella Sabatini?"

James has a question, though. "You mean if I was at a soiree, up in Pacific Heights, and there was Kim Basinger, leaning lonely against a wall, and there was Gabriella Sabatini in the kitchen with no-one to talk to, which one would I talk to?"

Silence reigns as they all look at him, as if he is dumber than they actually thought he was. They all answer in unison and with emphasis. "Yeesssss." (The "dumb limey prick" is implicit).

Mike Remo looks to TMan for his verdict. He answers immediately. "Gabriella." He looks at James, smiling.

Mike adds, "Well, I'm for Kim, as she was my pick."

James suggests, "Well, you two better get off up to the soiree then?"

They ignore him. Mike Remo looks to the two guys at the bar, and they both speak as one. "Gabriella."

Mike declares. "Gabriella Sabatini takes it. She's with Jimmy."

TheGnome sits back in his chair in abject disappointment. He bemoans, "No, no, no ..."

James is laughing now, as he thinks back to his father enthusing about Gabriella Sabatini. His Dad always loved tennis. She was gorgeous, though. His Dad once told him that she 'couldn't get enough.' When asked, 'How do you know?', his dad had replied, 'I read it in The Daily Mirror.'

"Fair enough." As Shakespeare would say.

"She will be good company." James smiles contentedly to himself.

Deirdre brings over the next round, and slowly walks away from the table, shaking her head in disgust.

TMan starts the next 'deal' with, "Claudia Cardinale."

James shakes his head. "Where do you get all these?"

"Did you not get an original copy of Blonde on Blonde, Jimmy Boy? Cos if'n you did, you would find that Bob had put a pic of Claudia in there. And why not? Not sure Claudia was impressed, though. She set her lawyers on him?"

TheGnome is next, and he is concentrating hard now. "Errrrrrrrrrmmmmmmmmmm ... Sandie Shaw."

Mike Remo smiles. "Hmmmmm, always something sexy about Sandie, for sure." He retreats deep into thought. Eventually, "Stevie Nicks."

James' concentrating face is on duty now, as he begins to rifle through his mental filing cabinets.

TMan intervenes. "No point, Jimmy."

"Whaddya mean? It's my turn?"

"No point, Jimmy. No-one can beat Stevie Nicks."

James looks around to the others for support to his objection. TMan asks the question to all assembled. "Can anyone beat Stevie Nicks?"

TheGnome shakes his head, Mike shakes his head. The two guys at the bar shake their heads. TMan shakes his head slowly. "Sorry, Jimmy that's one to Michael J Remo. Stevie Nicks is with him."

James accepts the ruling, reluctantly.

It's James' turn to start now.

He thinks, "... Chrissie Hynde."

The table goes quiet. The two guys at the bar are quiet. Everyone looks at James.

Eventually, Mike breaks the silence. Okay, that's another one to Jimmy English."

James asks, "How so?"

TMan slowly explains. "Well, no one can beat Chrissie Hynde. Keeerrrrissst, you limeys don't know what day it is, do you?"

James scratches his head, laughing now.

TMan asks everyone for confirmation. "Can anyone beat Chrissie Hynde?"

Everybody shakes their heads.

James laughs, shaking his own head. He asks, "What about Stevie Nicks?"

TMan looks at him, as silence falls. "Don't be fucking silly, Jimmy English. She's with Mike Remo."

They rock about, laughing.

TheGnome pronounces, "Stevie is not a two-timing bitch, Jimmy. How could you suggest such a thing?"

Deirdre appears with a jug of beer, shaking her head, but laughing too. "You guys are bad tonight. I'm seriously considering a ban. No Dirtkickers."

"Goddam right we are bad, Deirdre. So, keep the beers coming on in."

One of the guys at the bar asks, "What do you guys do?"

TheGnome says, "We purvey Skulk Rock to any enlightened listeners in the vicinity."

TMan adds, "Fuckin right we do."

The guy asks, laughing, "What the fuckin' fuck is Skulk fuckin' Rock?" (He is a particularly articulate fucker.)

TMan elucidates. "It's original songs with drive, with groove, it's loud, it's soft, it's always got groove, it's new, it's old, it's LoFi from on high, and it boldly goes anywhere we take it. But it's always got groove."

The guy laughs, and asks, "So, who are you?"

The Dirtkickers answer as one. "We're The Lowdown Dirtkickers, and we're out of control and coming your way."

The other guy asks, with a slight edge of sarcasm, "It's not mainstream then?"

The Dirtkickers go quiet, until TheGnome speaks, and with some considerable authority. "The damage the mainstream does will one day end. The earth will rid the plains and mountains of them. Their wicked machines that burn the air and choke their own children will kill them all. Their cities will crumble. Some of them have love in them but the force of greed rises too high within them. They have it within them to foresee their own end, but, still, they do nothing. Their thinking is lost. They worship fake gods. Evil machines have grown them too many. We can only watch for now, my brethren."

The two guys at the bar look at each other, before declaring, "That's right. The Mascara Snake."

The Dirtkickers are busy teaching the two guys the Skulk Rock salute, as Deirdre brings over another jug and makes a declaration.

"You fuckers want fucking locking up. And soon."

Chapter 18

Come Running

It's a bright day, and Marv walks out into his main workshop. He shakes his head as he sees an Angel flat out on the ground. The rising sun sends a shaft of light from a hole in the roof and puts the sleeping Angel in a spotlight. Marv lightly pushes the toecap of his biker boot into the Angel's ribs until he groans. "Another day, another dollar, Al."

Al groans and rolls over. Marv dials in Radio Castro and ambles over and lifts the hood on a V8 Pontiac he is working on. A Lowdown Dirtkickers' track is playing, and Marv sings along. The bright light from the main doorway is suddenly dimmed by an imposing figure. Marv senses a presence and looks up slowly. King Snake follows his shadow slowly into the workshop. He is followed in turn by Sly and Si.

Marv smiles. "How can I keep you guys rollin'?"

"I phoned about the old Dodge truck?"

Marv faces King Snake and frowns. "Goddam it. I sold it a couple of days ago. You never left me a number. That sonofabitch was here for months, and now two people are interested in space of a week. Don't worry, man, it was a real Dog and $2500 was a good price. Still, you know what they say? A fool and his money are soon parted. You don't look like no fool though, mister."

King is not impressed with Marv's double negative and emits a sound somewhere between a hiss and a gurgle. King doesn't seem to dwell on the personable phase of a conversation either. "I fuckin' rang you about that vehicle."

"So you said. I remember, you're from a long-ways away and I didn't think you'd wanna travel for a shitbox vehicle like that. I'd've rung, but you didn't leave no number Mr."

"Who bought it?"

"Some guy from outta town."

"Who did you buy it off?"

"Some guy from outta town." Marv is beginning to sound annoyed. "I'm runnin' a business here, man. Vehicles come and vehicles go."

There's a pause. King stares and nods to Sly, who walks over to one side. Sly Snake is obviously toting, as he wears a long coat on a hot day.

Marv looks un-phased. "So, if there's nuthin' else I can help you guys with."

King Snake lets out a slow hiss, and slowly pulls his chosen knife. "I think your mind is messsssed right on up with your fuckin' LSsssD, and whatever other ssshit you stuff up your city boy assssss. I'm gonna cut sssome information out of you."

He begins to advance on Marv.

Marv calmly puts down a spanner, and his hand re-appears holding a Glock 19, 9mm.

"What you gonna do, shit-kickin' country boy, stab my bullets?"

King laughs as Sly and Si Snake produce short barrel shotguns.

The tension is cut by a voice from a corner door. "Country boys with knives and shotguns make me fuckin' laugh."

Don Estrada moves forward from the shadows. He has a Winchester pump in his hands. As he moves forward, three more Angels appear, each similarly armed, their weapons trained on The Snakes.

"One wrong move and this place will be like a country butcher's market stall. You wanna end up in Ho Ming Chee's sweet and sour pork stew fat country motherfucker?"

Don moves forward. He sees Si Snake stood looking tense. Don raises his voice. "Alvin, there's a good old country boy out here that doesn't know he is gay yet. Can you get out here and see to him?"

There's a pause, before an overweight and less than good looking Angel rushes in, asking, "Where's that, Don?"

King slowly lowers his knife. "Okay, Mr Marv, I'm gonna have to believe you, for now."

"Your choice." Marv smiles.

King backs away, his hiss becoming a snarl. "I know you bought that truck off of a bitch called Lucy from Illinois, and I know she is still around here, and I know ... she is walkin' like a dead bitch."

Marv stares at King Snake without blinking, as Don walks forward, his pump gun trained on King Snake. The Snakes slowly back out of the workshop. More Angels appear, and they 'cover' the Snakes, herding them to their van. They keep weaponry trained on the van, until it is out of the gates and moving off up Illinois Street.

Marv lets out a long whistle. "Pheeeewwwwwweeee, thanks, boys. That's livened up my morning."

Al the Angel declares, "You'd be butchered meat with country cannibals fightin' over your bones, if we weren't here, Marv."

Marv smiles. "And you'd all be riding pushbikes."

The tension eases, and they all smile.

Don sounds genuinely friendly as he puts down his weapon and walks over to hug Marv. "When you need an equation you can depend on ... eh, Marv?"

"I always come running to you Don Boy."

The words cue movement in the assembled Angels and, as if by instinct, they walk to their musical instruments and begin to play.

Come Running

What if positivity can't save you?
When gravity makes you crawl?
What if electricity betrays you?
When you got to make your one last call?

When you feeling that lonely when you feel that all alone
God's looking for you with a nuclear drone
And all your tablets have turned to stone
Come running – come running to me
Come running right back to me

What if your religion is a ball and chain?
What if it never ever brings you back again?
And what if the next world is just the same?
None of your memories remain

What if x-rays can see your thought dreams?
What if they're featured in a medical magazine?
What if the doctor prescribes you pity?
Because you can't handle eternity

So if you're feeling that lonely if you're feeling that all alone
God's looking for you with a nuclear drone
And all your tablets have turned to stone
Come running – come running to me

When a Sultan casts you into a dungeon
When you need an equation you can depend on
When you got good reason to join the foreign legion
Come running – come running to me
Come running right back
Come running right back
Come running right back to me

The song rings in Marv's workshop. Marv and Don jive with each other. Their love and relief is obvious. As the song ends and silence takes over, they all walk to the tall fridge and grab beer.

"I hate those situations, Marv. We're getting too old."

"Tell me about it, Don."

Marv moves to a couch and sits as the Angels disperse, keeping an eye on the gate to the yard. Two of them stare down the Snake-Van as it slowly drives past one more time.

Marv holds his head in his hands. "Hey, Don, is that little Lucy still living with Ronee?"

"Yeh."

"We better keep a surveillance on that situation?"

Don Estrada's eyes narrow. "Daughters, Marv. They just give you worries."

Don paces, thinking. He asks, "Hey, Marv, do we have any of those electronic tracker devices still?"

"We don't, but I can soon get some more."

"We need to get one on their vehicle to keep one step ahead."

Prospect Al is listening. "Why don't we just kill the shit out of them, boss?"

Don and Marv look at each other. "He's got a point."

Chapter 19
Nothing You Can Do

James walks out of Doctor Charlie's medical practice and looks at the blue sky. His mind presents random flashbacks. For some reason, he has a desire to see the ocean. He hasn't seen it for some while. He walks two blocks south, crosses Fulton Street, and enters The Golden Gate Park. He breathes deep and treasures every breath. He sees birds he has never noticed before. The blue sky seems to be a different blue, deeper, richer, and clearer. He wonders if that is down to the drug program Doctor Charlie has put him on recently. He wanders westwards through the park, smiling at others. He wonders why he never spent more time over here. Time seems to expand around him, and the world suddenly becomes more intense than before. He loses track of time, as he wanders past lakes, across the golf course, as he begins to smell the ocean air. He sees a windmill in the trees and walks down the hill towards it. He hears the ocean now. As he passes the windmill and steps out of the tree line, the Pacific Ocean confronts him. Wide and tall rolling waves crash onto the beach, encouraged by an easterly wind. He crosses the highway and descends a ramp onto the beach. The warm breeze seems to electrify his skin, and yet more memories flash into his mind. He remembers family trips to Blackpool, England, when he was a kid. He remembers playing football on the beach there with his father. He thinks of his insignificance as he sits on the mostly deserted beach, watching the breaking waves. Point break. The phrase "Nothing You Can Do" jumps into his mind, and he begins to sing to himself.

Time is an inexorable flow, according to Newton. All James could think was that some of it had inexorably flowed past him. He has no idea how much, as he finally leaves the beach, with a song intact in his mind. His focus becomes that of getting back to Dirtkickers HQ before he forgets the song. His mind is solid and fully occupied with this urgent task. He sits on a crosstown bus, singing the song to himself, and hurriedly lets himself into the lockup. He scribbles down the lyric and begins to work on the chords. He wants a defiant groove, and more than just a rock/blues tune. He experiments with key changes and the song appears. He gets the warm contentment of having created something.

As James sits and makes himself a coffee, Mike Remo arrives. "Yo, Mr English. You look well."

"I been on the beach, Mike."

Mike smiles and sings a few lines from 'Surf's Up'. James laughs and tells him about the new song. Mike is keen to run it down. TMan and TheGnome arrive, and Mike insists they work on the song. It takes time to tame this one, as there are a few sections to it, but pretty soon the song is taking shape. Thunderman is his usual energetic self.

"Nice song, Jimmy E. We were worried about you. You not been your usual self?"

Mike Remo is quiet and gets everyone a beer. They all sit. Thunderman is irrepressible. "Those two women wearing you out, Jimmy?"

James remains quiet, as if lost in thought. Mike Remo looks at Thunderman, as if to tell him to ease off.

James suddenly speaks. "Something I need to tell you guys."

"What's that, Jimmy?"

"I will need to leave the band soon."

The guys go quiet. "Why?"

"Not that I don't love our skulk rock pioneering. I love it with all my heart."

"What is it then, Jimmy?"

"I have a medical condition."

Mike Remo's eyes slowly close as his head begins to drop.

Thunderman tries to make light of the announcement. "Have another beer then."

"Not that easy, TMan."

TheGnome is constructive. "We can score something stronger, if you like?"

James forces a laugh. "Well, Doctor Charlie has me on a pretty solid program already, so I'm feeling okay."

TheGnome continues. "What the fuck is the problem, Jimmy E?"

Mike Remo opens his eyes. He knows what is coming. He stares at the wall. He doesn't want to look anywhere. His own memories flood back. He feels Stella's hand on his shoulder before Jimmy speaks.

"Well ... it's known as death."

"What?"

"Don't make me explain. Please."

There is silence. Mike digs his nails into his palms and eventually asks, "How long?"

"Six months tops, but a rapid decline to pain and loss of dignity."

"Fuck Shit Piss, Jimmy." The MetroGnome looks down at the floor. TMan stares out of the window.

James lightens the mood, or at least tries to. "So, hey, boys, we need gigs and recordings as quickly as possible, and as many as possible."

"Fucking right, Jimmy."

"We got to commit to 'Skulk', with more purpose than ever."

Mike Remo takes a deep breath and reaches over and lays a hand on James' head.

"We love you, man. That's exactly what we'll do. We start now. And at Ho Far tonight. You feel okay for it?"

"You bet, Mike. Dr Charlie has me riding high. I need groove."

The Dirtkickers all do their best to lift the atmosphere, as they load the 'Tour Bus,. Otherwise known as the van, for tonight's gig. Soon the 'Tour Bus' is moving into Chinatown, with Mike at the wheel. Gigs clear the mind. James gazes out at the dead red chickens hanging in the windows. He wonders about the afterlife. The crosstown journey becomes quiet. Even Thunderman falls under solitude thoughts. James finds himself trying to cheer the others up. He asks himself how crazy that is. They pull up outside The Ho Far Bar, and a smiling Chinese guy emerges.

Mike Remo shakes his hand. "Ho Chi Minimum. How the fuck are you?"

Ho Chi smiles, and responds. "Sclew you, Mike Lemo."

They hug. Mike Remo sings. "Hey Ho Hey Ho, we gonna rock and roll."

Ho smiles. "Only two sets tonight, Big Mike. Big Boss has booked a new band for 3rd and 4th sets."

"Is there a problem here, Ho?"

"No ploblem, Mike Lemo, same money for 2 sets. And unlimited flee dlinks to compensate?"

"We can use house drum kit too?"

"No ploblem, as long as other band can use your amps?"

Mike looks at James and Thunderman. They nod. "It's a deal, Ho."

"Many toulists in town, Mike. Big Boss wanted four sets and late night."

"That's great, Ho. Better for us to have drinking time."

"I look after you, Mike Lemo."

The Dirtkickers quickly set up the stage and move to a quiet corner and get the beers in. They swap stories of past gigs, and James smiles and laughs with them.

The bar gradually fills, a mixture of tourists and locals, until

The Dirtkickers get the sign from Ho. Mike pulls the four of them together.

"Nothing matters but Skulk Rock boys. If they don't get it, we don't care. We don't play no covers. We play our tunes. We always do. We make no apologies. We never surrender. Nothing gets in our way. Let's shove some skulk into the space-time continuum. Our job is to put it out there."

The Lowdown Dirtkickers take the stage. Mike Remo steps up to the mic. This must be the thousandth time. Maybe more. "This is a song relating to the times in life you come up on situations where there is fuck all you can do. It's called 'Underwater in a locked car – At the bottom of a Reservoir – On a planet so far – Out of orbit round a black star'."

They look at TheGnome. Mike nods. Three clicks, a snare like a cannon, and they are in.

Nothing You Can Do

Like you're falling from a thousand miles
Like you lost your teeth and still want to smile
Unconscious pilot in a nose dive
Now you're dead you want to be alive

Nothing you can do
Nothing you can do

Like an outlaw with no alibi
Like a black cloud in a summer sky
Like a witness telling a lie
Or like a gun in the hand of a jealous guy

Nothing you can do
Nothing you can do

Well watch the stars revolve around a nighttime sky
And feel the gravity every time you try to fly
There is nothing you can do

A roulette wheel is bound to lose
I'm telling you all of this bad news
The worst thing is - it's true

You're falling from a thousand miles
No Samaritan you can dial
You're walking down the aisle
And your wedding dress just went out of style

Underwater in a locked car
At the bottom of a reservoir
On a planet so far
Out of orbit round a black star

Nothing you can do

The Dirtkickers really push it right on up. James' news, the beer, and the general atmosphere roll them along with a groove like never before. James adds a tense solo.

The audience sense it. You can tell when they get it. A light goes on somewhere in the universe, and it beams photons through every brain receptor. Tonight, Skulk Rock rules the airwaves. The audience draw energy from it. Immense energy. They love it. They want more. The situation makes them thirsty. The bar staff are suddenly occupied. Ho Chi smiles, as he has to recruit himself to help behind the bar.

Before the song even ends, applause vibes rule the atmosphere. The dancers want more. There are suddenly more people. The Ho Far Bar is rammed, and as Mike Remo unpacks his saxophone a buzz seems to go around the audience. James looks out over the crowd and spots Felicia, and her three friends, Amanda, Yolande, and Miranda enter the bar. As The Dirtkickers groove into the next song, the four supermodels also begin dancing. As usual, Felicia commands all attention. Her friends are loving it too, and dance provocatively with many of the good-natured groovers at the gig.

The whole holy vibe never diminishes. Mike Remo uses every trick he knows. He faces down fate like a fusion bomb. He tells it to 'fuck off'. The audience love him. James watches him work the audience. James loves it too. He smiles at Mike, TMan, and TheGnome. He loves these guys. He takes one more of Dr Charlie's tablets during the break. So many people in, he can't even get across to speak to Felicia. He smiles over. She waves. The disturbance of the air from her hand reaches him like an affection-tsunami, and he is electrified. Ho Chi is loving it. He struggles through the crowd with two jugs of beer for the band and places them on the stage. One of his waitresses brings two more. A slim Chinese girl with amazing cheekbones and lined eyebrows that make James' eyes swim along their wavy lines. She smiles at him, as he thanks her for the beer.

Ho enthuses like never before. "Mike Lemo, you lock. You lock like fuck. Big Boss say I can pay you more tonight."

"Thanks, Ho. We appreciate you giving us gigs. We really do."

"We buying bigger bar, Mike Lemo. It will be Skulk Lock HQ."

"That's the truth, Ho. The whole truth and fuck all but the truth. Now we are 'sworn' to it."

Ho Chi Minimum gives Mike the Skulk Rock salute.

Time hurries. The band could play all night. As the 2nd set approaches the finish, the audience calls for more. Mike Remo thanks them and tells them, "Thank you all, Skulk Rockers. We will see you next time. But don't leave. There is another band to play a set in thirty mins or so. How much pleasure can you handle? We need to concentrate on some serious drinking time now."

Still, the audience call for more.

Mike Remo calms them down. "Hey, Skulkers, it's well known that this is the best rock bar in SF, and Ho Chi has booked another real good band for your entertainment."

He calls over to Ho. "What are they called, Ho?"

"The Snake Blothers. Flom Montana."

The audience gradually calms. The Dirtkickers move into a rear bar and sit enjoying a drink. They all embrace James.

As they sit, James asks. "Hey, Mikey, did Ho say The Snake Brothers?"

"No, The Snake Blothers." Mike laughs at his own joke and hugs James.

"Ha haaaa. Oh fuck, I've heard they are trouble?"

"Never heard of them around here. A bunch of country shitkickers probably. Anyway, they gave us some drinkin' time and free drinks. Let's move through to the back bar."

They struggle through the crowd to a private rear bar that Ho uses as a 'Green Room'. James makes signs across the room to Felicia, in order to indicate their destination. She nods. Jugs of beer are waiting for them. The Dirtkickers stand to attention and give each other the Skulk Rock salute. Felicia's smiling face appears around the door frame, and she walks in with her three friends. Felicia introduces Amanda, Yolande, and Miranda to the band. The Dirtkicker's mood lifts even more. TMan tells TheGnome, "We're in Babe Basement, but these ain't no bargain broads, Baby."

The mood relaxes now as they all sit and share jokes. A couple of rounds of drinks later, they hear the next band start up. Crazy as it sounds, the rhythm slithers and menaces. It seems to slide into every corner of the rear bar, as if seeking out listeners. It demands attention. Amanda begins to dance in her seat, and finally grabs Mike Remo's lapels and teases. "I neeeeeeed to dance." The two of them wander through to the main bar, just in time to hear King Snake introduce the next song. Amanda looks a bit taken aback by the manifestation of 'The Snake Brothers'. Mike Remo also stops in his tracks. The music is hard to categorise; loose rhythms and a very bass rich sound with a mixture of blues riffs and melodic scales, that seem to worm their way into the listener's very existence.

All the Snakes seem truly scary. Singer/Frontman Snake is built solid, with a thick, dark, tattooed neck. He has thick curly greased hair, slightly grey from red, swept back, and the thick skin around his neck almost looks like some kind of 'hood'. He wrings strident chords from a tobacco sunburst Les Paul guitar. His guitar strap is snakeskin, and there is what looks like a large hunting knife sheathed on it. Mike Remo giggles to himself and sees him as a King Cobra. Drum Snake is similar, except slimmer and taller, his long limbs seeming to have extended reach. His 'sound' includes percussion effects that resemble rattlesnake rattles, and they are seamlessly incorporated into his grooves. Second Guitar Snake is sturdily built, like King Cobra Frontman, with thick stubby fingers moving efficiently over his black Les Paul guitar. His overdriven sound seems to place a 'hiss' on the edge of each note he exudes. As he plays, his tongue darts in and out of his mouth. Mike wonders to himself if they worked this 'snakiness' up, or whether it is actually how they are? Has evolution played a strange trick here? Missing links of some sort? Bass Snake is different, though. She is a slim athletic girl. Her raven black hair hangs in curtains, tending to obscure her face from the many gazes that she draws. She plays a black Fender Precision bass. She wears a black leather skirt and black/grey snakeskin jacket. Her long, slim fingers are adorned in silver jewellery. Her bass lines are integral to the sound. Unexpected, but always grooved. Mike characterises her as more birdlike than reptilian. The spotlights accentuate her collar length black hair and seem to reflect in rainbow colours from the darkness. She is a raptor, for sure. She draws his eye.

The frontman introduces himself as 'King Snake', in a voice that is both grunt and hiss. The audience are shocked into some kind of trance stance already. His manner is ugly. His words are chosen to alarm. Whether by design or by nature, King Snake and his 'band' create a negative tension. The rhythms are seductive, but the tension is inhibiting. It pulls and pushes the audience, who still want to dance, but only the drunken-most are left in gyration. Most now just stand and watch. Mike notices how strange that an electric atmosphere of good will can change into negative charge so quickly.

King Snake makes a strange gesticulation to the audience, as if to mesmerise them, his hand raising slowly upwards like a snake's head. He rings some boogie chords from his Les Paul.

Hypnosis

It's takin place - In a purple haze

Listen to what I say - As you drift away
Watch my swinging gold watch - You're gonna like it a lot
I'm taking control - Of your body and soul

**I was a superhero – but I quit
I was a hitman – 'till I got hit
Now I'm a mind reader – I got your mind and I'm lookin at it
You can't resist
You know you can't resist
No woman can resist
My hypnosis**

So you can relax - You know I'm gonna bring you back
I will count to ten – Snap my fingers and then
You will feel secure - No worries anymore
The future is my design - No point in you tryin

*To resist
This is how it is
Looking into an abyss
It's hypnosis*

**I was a superhero – but I quit
I was a hitman – 'till I got hit
Now I'm a mind reader – I got your mind and I'm lookin at it
You can't resist
You know you can't resist
No woman can resist
My hypnosis**

*You are feeling sleepy,
I know I'm sounding creepy*

**But I hope you understand
That I am in command
You are in safe hands
I got no evil plans
It's hypnosis
It's just hypnosis**

Mike Remo and Amanda are the only people dancing now. Mike is hardened to these atmospheres, and Amanda is buzzing on wine and whatever else. Maybe she truly is 'hypnotised'. They say some snakes can, and do, hypnotise victims of venom. Mike smiles at her but knows that women like Amanda won't stick around. Nevertheless, he likes her and is enjoying her temporary attachment to him. The song grooves, but somehow The Snake Brothers seem to exude too much menace. Amanda sinks into the music and is swept along, and she begins to enjoy being on display. Someone in the crowd distracts Mike, and he steps over to chat as Amanda continues to dance alone for now.

Noticing her dancing alone, Second Guitar Snake steps down from the stage and gyrates with Amanda as he riffs his guitar. As the song finishes, he leans forward with a leery whisper into Amanda's ear. Amanda looks shocked and pushes him away. He moves to walk away but, as if by a considered response, he turns and head butts Amanda, who immediately goes to the floor. The room gasps. Mike Remo turns around and sees Amanda on the floor with her nose smashed and bleeding. The audience are quiet, and in shock.

Mike Remo looks at the stage. "What the fuck?"

Yolanda and Miranda appear and help Amanda to her feet. King Cobra Snake now moves forward, looking directly at Mike Remo, hissing and grunting into the mic, his 'hood' enlarged. "Do you want the sssame shit, cssity boy? Because, if you do, stick around. Otherwise, take your city assss and your city tart and fuck right on off into the night."

Mike Remo calmly looks at King Snake, not moving an inch. From nowhere, he pulls a handgun and shoots. The shot is followed by a loud overdriven discord. King Snake staggers and looks down at his guitar.

Mike has shot his guitar and the slug is embedded in the maple capped mahogany body. Everybody is stunned. Silence reigns, until Mike Remo breaks it.

"I always wondered if a Gibson Les Paul in Tobacco Sunburst would stop a bullet?"

As King Snake steps forward, Mike Remo stares him down. "Good job you don't play an SG fat overgrown bullhead piece of shit, country boy. Will your gut smother a bullet?"

King snake shows no sign of backing down, and now has the large knife from his guitar strap in his hand. It glints under the house lights, reflecting menace. The only sound left is decaying exponentially until a loud shotgun blast shatters the airwaves, as well as the ceiling plaster above King Snake's head. Dust and debris fall down onto and all-around King Snake.

Ho Chi steps forward with a Winchester Pump in his hands. "Get the fuck out of my bar, you countly plick."

King Snake looks momentarily stunned. He is now surrounded by Ho's smartly suited muscular doormen, all in an understated martial arts pose, but coiled and ready. After some thought, however, King Snake sees the sense in Ho's suggestion. The Snakes unplug their instruments and slowly leave the bar, walking past Amanda, who is receiving attention from Felicia and her friends.

As the dust settles and Mike Remo walks over to the girls,

James sits in a corner alone, staring ahead. His face is pale in the moonlight beam through the bar skylight. He looks like a ghost.

Chapter 20
Speed Gun

James walks through a misty San Francisco morning. He takes in some views and sings to himself. As he walks across Haight, a female traffic cop manifests herself from a concealed doorway. She seems somehow full of life and energy. She is not inhibited by people on the street, as she points an electronic device at a high revving sports car with an impatient driver.

She speaks to herself as James passes. "Sonofabitch."

"Did you get him?"

The cop turns and smiles enthusiastically. "He's been hit by a speed gun."

"You a good shot with that thing?"

"I never miss. I'm the grim reaper of speed."

She points the speed gun at James and makes a gun/ricochet sound, and then 'blows across the barrel' in a mimic western style.

She smiles at James. "You better not speed around while I'm in town."

Her countenance is irrepressible, and James can't help but smile. He thinks to himself that in different circumstances he would stop and try to engage her in conversation. Maybe even get to buy her a drink when she is off duty. Maybe even get to fall in love with her. Maybe even get her to wear her uniform in private for him. He'd take a taser from her or for her, for sure. Somehow, though, his present condition doesn't seem to allow him that freedom. He tries to say all that to her in a smile, and he thinks she gets it. Telepathy is a wonderful talent that he has, especially with women. She has the female equivalent too. Their instant love affair cheers him as he steals himself the energy to walk up the hill to Ronee and Lucy's door. He rings the bell, and a Beefheart riff sounds.

Lucy answers the door, wrapped in a blanket and looking sleepy. "It's you."

"Yup. Can I come in?"

"S'pose."

"Had a heavy night?"

"I had a gig over in Oakland. Late back."

"How'd it go?"

"Good, real good."

She makes him coffee as he looks out over the rooftops. "Hey, Lucy, where's your guitar?"

From the kitchen. "Next to my bed."

James picks up the guitar and starts a chord pattern in a swing groove. He sings. "Time is upon me like a pack of wolves, Graviteeeee like an avalanche."

Lucy appears from the kitchen. "And I got sins I can't absolve, just like everyone."

They smile and both say together, "It's a keeper."

Lucy produces a pad and a pencil.

James adds, "Got a chorus start." He messes with chords. "I been hit by a speed gun - Time is a policewoman..."

Lucy contributes. "We're all on the run. The bitch is after everyone."

They laugh as they write it down.

"Let's give it some class with a key change."

"Let's give it two."

"Yeh, man."

James and Lucy are lost in a song creation whirlwind. The clouds pass by outside. They pass the guitar.

Eventually, James sings this song alone to Lucy.

Lucy smiles as if the song were a new child born to them.

Speed Gun

Time is upon me like a pack of wolves
Gravity like an avalanche
These are problems I can't solve
And I'm not the only one

Cinema in the back of my mind
Keeps replaying all of my crimes
Memories malinger
Like death's cold finger

I been hit by a speed gun
Time is a - policewoman
We're all on the run
The bitch is after everyone
Time bomb · time bomb – time bomb
Weapon of mass destruction
Fall asleep and you wake up
Fall asleep and you wake up
Fall asleep and you wake up gone

All of your memories - erased for good
By time's fell hand defaced –
In cold cold blood
I wouldn't bullshit you
Everything I say is true   .
And I'm not even tellin you
The lies you want to hear ?

How did I ever get in this condition ?
The last thing I remember was the foetal position
In a care home waitin' to die
I can still hear My Mother's lullabye

I don't think of that - just you
Our time bomb was for two
We can still escape
Better not leave it too late

We been hit by a speed gun · speed gun
Time is a - policewoman
We're all on the run
They are after everyone
Time bomb · time bomb – time bomb
It's a big explosion
Weapon of mass destruction
Fall asleep and you wake up
Fall asleep and you wake up
Fall asleep and you wake up gone

"Hey, Jimmy, that's a good song."

"It's our song, Lucy."

"Well, Jimmy, the ideas were yours."

"Wish they weren't."

"Don't say that, Jimmy. You have a keeper there."

"It's the only song I ever made up that has any truth in it, Lucy."

"I don't understand."

"Well, mostly my songs are bullshit items."

Lucy laughs. "And this isn't?"

"Nope."

"You mean you got a speeding ticket?"

"From the doctor. Yes."

Lucy partly realises his meaning, and asks, "What's the problem, Jimmy Smith?"

"Three months."

"Three months? You're not making sense."

"Six months, three months. It's how long I got."

Lucy is shocked. Her eyes fill with tears. Silence besieges the room. Eventually, James tries to be jovial. He fails miserably. "Who gives a shit? We all got to go sometime."

"I give a shit. I'm pregnant."

Silence takes over more. Neither of them says anything as they run all the cliché conversations in their minds. Eventually, Lucy walks over to him, and they embrace.

Lucy begins to sing (Smith's tune). *"What a mess I've made of my life ..."*

James replies, "No justice, is there?"

"Well, we know I'm an evil person, James. Looks like what goes around comes around? It should be me who is terminal."

"We're all terminal, Lucy. Just wish it wasn't so close."

"We need a Sydney Carton."

"We sure do."

"Do you know any Mr Darnay?"

They stare from the window.

Neither of them is emotional. James muses, "Fucking tough to make a living out of music."

He pauses. "Lucy, don't bite my head off, and I don't want to panic you, so stay calm. The Snake Brothers turned up at Ho Chi's Bar last night."

Lucy staggers and turns pale, as a black cloud passes over the sun and shadows weaves into the room. She moves away from the window and actually cowers in the corner. She slowly sinks down on her haunches. "You didn't think to tell me?"

"I just told you."

She bursts into tears. James tries to comfort her with, "We can sort this out."

Through tears, she replies, "How the fuck can I sort this out? Kill them all?"

They look at each other and manage to laugh. Lucy looks thoughtful. "Guess I'll have to move again. Fuck. I love it around here. Can you teach me the language for Manchester?"

"That's a big ask, Lucy. Maybe I can be Sydney Carton."

"You mean you'll confess to killing Seth and take my rap?"

"Wouldn't work, Lucy."

She musters a laugh. "C'mon, Jimmy English, do the decent thing."

There's another silence before Lucy adds, "Guess I could kill them all. I've already gotten one."

"Wouldn't work, Lucy."

"Oh, listen to Mr FuckinItFuckinWouldn'tFuckinWork. Why wouldn't it work? I'm already a killer."

"So am I."

Lucy stares at him incredulously. "How so, Public Enemy Number 1? Don't tell me you still think you killed your dad?"

"I did."

"You fuckin' didn't. You had an argument and, okay, used a bad word in a bad way. You never saw him again. Hardly a case of ultra-premeditated-violence."

James stares.

Lucy descends into sarcasm. "Killing someone properly needs some kind of weapon. Don't tell me you are trained in a verbal martial art and your words are officially weapons."

James enters the sarcasm war with an irony torpedo. "Well, such is the power of my poetry I can reduce living beings to rotting carcasses with carefully chosen word bolts."

James is anything but jovial. Tearful would be closer to an apt description. He disguises it well.

Lucy manages to regain some self-awareness and goes for fake bravado. "Get over it, you lily-livered limey."

James follows suit. "Sonofabitch took my guitar and smashed it."

Lucy's mind is immediately transported back to Montana, and tears roll down her cheeks. "I know that feeling. Any jury would return not guilty verdict. Extenuating circumstances."

Unexpectedly she holds him. Safety in numbers.

James carries on. "I should never have left home."

Lucy calmly replies, "Yes, you told me."

James rambles. "Carousel was my dad's favourite musical."

There's a silence. Lucy holds him, then she softly sings:

'If I loved you, words wouldn't come in an easy way…'

James responds by singing some of Billy Bigelow's lines.

'You can't hear a sound, not the turn of a leaf

Nor the fall of a wave hittin' the sand.

The tide's creepin' up on the beach like a thief,

Afraid to be caught stealin' the land.

On a night like this I start to wonder

What life is all about?'

"We don't know what love is about either, do we, Jimmy Smith?"

"Love is looking after kids, Lucy Smith. All that's left of us is love."

"Well looks like we need a Sydney Carton and a Billy Bigelow and a Phillip Larkin?"

"Or, more realistically, maybe I'd better just leave town."

"No. Leave it with me, Lucy, and I will sort this shit out."

As they embrace, two ravens stand silently on the ledge outside the window, their blackness scattering sunlight into shards of silver and frozen blue.

Chapter 21
Hound Dog Man

James lies in bed. It's Monday morning. He listens to the city sounds drifting across rooftops and up the hill to his flat. Life has been different since his condition became known to his friends. They all make time to see him and talk or, more importantly, listen. So much so, that sometimes he enjoys his downtime alone. This morning, he watches a disc of light progress across the wall, plotting its arc in his mind. It reminds him of his bedroom at home. He kills those thoughts and gets out of bed. He makes himself a pot of tea and goes through the ceremony of Doctor Charlie's medicines. He hears a Harley pass by outside. A few minutes later, there is an irregular thumping on the door, a few flights of stairs below. As he negotiates the stairs, he is reminded of the old 'drummer at the door' joke. He giggles as he remembers trying to use that joke on TheGnome one time.

TheGnome had asked him, "What's the difference between a gynaecologist and a drummer?"

"Okay, Gnomio. What is the difference between a gynaecologist and a drummer?"

"A gynaecologist only works with one cunt at a time." Followed by TheGnome dance.

That must be why he now expects to see TheGnome accentuating an irregular door knocking. His expectations are proven wrong as he opens the door to the spectacle of Marv in full Angel regalia, complete with red bandana.

James blurts, "I got the $1400, Marv. I just haven't had chance to bring it over."

Marv smiles. "No worries, James English."

James laughs.

Marv continues, "But a coffee would be nice."

Marv follows James upstairs. As Marv sits, he produces a hip flask and adds some liquor to his coffee. He offers it to

James, who figures it might be polite not to refuse. Marv does the honours.

"Michael Remo tells me you had some trouble with those Snakefuckers the other night."

"We surely did, Marv. Mike pulled a gun."

"His Ma always took a gun to gigs. Looks like she trained young Michael well too? You can never be too careful, Jimmy."

Marv sips his coffee and makes a "chaaaaaaa" sound of satisfaction. "Thing is, Jimmy E, you can forget the $1400. We can call it quits, if you can do a little job for me and Don?"

James is somewhat relieved, as he isn't quite sure he can lay his hands on $1400, without asking Mike for help.

He smiles. "Sure thing, Marv."

"We don't like those Snakefuckers one little bit either, and we need to get a tracker on to their vehicle, so we can locate their whereabouts at any time."

James nods, in awe of Marv. He is being ushered into a higher echelon in the Kingdom of Marv.

Marv confides, "We figured you might know the places they might be gigging and could find an opportunity to deploy a tracker for us."

Marv produces a small device with a magnetic base. He walks over and sticks it to James' fridge.

"I'd be happy to, Marv. But what is your interest?"

"They behaved in a threatening manner to us. Big mistake, Jimmy. Don is worried they might find out where little Lucy lives, and, as you well know, she lives with Ronee. And you know Ronee is Don's daughter?"

"I didn't know that Marv."

"Well, there you go. We would just be happier if we knew where they were. Bringing up kids is tricky for me and Don."

James nods again. "I'd love to help Marv. I need to know where they are too."

Marv smiles. "Marv's Motors have the technology, Jimmy."

He looks out of the window. "Nice view, Jimmy E. Nice day for a ride out to Marin. Let me know."

James nods again, and they shake hands. He feels honoured somehow to be given a task by Marv. Not to mention the cancellation of his debt. He shows Marv to the door and stands watching as Marv kicks his Harley to life. The engine grooves a slow tempo initially, until Marv kicks its song into a faster beat, and accelerates away up the hill. James returns upstairs and looks in his various underground music press mags.

He speaks to himself. "Okay, Mr King Snake and The Lowdown Snakefuckers, where are you sons of bitches playing next?" He spots an ad. "Ah-ha, Mad Lennie's Bar."

James thinks to himself what a nightmare gig that will be. Mike Remo hates the place and won't book the Dirtkickers there. Too much tension, too much anger, and too little security. San Francisco's underground post punk, melt metal, trip tide, gothic groove, psycho soundscape scene. It's a nightmare for drugs, violence, and shit-rock.

"Best place for The Snakes, though," James muses to himself. "Maybe they'll get massacred."

**

Fate decrees that the night of the The Snake's gig is a no-gig night for The Dirtkickers. James ostensibly fixes with Mike to borrow the Dirtkicker van to take Lucy to Sausalito for a meal in the Muso Café they both know. In reality, he motors across town and sits in the Dirtkicker van at the rear of Mad Lennie's Bar. He feels guilty to deceive Mike Remo. Needs must. The clientele spill onto the streets. Some fight, some stagger, some puke, and some zone out to a twilight world of dark lights and even darker shadows. James watches impassively. Two younger guys stagger past.

He exits the van. "Who's playing there tonight, guys?"

"The Snakemen or something. Wild night. Too much for us."

"Have they finished?"

"Nah, there's another set yet. Way too crazy for us."

James climbs back into the van and waits until he hears the set start. He recognizes the bass lines escaping the building fabric. The bass can always find a way. It's later and the surroundings are otherwise quiet. All the clientele has moved back into the venue. He picks up Marv's tracker. He walks around the venue to the car park and loading bays. He sees the Snake-Van, as described by Marv, parked close by a two-storey brick wall. He checks no-one is around and quickly lies on his back, attaching the tracker device to the concealed side of a structural chassis member. He checks it is stable and safe. As he carefully rolls out from under the vehicle, he hears a faint fluttering noise. He is panicked a little, although he disguises it well. Nevertheless, relieved to find no-one there. He stands and looks around, with his back to the van, assuming the noise to have been the breeze blowing something around. He turns to take one last look at the Snake-Van, and staggers in shock as

he looks up to see a bird the size of turkey perched on the rear of the vehicle. His stagger forces him backwards to stumble over a kerbed walkway and onto his ass. He now realises that the bird is no turkey, as it opens a vast wingspan and floats to the ground. He thinks to himself, "It's a fucking eagle!" His mind panics. The eagle bends his head under the Snake-Van, as if to see what James has been doing. The bird then walks slowly towards James, who is frozen. It turns its head to one side and stares. He feels like it is staring into his mind. The eagle now turns and runs two or three steps, before becoming airborne.

James shakes as he regains his feet, tries to slow his heart rate and trembles his way back to the parked Dirtkicker van. In the van, he shakes as his composure slowly returns. He wonders if it was a 'vision' induced by his 'medication', but he takes another 'Doctor Charlie' anyway.

In time, the bass groove fades to a long decay, and clientele begin to spill out of the club. They mill around, slowly disappearing into the night. Eventually, he sees King Snake standing on the sidewalk outside the venue. There is a full moon over his head and his aura reaches out scarily. James shrinks further into his seat and watches impassively from the van, his eyes just above the dash. He sees the other Snakes appear as they load instruments back into the van. Then, there is a deep throated diesel sound as The Snake-Van starts and moves around to the front of the club. The tall, slim figure of the female bass player appears from a rear door, as King Snake wanders back into the club. James once again notices how slim, athletic, and attractive she is. The moonlight suits her. A few minutes later, King Snake reappears from the club and climbs into the Snake-Van. It moves off. James grips the steering wheel of the Dirtkicker van with white knuckles as he starts it up. He follows the Snake-Van at a safe distance. This was not in Marv's brief, but James is wired for the task. Good old Dr Charlie. The Snake-Van travels out of town, west towards the ocean.

Hound Dog Man

There was a tear in my eye – but it long since dried
I said goodbye – but it was a lie
Hear me howl like a wolf – a wolf in the night
Hound dog dreams never turn out right

They look for me - but I can't be found
They want me gone - but I'm still around
My hound dog heart beats with no sound
I bury my hound dog bones – deep underground

I'm a hound dog · I'm a hound dog man
I'm comin for you · Just as fast as I can
I'm a hound dog · I'm a hound dog man
I'm comin for you · Just as fast as I can

I follow rivers and drink from lakes
I watch and I wait – until I get my break
I'm always on the take
I got a million dollars to make
Ice turning black no turnin back on this highway
This is no place for a cry baby
Fate is a gambler – he will deal your hand
You always need an alternative plan

Cos I'm a hound dog · I'm a hound dog man
I'm comin for you · Just as fast as I can
But I'm a hound dog · I'm a hound dog man
I'm comin for you · Just as fast as I can

So I'm steppin off a plane In your neighbourhood
I find my way Through the darkest wood
So I'm on a ship The stars are looking good
I'm on your scent I can smell your blood

I'm a hound dog · I'm a hound dog man
I'm comin for you · Just as fast as I can
I'm a hound dog · I'm a hound dog man
I'm comin for you · Just as fast as I can

He follows at a distance for a streetlight hour, until the Snake-Van pulls into a high fenced rental property. James pulls off the highway nearby and makes full note of the location. It's useful information, but his mind has no plan, yet.

It's a clear night, and whatever Dr Charlie has him on shows no sign of abating. He should never have taken the extra dose, and he mentally blames the eagle. He decides to look out over the ocean once again, as it is nearby. He gets back on the highway and heads west. As he cruises the coastal highway, heading south, he sees a 'viewpoint' sign and turns down an access road. The road leads him to a secluded car park, with the ocean laid out in front of him. The moon hangs on its gravity and stars are visible. James gets out of the van, and the sound of the rollers breaking obscures the noise of any traffic on the nearby highway. As he turns around, he sees a steep drop to the beach below, probably about fifty feet. He looks at the drop and notices sail boats parked on the beach below and to the left.

He wonders how you would get a boat down there and eventually discovers a zig zag ramp at the far end of the viewpoint parking area. A tractor is parked nearby. Looking to his left, a dirt road runs steeply upwards, behind a row of poplar trees, to some rough agricultural land. He wonders to himself how long it will be before that is developed for yet another coast side resort. He walks over and looks at the land. As he walks back to the Dirtkicker van, a plan does begin to form in his mind.

**

The following day finds James driving The Dog cross town once more heading for Marv's Motors once again. Marv looks out from the workshop and walks out half glaring, half staring at James.

"Fuck me, Jimmy E. Thought I'd seen the back of this old 'Dawg'."

"Hey, Marv. I deployed the tracker, but I got another problem."

James tells Marv selected details of The Snake problem. He tells him that circumstances have changed, and Lucy is pregnant.

"Congratulations, Jimmy English, we heard you are always falling in 'lerv'. Now you will find out about the associated problems." Marv seems more patient than usual.

James laughs but tells Marv he needs rid of The Snakes once and for all. Marv is now a little more edgy.

"I don't know any hit men, Jimmy E. Maybe, just maybe, you might tell the 'authoriteeeeees'?"

"Can't do that, Marv, and it ain't the advice I would expect from you."

Marv suddenly stops in his tracks. He looks around his yard, as if trying to get his bearings. He seems to suddenly return from his mental excursion, and he turns to stare at James.

"Goddam. You're right, Jimmy English. What was I thinking and what was I saying? What the fuck came over me?

Strike all that from the record. Next time you hear me talking complete shit, Jimmy English, I want you to kick me in the nuts. And hard."

James laughs. "Not sure I could do that, Marv. Maybe a polite reminder that you are talking like a pillock."

Marv becomes silent, and slowly turns to stare hard at James. James is faced with a decision. Does he try and bluff this out or does he run like a motherfucker before Marv pulls his head off, or worse? What could be worse? James is sure Marv could think of something.

"I ain't never been called a pillock, Jimmy English. What is it?"

James struggles to find an answer. "I'm not really sure, Marv. It's a word we used in England. Not very complimentary, and I apologise."

"Apologies not necessary, Jimmy Boy. Marv was talking like a 'pillock', for sure."

"I'm sure it won't happen again, Marv."

Marv laughs. *"That's right The Mascara Snake – fast and bulbous."*

"Bulbous also tapered."

"Also, a tin teardrop."

They both laugh at the Captain Beefheart quotes, until James turns serious. "Hey, Marv, I'm gonna ram the shit out of them."

Marv laughs. "That's my boy!"

James continues. "I need an edge, though. Can you fit me a super-safe and shock resistant driver seat into The Dog?"

Marv looks vacantly and puzzled at him.

"Please, Marv, I'm serious here."

Marv seems perplexed, rubbing his chin. "You wanna waste your time and money on crazy schemes, Jimmy, I'll take your money. I can put a drag racer's bucket seat and shock mount it for you. 250 bucks. Come back in two days."

James realises Marv wants the conversation over. He confirms his requirements and counts out the money. James walks out of the yard and Marv watches him go, shaking his head.

**

James is floating now, as he crosses town. His thoughts blur and whirl. He thinks of Lucy and worries about how he left her tense, by mentioning The Snakes. He hopes she hasn't done anything crazy, like left town. The worry builds in his mind and he panic-rushes over to the house. As he rings the door chime, there is no reply. He shouts through the letter box. Eventually, the door slowly opens, and Lucy's nervous face manages a smile. As she invites him in, he sees her rucksack in the centre of the room and the Nick Lucas case nearby.

"Lucy, you can't leave town."

"I have to."

"No. I'm going to sort this out."

She holds him. "You can't, and it's not your problem, is it?"

"Yes, it is my problem. It's our child, isn't it?"

"Yes, it must be. Unless it's the new Messiah."

"The Manchester Messiah. Rock and Roll."

They fall silent and Lucy makes coffee. As James sits on the couch, he moves a box to one side and notices its weight. Curiosity makes him lift off the top, and he sees Howard's gun in there, along with the ammunition.

As Lucy returns, she sees him looking at the contents. "It was a gift."

James looks open mouthed. "Hey, LuLu, we don't want to do anything stupid here. Do we?"

"You tell me. You're the one being stupid thinking you can 'negotiate' with The Snakes."

"No, I have a plan. No negotiation."

Lucy looks at him and shakes her head. "There's nothing you can do James. Nothing!"

He stares back with madness in his eyes. "Give me a few more days."

Her emotions take over and her tears flow. She collapses on the couch beside him. James holds her. Maybe it's Doctor

Charlie's treatment plan, or maybe the circumstances, or maybe both, but his mind brings everything into sharp focus. It must generate a confident tone in his voice because she calms down and agrees.

"You won't do anything stupid then, Jimmy Smith?"

"Of course not. But could I borrow your gun?"

She turns in fake shock now. They both laugh.

"I really do have a plan, Lucy."

She nods in implicit agreement. Together, they work out how to load the gun. As James slots in the last cartridge and clicks the barrel closed, she says, "We're children in a grown-up's world here, James Smith. But it's grown-ups who have fucked this world."

"We're growing up fast here Jimmy."

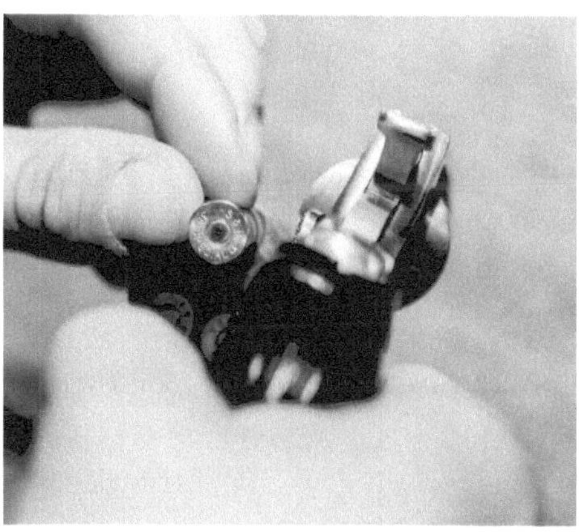

Chapter 22
Park and Ride

Marv has the dragster bucket seat in the middle of the yard, as Don rides in on his Harley 'Softail'. "What's goin' on, Marv?"

"You wouldn't believe me."

"Try me."

Marv continues attaching the seat to a steel frame with resilient shock mounts, as Don walks around the job.

"Not another drag racer, Marv?"

"Nope, young Jimmy English from The Dirtkickers says he is gonna ram the crap out of the Snakefuckers!"

"What?"

"Oh yeh, man. He reckons he needs rid of them. Says he's gonna ram them." Marv giggles. "And he needs a safety seat in his truck."

Don is laughing. "Well, I suppose it would solve our problems."

"Not sure it would solve his. Since Mike Remo told us about his illness, I figured I might cut the little limey some slack. Having a 'project' to work on might take his mind off things."

Marv and Don look at each other, and then nod in agreement. "He's not your average stoner."

"He tells me his little girlfriend Lucy is gonna have to leave town, if he don't get these guys off of her back."

"Awwww, he's in love again."

"Sounds like it. She's pregnant to prove it. Mike Remo does say he is a sucker for the women. Dumb limey. I dunno, though. He is a good kid."

Marv bolts up the resilient shock mounts and wobbles the seat in the frame to check everything. Don helps. They work efficiently together.

"You know what, Marv, I kinda like that little Lucy."

"Reckon so. Mike Remo has got her onto the music circuit. That's how English Jimmy met her. Fate fucks us all about."

"Yup. There's something else going on here, Marv."

"Right enough. Anyway, he did tell me he'd fitted that tracker."

"Daughters, Marv. You gotta love 'em, but they are a worry all your life. Can't leave anything to chance."

"Goddam right. Maybe we'd better keep a good eye on this situation."

Don and Marv continue fitting the seat and frame into The Dog. It's an ugly fit with visible bolt-work out of the roof, but it seems to work well, as Marv tests it with a few emergency-stops around the yard. On Don's suggestion, they also weld on a heavy set of bull bars to the front.

"It's a tank, Marv."

**

Across town, James meets Felicia once more in Boudin's. The electricity's somehow gone from their secret liaison. "Hey, Flea. How's the fiancée?"

"Rich is out of town for a week or so."

"How is Amanda?"

"Broken nose. Got reset. She has good cover."

"I'm so sorry."

"She lost one of her modelling contracts."

James repeats. "So, so sorry."

Felicia smiles. "Not your fault, Jimmy E."

Felicia's gaze moves slowly around, and out across the Bay. Her expression is cold, like James has never seen before.

"Who were those snake guys? I hate them."

"Long story, Flea. I need to deal with them. Could use your help."

"Count me in, Jimmy E. I need an adventure."

"Could be this Friday, when they have a gig over at Fisherman's Wharf."

"And your plan is?"

**

James arrives back at Marv's Motors, later that day. He is absorbed in his circumstances. Tunnel vision. He stares straight ahead, walking into Marv's office. Marv and Don are in an embrace, and James does not even notice.

"Don't you fuckin' limeys ever knock?"

James apologises. Marv laughs, and the three of them walk out to where The Dog sits in the yard.

"We put some crash bars on the front there. Thought that might be useful too."

"Oh, wow, never thought of that. Do I owe you?"

"On the house, Jimmy E. Here's your $250 back. You'd be helping us out if this goes down according to plan."

James tries the seat. Marv and Don look at each other, with puzzled expressions.

Marv asks, "When is your big hit taking place, Jimmy E?"

James is a little lost in thought, as he struggles with the pilot style safety harness. "Their next gig will be their last."

"When's that?"

"Tonight, at Bay Sounds on the Wharf."

Marv and Don smile at each other.

Don asks one last question. "Hey, Jimmy, those snake guys don't know where your little girlfriend lives, do they?"

"No, and they never will."

Don walks to James and put an arm around his shoulder. "You take care, Jimmy. Not everybody is up to this kind of work. No way of really telling if someone has it in them. It's a little like a gig, Jimmy Boy. When you're up there, you got to go for it. Half measures don't work. It's your gig and no-one else's. No half measures. No room for Jimmy Nice-Guy on this job."

James looks at Don. His self-esteem is heightened by this friendly 'advice'. He has been inducted. He's not exactly sure what he has been inducted into, but it expands his confidence.

Marv and Don look at each other as James drives out of the yard.

"Do you think he can pull this off?"

"Could be a gig too far for young Jimmy."

"We'd better keep a good eye on this one Don."

**

As the evening arrives, James parks The Dog on the street, just along from the Bay Sounds' venue. He walks up to the venue and hears the muffled Snake-Rock from within. He thinks to himself. *"Love those bass lines."*

A guy staggers out of the venue, with blood pouring from his nose. James asks the doorman what time the gig is due to end. He goes back to sit in The Dog.

An hour or so later, Felicia's Porsche pulls up behind him. Felicia has changed her hair and outfit, and looks her usual stunning self, if a little different. She looks just a little too overtly sexy, in James' opinion.

"Don't worry, Jimmy E. I do know how to pull dumb guys as well as rich guys." She smiles and giggles, although James detects her nervousness too.

"You do know where you've got to take them, Flea?"

"Of course. You showed me."

"Any problems, bale out. If you're not there by 2:45am, abort the mission."

"Acknowledge, Affirmative, Roger, Over and Out." Felicia is good at mischievousness.

James looks at his watch. "It's about time."

He kisses her on the cheek, and she confidently descends from the Dog and walks to the venue. James sighs as he watches her walk (like only Felicia can walk). He sees her walk

to the Bay Sounds' entrance and enter. The door-guy can't help himself look her up and down. She enters the gig, buys a wine, and works her way to the front. As she emerges from the front of the mosh, Jake Snake immediately locks his stare onto her. Felicia stares back and wins 'Round 1' of the psychological cage fight, as Jake is the one to look away first.

His guttural, hissy patter over the mic seems to command a silence. "This-sss is our las-sss-t groove for tonight. You CityBillyMotherFuckers don't pay enough for any encores. You been 'sssss-naked', though."

He looks at Felicia once again. "If'n you want more sssssss-naking ... you're welcome."

His eyes narrow and his tongue darts in and out. Felicia shivers, but she doesn't let it show.

King Snake continues. "Thissss one is called Park and Ride."

His black eyes seem to burrow into her mind as he stares at her, before Sly Snake drumlicks the song into life.

Park and Ride

Why don't you and I try park and ride
All you gotta do is step outside
Come and see what I got
It's waiting outside in the parking lot

I got a line laid out on the dash
You got time and I got cash
Baby, you got that touch of class
You are a fine piece of ass

**Why don't we try – park and ride
Time is never on your side
How do you know if you never tried?
Why don't you and I try park and ride**

I run a Gold Buick Six
I like to ride and I need my fix
My bullshit – is bonafide
I'm the only prophet who never lied

**Why don't we try – park and ride
Time is never on your side
How do you know if you never tried?
Why don't you and I try park and ride**

When I got my black Cadillac
I told my Daddy I'm not comin back
There's a highway right outside
The stars will be my guide

As the rhythm kicks, the audience start to groove. The Snake Brothers have quickly built a following. The audience have a 'snake dance'. Stoners, pissheads, musos all enter the spirit. Felicia joins but doesn't join. Her charisma can look after itself.

Jake Snake keeps staring at Felicia. He can't resist. She holds his gaze, as she sways to the music. He plays a guitar break, without losing his eye-lock on her. She keeps cool and her aura matches his. Inwardly, she struggles, swearing at him beneath her breath. Her skin crawls and she wonders if she is turning into a snake herself. She fights his mental probing until the end of the song.

As the song ends in crescendo, Jake Snake launches himself upwards and forwards from the stage, and lands with the precision of a gymnast directly in front of Felicia. Still, she stares him out. The audience is silent and watching. Jake seems to expand the loose skin behind his neck, and hisses as his tongue darts in and out.

As he stops, Felicia leans forward and whispers, "I know the perfect place to park and ride. I can show you, if you're outside and ready to roll in thirty minutes?"

She turns and melts into the crowd. King scans the mosh and sees her disappear through one of the exits. He turns and tells Sly, Si, and AJ to pack up quick. "Fucking quick."

Jake explains, "The bitch in the mosh wants snaking, and King Snake is on the case."

King finds the promoter and picks up the $1400 they had agreed. The promoter tries to shake his hand. King ignores him. "Next time, the price is $2000."

The promoter nods.

King adds. "$3000, if you want to spend time with AJ on bass?"

The promoter laughs, but King just stares. "Think about it. Sssssssssssssss."

The Snakes quickly pack up their equipment and pack it into the Snake-Van. As King checks his watch, he drives slowly out of the parking lot, scanning the street. He suddenly spots Felicia waiting in her open top Porsche parked on the street. She pauses to give a wave and accelerates away from the kerbside. The Snakes 'whoop and holler'. They sing 'Park and Ride' in the Snake-Van as they follow. Jake Snake grips the steering wheel tightly, his eyes locked in concentration. Felicia alternates her speed.

Sly Snake warns. "The bitch is winding you up, Pa."

"No, boy. She's hot for it. Believe me." He shakes his head and flaps the loose skin behind his neck.

"Pa, she could take us miles out of our way?"

"I don't care. I'm hot tonight."

Si Snake shouts excitedly from the back, "Can I go in after you, Pa?"

"You could, boy, but I'm going to destroy her."

In the back, AJ looks up with a frown.

Si asks, "Really destroy her, pa?"

"Enough that she don't forget the experience forever, boy."

Si lets out a hiss-whistle. "Make it permanent, Pa."

Sly looks across and hisses too, "Yeh."

The three of them are focussed now. AJ shrinks into her seat in the back. She's never seen them this bad. As the Snake-Van reaches an elevated highway, she gazes out of the window to her right. The moon hangs low, and she sees an eagle against its disc of silver light. The speed of the eagle seems to match theirs, such that it stays over the moon disc. She mutters to herself,  "Ooljee, Ajei, Atsah." (In Assiniboine, her mother's name, her name and great eagle). The eagle looks over at her.

**

James reaches the viewpoint car park and is relieved it is deserted. He carefully backs The Dog about one hundred yards up the dirt track, under cover of the poplar trees. He is strapped into the pilot seat Marv has welded into the Dog Truck. He looks at his watch. He keeps the engine running. He takes one of the pills Doctor Charlie has given him. Moonlight reflects over the water. The breakers crash in with a regularity tonight, creating a broadband wash of sound. There is not much wind, but there must have been a storm, miles out in the ocean. He thinks of Lucy and her stories about the moon. He looks at his watch. It's 2:35. He worries about Felicia. He worries about his plan. He checks his safety harness clips. He checks the safety strap Marv has fitted to restrain his forehead. His heart beats out a fast shuffle rhythm, and the breaking waves like crash cymbals, accentuating his thoughts. Could this really work? Doubts crawled into his mind. Too late to stop now (wasn't that a Van Morrison album?). His fingers cramp up as he tight-grips The Dog steering wheel. He keeps the engine ticking over.

**

On the coastal highway, now. Felicia keeps her speed to regulation 55mph. She keeps a vigil on the Snake-Van behind. It stays a steady 30 yards behind.

Sly Snake watches her intently from the passenger seat. "Don't lose her, Pa."

He looks over at Jake Snake, and two veins bulge on his moonlit forehead, as Felicia reaches the sign for the viewpoint. Jake laughs. "This is so convenient. Not a long drive home after she's dogmeat."

"You gonna be tired, Pa?"

Si snake is excited now. "Bet her husband bought her that car too."

"You bet he did, boy."

"We gonna teach her a few more tricksssssssss tonight."

Felicia rounds a final corner and slows. She turns into the viewpoint, about 50 yards ahead of the Snake-Van. As she halts the car, she looks to her right and sees the row of poplar trees. She adjusts her parking position forward by a few yards and looks in her mirror; exactly where she and James had planned.

James sees her headlights coming down the access road and revs The Dog ready. He checks the restraint around his forehead. He sees The Snake-Van behind her. His mind buzzes. The Doctor's pills work just fine. His thoughts are clear as the moon, clear as a wavy bend. He accelerates. He hits 50mph, as The Snake-Van pulls up behind Felicia.

Jake Snake's window is down, but he doesn't hear The Dog screaming down the hill, because of the sound of the ocean rollers breaking on the moonlit sand, 50 feet below.

Jake sees Felicia turn her head, and tells Sly, "She's mine now, boy. Told you she wanted snaking. Sssssssss"

As he turns to open the door, it's too late.

James hits 60mph, as he switches on the headlights. He sees King Snake turn his big head. Time seems to freeze as he sees King Snake's eyes narrow and his tongue dart. James must be 6 feet from King Snake at impact. He doesn't remember much else, other than opening his eyes again as he slams backwards and forwards in Marv's safety seat. The Dog has stopped dead at impact. As he focusses, he sees the Snake-Van catapult to the cliff edge. It is almost stopped by a row of low rocks that tourists can sit on looking out to sea. It teeters, and then rolls over and out of sight, down the cliff. Amazingly, The Dog's lights still work, and their beams shine out over the cliff and the ocean.

**

The Dog oscillates back and forth on its suspension, and the Snake-Van has disappeared into the void. A dust-cloud is all that remains. Felicia, out of the Porsche now, walks forward to the edge, just in time to see the Snake-Van bounce down the rocks and onto the beach. She watches for a while, before turning and looking at The Dog. James sits in the pilot seat, looking shocked. Felicia looks in through his window. "You okay, Jimmy E?"

"Think so."

"Mission accomplished."

"Looks that way."

"It's put Snake Rock back by 10 years."

"It is history, Felicia."

"So are we, Jimmy E. We better be gone."

"Are you okay, Flea?"

"Yeh. Not the first guys I killed. Sexist bastards."

James looks a little surprised.

Felicia finds a smile. "Only joking Jimmy E, but don't worry, I love you." She walks forward, kisses him and, as she begins to walk away, she turns. "We're so bad, Jimmy English. Aren't we?"

Before James can formulate a reply, she is back in the Porsche and disappearing away up towards the highway. He manoeuvres The Dog into a parking position and switches the headlights off. He feels some kind of relief as the thought of telling Lucy that he has solved her problems, begins to seem a possibility. It circulates in his mind. He walks forward and looks over the cliff edge. The Snake-Van is upside down on the beach, steam rising from it. Shouldn't it have burst into flames like the movies? As he stares, a shadow crosses the moon, and he looks up to see the eagle. It takes his eye, as it glides slowly downwards, zig-zagging as if checking for a safe landing. It lands on a rock near the Snake-Van and, as James' eyes follow it in amazement, he double-blinks as he discerns a movement from one of its doors thrown open. He looks more closely, closing and opening his eyes as wide as he can in an effort to improve his vision. His heart thumps like a kick drum through a reflex bass cabinet. He senses panic rising. He looks one way, and then the other. He remembers Lucy's gun and walks quickly over to The Dog. He looks on the seat where he had left it and is shocked to find it gone. His mind jolts in panic, before he realises it must have been thrown forward in the impact. He finds the gun in the passenger side footwell, with a scattering of shells around it. He picks up the gun and walks to the cliff edge again. Two figures are now visible, crawling from the wreckage below. He walks quickly to the path beside the access ramp and begins to descend to the beach below.

The path leads to the beach, about 50 yards south of where the Snake-Van has landed. James cocks the pistol and slowly walks towards the upturned vehicle. As he walks, he sees two figures on their feet and slowly pulling a third person from the wreckage of the Snake-Van. His mind whirls. *"This was not part of the plan?"* For some strange reason, he admonishes himself for stating the obvious. The ocean rollers make a loud noise but, even so, he slows his walk, as if to remain undetected. He realises he is shaking. With no logical reasoning, he holds the gun out unsteadily in front of him. As he gets to some 25 yards from what are now three people standing, Sly Snake looks along the beach and wipes blood from his eyes. He blinks and stares at James. James stops in his tracks. As James is frozen, Sly turns and taps King Snake on the shoulder. King slowly turns and his stare hardens on James. James freezes, as he seems to see the skin behind King Snakes neck expand. A voice in his head screams. "Oh fuck, oh fuck, oh fuck." He sees King Snake speak to Sly and Si. They immediately separate, standing three or four yards from each other. James notices they are all limping badly. He doesn't know which one to point the gun at, and eventually he settles for King Snake. King Snake's deep-hiss voice induces a shock through his whole body and consciousness.

"Where is the Woodpecker?"

James wonders if he is hearing correctly. *"Woodpecker? What the fuckin-fuck is he on about?"*

Sly and Si are scanning the objects that were in the Snake-Van, but which are now strewn over the beach. James tries to work out which one to shoot first, but his mind is frozen. His consciousness begins to sink. His mind swims in random thoughts. In the midst of this, his eye is taken by another movement at the upturned Snake-Van. A long, dark shadow begins to emerge from the rear of the vehicle. Time itself freezes, his mind freezes, and the gun in his hand seems to double in weight. He tries to point the gun at the shadow. He hears Sly Snake shout, "SnakeDog." The shadow suddenly swivels, and James realises it is some kind of dog. He is now convinced this is a nightmare and he can't wake. SnakeDog is long and low slung. Some crazy muscular attack daschund, its black coat shining in the moonlight. He hears a voice shout. "SnakeDog, kill." He sees the dog scan around, until its eyes lock on to him. It then rapidly accelerates towards him. The dog's white teeth are clearly visible as it emits a strange hiss-growl. Whatever, it triggers some kind of wakeup call in James' mind. Some remnant of Doctor Charlie's medication kicks into gear. James points the pistol at the advancing dog. He fires once, and the dog keeps coming. He fires again, with the same result. He whimpers, as he fires a third time, with the SnakeDog about ten yards away. The bullet finds a mark on the animal's back. It howls and falls. It rolls, and it seems its rear legs are paralysed. It truly slithers like a snake, screaming at James. As it gets closer, James finds the presence of mind to wait until he can't miss. He fires a fourth time, and SnakeDog is quiet and still, with a bullet through its head. It is frozen motionless in the soft sand.

"Welcome to San Francisco FuckingSnakeFuckingDog."

King Snake is now limping slowly towards James, his 'hood' massively visible. James burns in the gaze of his red eyes. Sly Snake is also approaching, having found a large hunting knife amongst the debris. Si Snake is still looking around amongst the flotsam items. James points the gun and tells them to freeze. He hears his own voice sounding ridiculous and having no effect on either King or Sly. Instead, he is the one who freezes.

The sound of the ocean seems to change its timbre now, for no reason. So much so that everyone stops. As the noise gets louder, James realises it is an engine. He swivels to look behind as one, two, and then three Harleys swing around from the ramp down to the hard sand, lower down the beach. Each of the riders produce sawn off shotguns from somewhere on the bike, and before James can think they are past him. Three blasts in quick succession shock his sensitive musician's ears. Sly Snake flies backwards and hits the sand, and Si Snake shortly afterwards. King is hit and staggers to his knees, before falling onto his back. James sinks to his knees in shock, as if he's been hit himself.

The bikes sweep around on the hard sand and move towards him. They stop their engines, and Don, Marv, and Al step off. Al and Marv check on the fallen bodies. Don stands over King Snake and a fourth blast makes his body jump. James sinks further to the ground, as King Snake seems to make one final effort to get up. Then, one last long gurgle-hiss, before he lies motionless on the sand.

Chapter 23

Last Pistol Shot

James slowly tilts forward, until his elbows hit the sand. He grips Lucy's pistol, his breathing quick and shallow. Marv walks over to him and helps him to his feet.

"Well, you certainly got some balls, Jimmy E." He pauses, before continuing. "You'd never make an Angel. But you do got balls."

Don laughs. "We are guardian Angels, Jimmy Boy."

Angel Al is wandering around the beach, looking at the detritus. He bends to retrieve an object, and then walks over with a strange boxy-looking weapon.

Don is immediately alerted to it. "Al, you be careful with that thing."

Al points it to the sand and pulls the trigger. It begins to jump in his hand, sounding like a woodpecker. James then realises what King Snake had meant when he was asking where the woodpecker was. Al manages to control the gun, and Don walks over and takes it from him.

A slight movement from the upturned Snake-Van alerts them all, as AJ Snake's head emerges, and she slowly crawls out of the rear of the van. Blood pours down the side of her face from a head wound. Her straight black hair reflects the clear moonlight. They watch her struggle to her feet. James automatically walks over to help her. She looks at him in dazed surprise. As she looks around, she sees the bodies of the two dead Snake Brothers. She looks down impassively. Don pumps his Winchester to put a cartridge into the breach. James supports AJ as she stumbles towards the body of King Snake. She looks down at him for a few seconds, before spitting on his face. Marv flinches.

Don is first to break the silence. "She's got to go." He looks at Marv, as if seeking confirmation.

James immediately stands in front of her. "No, enough madness."

Marv laughs. "Jimmy English, a gallant English knight."

Angel Al begins to raise his weapon, still complying with Don's last instruction. There is what seems at first like a gust of wind, a sound like paper blowing in the breeze; enough to make them all turn their heads. A shadow passes across the moon and Al is suddenly enveloped by a large, feathered bird. He shouts and struggles but loses the battle and finishes flat on his back on the sand. The eagle flies off with Al's Winchester pump gun in its talons. It soars into the sky, and then out over the bay. From about 100 metres height, and clearly visible in moonlight reflecting off the ocean, it drops the shotgun into the middle of the bay.

Al stands up, indignant and embarrassed. "Goddam fuckin' duck."

AJ turns to face Don. She looks straight into his eyes, as she uses her hands to move the curtain of hair away from the blooded side of her face. James looks at the wound. He takes his handkerchief out and dabs at the wound. AJ grabs the material and holds it to the wound. "I'll live."

She stares at Don, selecting him as the leader, before continuing, "They're gone. I'm glad."

She pauses again. "I am my mother's daughter and that (she points at King) was never my father, nor them (she gesticulates towards Sly and Si) my brothers. They have owned my mother and I for as long as I can remember. I am Ajei and my mother is Ooljee. We have sought freedom for years. My mother has paid with her youth and beauty."

She staggers. James quickly helps her. Don still stares, holding his weapon.

Ajei makes a kind of yodelling sound, part music and part wail. There's a fluttering sound from above and, again, a shadow crosses the moon. The large eagle lands on the upturned Snake-Van and stares at Don. Don Estrada seems to be eye-locked to the eagle. Don is speechless and offline.

Ajei breaks the wordlessness. "White man want ... the money?"

She staggers to the rear of the Snake-Van and retrieves a metal suitcase. She throws it onto the ground in front of Don. It somehow seems to break Don Estrada out of his comms with the eagle. A quick blast from his Winchester blows the padlock away. Don opens the case to reveal banded sheaves of high denominations. They stare.

Ajei continues. "White man powder also."

She retrieves a second case and drops it next to the first one. Don opens this to reveal it packed with bags of white powder. Marv and Don load the drugs into their pannier bags, pausing only to throw one bag onto the floor around the bodies. They leave the opened case near one of the bodies. They split the cash, taking ten or so sheaves, and leaving the rest in the case.

Marv looks at Don and Al. "Time we weren't here. The rest is yours, Jimmy E. Time to get outta here, now!"

Don uncocks his Winchester and they move to their Harleys. They holster their weapons, except for Don, who lingeringly stares at the eagle. Marv snaps him out of a trance. "C'mon Don Boy."

Don breaks free of his trance and the three angels ride off along the beach, up the ramp, and away into the night.

James looks at Ajei. She speaks in dialect to the eagle. She moves around the back of the Snake-Van and retrieves her bass guitar in its hard case and a rucksack. The eagle looks intently in the direction of the moon and out to sea. James turns to look also and sees the blood from three bodies carried in rivulets to the sea. Under the moonlight, it looks like snakes slithering into the sea. Ajei speaks to the eagle once again, and it soars away.

James supports Ajei up the path to The Dog. He puts the case of remaining cash on the seat between them, and they drive off. They drive in silence, other than James' shivering and coughing. At one point, Ajei retrieves a small pouch from her rucksack. She wets a finger in her mouth and then dips it into the pouch. She paints the dark powder on her tongue. She waits a few seconds, before sighing in some sign of contentment. She then looks at James with concern. She licks her finger again and dips it into the pouch. This time, she leans over and puts her finger to his lips. He opens his mouth, and she slides her finger slowly in and along his tongue. He licks and swallows. As the urban streetlights now slide past, he feels some strength return.

As they hit town, the sun is rising. There is no conversation with Ajei. James drives through the quiet city streets, trying to remember the way to Folsom Street Bus Station. Ajei gazes from the windows of The Dog, transfixed by the city. The watered low morning sun catches her raven black cropped hair. It seems to act like some kind of black body radiator. It accepts all light falling on it, and then emits subtle spectra, depending on the tilt of her head. James sneaks more and more glances at her. Eventually he parks on Beale Street, opposite the Greyhound Bus Station. He turns to look at Ajei. He finds it difficult to speak, but eventually says, "Sorry for the way things went down."

She slowly turns and fixes his gaze. Her face looks different, as she has stopped the head-wound bleeding and cleaned much of the blood. She looks at the cityscape around her.

"White settler parasite immigrants have changed it all."

James looks away, hiding his desperate need to look at her more. He opens the case between them. Ajei looks at the money with disdain. She looks back at James. She takes six wedges of high denominations. She also takes a few loose hundred-dollar bills from the case. She stares at James, looking deep into his eyes. He can't look away. Eventually, Ajei's eyes slowly close. James' eyes remain open. He is transfixed. Marv was right. Her eyes open, and she gives him the leather pouch, full of black powder. She slowly slides her finger into her mouth to remind him how to use the powder. He wonders if she is torturing him. She takes a hooded sweatshirt from her rucksack and slips it on over the black/grey snakeskin jacket she is still wearing from the gig.

She speaks. "Many evil people in this world. Less today than yesterday."

She opens the door and athletically steps down to the street. Her graceful movements have fully returned. She reaches behind the seat and retrieves her bass guitar. James aches for her to stay. She looks at him one last time. "Foreign whiteman might want to look in spare tyre of The Dog truck."

James watches Ajei walk across Beale Street and into the bus station. He seriously considers he is in a dreamscape. His life has changed so much in the last few months. Who would consider a nobody kid from Manchester England could have such an adventure?

**

It's not a long drive from Beale Street to Marv's Motors. Not at this time of the morning. James figures he'd better get The Dog off the streets in case there have been any 'reports' of criminal activity. Christ there should have been. It's early and no-one else around except Marv, Don and Al sat in the "office" looking at sheafs of money and taped bags of, presumably, drugs. James shudders. Still, he didn't make the world? That was grown-ups.

Marv looks up. "Jimmy English. Where's your new lady-friend?"

"Taking the bus back to where she came from Marv."

"You did well Jimmy. Real well. Good job we were around though. That tracker you deployed was a real winner."

"No problem Marvo." James is pleased to have called by a slight nickname. Nobody bats an eyelid. James feels like an honorary angel now.

Marv continues. "You know there were two other hoods following The Snakes as well. Big black Lincoln with South Dakota plates."

"Really?"

"Yeh Jimmy really. Not sure what we could've done if they'd got to the scene too."

"'Kin 'ell Marv. I had no idea. Who were they?"

"No idea Jimmy. Darndest thing happened though. We were just following at a discrete distance trying to work out a plan when their car suddenly swerved into a runoff ditch. When we got there, there was a big rock through their windscreen. No fuckin' idea how that went down?"

"Maybe they were after the drugs? You sure they were bad guys?"

"Soldier hoods Jimmy. Tell them a goddam mile off."

Don Estrada laughs. "Unconscious soldier hoods now and with a wrecked car."

Marv retrieves a bottle and four glasses. He pours measures. "Here's to a good night's work."

The four amigos raise their glasses.

Don Estrada adds, "And, a good old profit."

James gains in confidence. "Marv the money man."

Their laughter rings and slowly subsides.

"Bet you were sad to see your sexy Sioux depart eh Jimmy?"

Before James can reply Don speaks. "She is Assinibone."

"How do you know that Don?"

"I know it from when I was a kid in Arizona. Lived on an Apache and Navajo reservation for a time as best I can remember. We knew various tribes."

James suddenly remembers. "Hey, before she left she did say one thing. She said I should look in the spare tyre of The Dog."

The compadres go quiet until Marv slams his glass down. "Let's go do it then."

They walk out to The Dog and Marv goes straight to the spare compartment. He looks in and recoils. "No spare Jimmy E. You used it or sold it or something?"

"No way Marv."

Marv goes quiet. Walks in a circle holding his beard until he suddenly remembers. "Oh Yeh. I took it out when I was working on it. Now where did I put it?"

Al makes a suggestion. "Maybe on the scrap tyre pile Marv?"

They walk over to a big pile of old tyres and wheels in the corner of the main shed. Don and Al move tyres until Marv sees it. "There see. Wheel was corroded and useless. $1400 for that piece of shit."

They lift the spare wheel and tyre onto the central workbench. "Well there's only one place to look."

Don Estrada produces his hunting knife and pierces the tyre wall. He easily slices around find the tyre packed with similar packages to those they got from the SnakeVan.

"Jackpot. YeeeeHaaaa"

Marv calms Al down before speaking. "Jimmy English that is beginning to look like the best $1400 you ever spent."

James looks downwards. Lost to thought. The three angels give him space until he speaks.

"Marv, I don't have any time left for this."

Marv looks at Don, both speechless for a moment. "We did hear that you had those problems Jimmy ... I gotta say son ... you have faced them down – fuckin' big fuckin' time. Respect. You don't take no shit from Dr Death Jimmy English. You just keep on fuckin' rockin'. KOFR Jimmy."

Don and Al harmonise a big "Yeh".

James feels a pride-warmth inside him. It glows and energises him. His chest expands.

Marv speaks more. "Jimmy, you know when I said You'd never make an angels Jimmy – I was wrong. I was wrong big time. So, you are in."

The four angels shake hands. Rock and roll. No going back.

James makes one request. "You guys know that Lucy is going to have a baby."

"We did hear that, Jimmy."

"Will you make sure she's got somewhere nice to live?"

"You got it Jimmy. You got it."

**

"Jimmy, you can't do this."

His heart leaps. That's the first time Lucy has called him Jimmy. He aches to stay.

"All my life people have said that to me."

Lucy smiles and holds his hand.

He just carries on. "Even my mum once told me I'd never rock on the west coast of America. Where am I Lucy? And what is Skulk Rock?"

"It's the new wave Jimmy."

"Sure."

They both giggle. Tinged with sadness.

"Seriously LuLu. I'm going down. Doc Charlie says it will be soon."

"You need care Jimmy."

"I've had the best care anyone could have. Mike Remo and TMan and TheGnome and Doc Charlie ... and you."

She grips his hand tighter.

"Not to mention Marv and Don. Hey LuLu ... did I tell you I'm an honorary angel!"

She laughs. "Yes James, once or twice you mentioned it."

"Not many neckenders from Manchester have achieved that status ... so ... don't tell me 'you can't do this'."

"Point taken Jimmy E."

They are sat in The Dog and look around Florence Street.

"Wow Jimmy, this is a nice area."

"Marv and Don say they have an option on a property around here, when time is right. You and Ronee and Little Joan could be very happy."

"You know what Jimmy, I once sat in a diner car park in Malta Montana and dreamed of a house on top of a hill in San Francisco. Views over the bay and all that."

"Well, here we are."

"Are Marv and Don serious?"

"Yes. There was a lot of product in The Dog's spare wheel and a lot of cash liberated from the SnakeVan. We've done ok in the motor trade eh? Keeps America Rolling."

"Is it not evil money James?"

He notices she has gone back to 'James'. "James didn't make the world LuLu."

She giggles. "Listen to the murderous Lucy Smith admonishing you."

"Leave all that to Marv and Don and Ronee? You've done enough soul-searching LuLu. Time to concentrate on Skulk Rock."

"For damn right sure thing JimmyE."

James starts The Dog and drives around a few corners and parks at the top of Taylor Street next to Ina Coolbrith Park. James and Lucy look at the bay in the distance. Alcatraz – the reminder of all sins.

"I love it here Lucy. Ina Coolbrith has the poetry vibe and us being top class lyricists too."

"Still got your talent for self-deprecation, eh, Jimmy?"

As she turns to him, he sees a smile he's never seen before. Maybe behind her eyes. Maybe he is beginning to see what Ajei sees? Maybe it's the powder she gave him that he is now using regularly. It's running low though.

"Where you gonna go, Jimmy Smith?"

"Figured I'd go north."

She holds his hand. Highway 101 runs through her mind. "You take care."

"Hardly necessary now."

"Apart from the fact that you will have lawmen and bounty hunters on your trail."

"You love law breaking iconoclasts like me don't you Lucy Smith."

She laughs. "Not now I'm going to be a mother. Anyway, you're just a soft-hearted limey Jimmy Smith, and, full of shit too."

They both find laughter, until James unexpectedly breaks down in tears. Lucy looks at him, holding his hand in silence, as he regains his composure.

He asks, "All that's left of us is love?"

"Still making up songs, Jimmy Smith? You and Morrissey are my favourite Englishmen."

"Well, that one is Philip Larkin."

"Who's he?"

"The greatest."

He smiles, as a beam of sunlight now illuminates The Dog. "I got to go now, Lucy Smith. We've had all the time we are going to get. This last week has been so good."

She nods. "Yes, it has."

They step out of The Dog and breathe the fresh Pacific air. They slowly walk around The Dog. He steps onto the sidewalk beside her. She pats The Dog's hood.

She turns to James. "Never in the history of transportation has so much been owed to such an old shitbox truck."

They laugh, until James speaks. "Remember me to Nick Lucas, Lucy."

"Sure."

"No long goodbyes for this boy. We did all that the last week, but ... will you do something for me?"

"Sure."

"Look after our little girl."

"How are you so sure it's a girl?"

"I know. She will be our Little Joan."

James moves towards the Dog. She holds his hands. She wishes, with her whole heart, for Boris the Cranium's time machine.

"I mean it, Lucy Smith. No long goodbyes for me."

Lucy is dazed. James climbs into the truck seat. He winds the window down. "My Mum is called Joan. And she will love Little Joan."

Skulk Rock Originator and Honorary Angel James Smith, in a beat up old Dodge truck, drives off alone. As alone as you can be. The last she sees of him is a left at the bottom of the hill and west on Union Street. Heading for Highway 101 and end of land. His eyes on the street and bent to it again. The bay air and white cloud dreams of San Francisco all around. The lands of rock and roll. The lands of angels. The lands of love. The lands of last night's dreams. Aspiration and ambition scattered and decayed, for now. All is temporary. But, once again the stars will soon be out, and other soldiers will plot new happiness and beat back the darkness of the world that Jimmy Smith did not make. Nobody, no-one but the angels of fate, ever know what is going to happen to anybody anyone anywhere. Jimmy Smith, locked forever in memory and history. A bright star in the pacific sky.

Lucy walks into the park and sits. She stares at the day. Shadows and dark clouds begin to clear from her mind. She thinks of James, she thinks of her mum, she thinks of her dad. She thinks of Little Joan. Her tears run like a clear mountain stream.

**

James drives across town once more. He walks into the Dirtkickers HQ. Thunderman and TheGnome stare at him. Mike Remo appears from the back room. They look at each other in silence.

TMan breaks it. "Great gigs last weekend Jimmy E."

"Most certainly TMan. It's been my life's ambition working with you guys. We packed so many lifetimes into these few years. I owe everything to you guys."

Of all people, Mike Remo breaks down and sinks to his knees. In seven years, James has seen him handle anything an audience could (literally or otherwise) throw at him. It shocks James to see him like this. James walks over and sinks to his knees, embracing Mike. The other two Dirtkickers join them.

When Mike regains himself he walks over to the beer tap. Ho sent over a barrel of his best. He pours four glasses of IPA.

They sit and savour the beer and reminisce some of the finest moments of Skulk Rock.

Until it's time to go. Inexorable time.

As James makes his way to the door, he gives Mike a cassette tape. "Here's some songs." At the door, he turns. "You need a new guitar player, why not try Lucy?"

James walks quickly out and fires up The Dog. The three Dirtkickers follow and are now stood at the door. James winds down the window and smiles. He gives the skulk rock salute and shouts out the skulk rock mantra.

"KEEP ON FUCKIN ROCKIN."
They laugh through tears.
"Keep on fuckin rockin - limey bastard."

**

James cannot resist driving over to Felicia's apartment. He feels guilty for doing so, but he's not seen her since the Snake's demise. He see's her Porsche parked outside with a Lam-bore-fuckin-ghini parked behind it. *"Rich Fuckin' Guy."*

James remembers the first time he set eyes on Felicia. It's burned and engraved and baked onto his memory. That moment and many other moments since.

He puts The Dog into gear to drive away, as the apartment door opens. He pauses. Rich and Felicia exit and walk around to his car. As always, gravity and aether are disturbed. Scattered light from her is tunnelled into his vision. Gravity pulses his chest.

As Felicia sits in his car, she glances over and their eyes lock. It's immediate. It takes him back to Susanville and all the moments in-between. The reflected spectrum from her hair. Every small movement adds to her portrait. Leonardo, Michelangelo, Caravaggio could never capture it.

There's an infinity in that moment as Rich smiles to control his piece of status-symbol-shit. Their telepathy transmits on a bandwidth so wide that all time is irrelevant.

James thinks of the time Mike Remo told him she was just like all the others. *"This was fuckin' different."*

She smiles to him as Rich drives away. A smile locked into history. Bolted tight in incorruptible stainless steel.

**

He drives The Dog over The Golden Gate, heading north. The scenery of Highway 101 unfolds in front of The Dog one more time. As evening falls, he makes Crescent City. He finds a Hotel on Main Street, with a window overlooking various revelry bars. The receptionist looks at him suspiciously, as he pays cash in advance with a large denomination bill and tells her no change is necessary.

In his room, he looks in the mirror and is shocked by his current appearance. No wonder the receptionist looked suspicious. His breathing is shallow and desperate. He resorts to Dr Charlie's stronger medicine and two fingers of Ajei's black powder. The joint medication beats back the evil.

He phones his Mum in England. She's so so happy to hear from him. She tells him how she is busy these days and has lots of friends. She goes for coffee with her friends three times a week. She has trips to the cinema. She helps with the local amateur dramatic society. She tells him that cousin Jill is finally getting married to a guy from Oldham. He's got a good job in sales, although she doesn't quite know what he sells. Aunt Clara has bought at least four 'Mother of the Bride' dresses, because she can't decide which one suits her best.

Details that would have driven him mad with boredom, now seem so important to him. He wants the conversation to last forever, but it has to end. He tells his mother how much he loves her and how he thinks of her every single day.

He puts the phone down and smiles. He thinks of her smiling face.

He is calm now as he reaches into his rucksack and takes out Lucy's pistol. There is one cartridge of the five it holds left in there. He shudders as he remembers firing the other four at the SnakeDog. He clears his mind of those thoughts. He thinks of some of his songs. He thinks of Lucy Smith. He thinks of Felicia. He thinks of Mike Remo. He thinks of Thunderman. He thinks of TheGnome and his strange dance. He thinks of Ajei, he thinks of his Mum. He thinks of his dad. He thinks of Bob Dylan. He thinks of Gabriella Sabatini. He thinks of Stevie Nicks and Chrissie Hynde. He thinks of Dr Charlie. He thinks of Lucy. He thinks of Little Joan. He thinks of Lucy again. He imagines what little Joan will be like. He thinks of Felicia. Again, he thinks of Mike Remo, TMan and TheGnome. He gives the Skulk Rock salute. His other hand feels the cold cruel stainless steel of the pistol.

On the street below, revellers gather under cover, outside a rowdy bar, as a clear moon is visible between heartless black rain-bearing clouds. The summer is gone.

Last Pistol Shot

The rain beats on a hotel window pane
And laughter in the street below
Life goes on like a hurricane
But for me it moves so slow
One more dream and one more pill
I'm thinking back – what I had and what I got
The clock ticks but time stands still
I'm looking down the barrel
Of my last pistol shot

I wish that the stars would turn around
My dreams are all twisted
My gravity is sinking down
And time is telling me that I never existed

The world is turning still
I'm looking at your picture and I still like it a lot
I'm still here but I'm still ill
I'm looking down the barrel
Of my last pistol shot

None of the revellers below hear the dull boom of the pistol. None of the revellers notice the flash of light from the second-floor room.

Life goes on.

Chapter 24
Starkeepers

A wooded glade with shafts of sunlight streaming down. A figure sits on a log. An older man walks through the woods and into the glade. He approaches the sitting figure from the rear. The sitting figure is gazing down at his hands, and not moving. The older man stands behind him in silence for a while, before speaking softly.

"James?"

The sitting figure is James, and he turns in surprise and amazement.

"Dad?"

"Yes."

"What are you doing here?"

"Well, I'm a 'Starkeeper' now," his father beams.

James looks shocked.

The Starkeeper continues. "I know it's a surprise. I had a similar surprise."

"Am I dreaming?"

"Nope. You're what we call a 'waiter'."

"What the fuck?"

"Language, James." The Starkeeper admonishes him, before continuing. "It has been deemed necessary that your situation is to be considered further, before your full admission to the starlife."

"Hey Dad, don't bullshit me."

"Golly, James, you even talk like an American these days."

James stares at his father for an extended period, before his tears arrive. Then, he rushes forward to embrace him.

"Dad, I'm sorry."

"I'm sorry too. I was single minded about your future. And sorry I didn't appreciate your music. And sorry I was too protective."

They smile in silence.

James speaks first. "So, after all the bollocks religions on earth, it turns out that the universe runs like the gospel according to Rodgers and Hammerstein?"

"Bluntly put, James, but, nonetheless, accurate."

"Carousel always was your favourite, eh?"

"Well, yes it was." The Starkeeper breaks into song (badly). "When you walk through a storm. Hold your head up high ..." He does a little dance, and smiles. "You see, you got your skulk rock talent from me, 'Jimmy English'."

They laugh.

Mr Smith suddenly turns serious. "The thing is James, you have been ... well, what some people might deem naughty. There is a debate over cheating death by suicide." He wags his finger. "The Powers that be have decided you can remain a 'waiter' for now and, if you prove yourself diligent, then they will reconsider your situation."

"What the fuck does that mean?"

"For a start, it means you can mend your potty mouth, young man."

"Sorry."

"And the rest of the time, you are to watch out for your friend Lucy. And, of course, for Little Joan."

James looks confused, but then asks tentatively. "Little Joan is my daughter?"

"Yes, James, and you are to stand guard until she comes of age."

"Yes, of course."

"She is three and a half now. Your case has been a tricky one."

"When can I see her?"

"I will take you there now, but your task will be to keep 'The Night Shadows' at bay."

"The Night Shadows?"

"Yes, they bring a variety of evil to the world."

"How do I spot them? And how do I protect her?"

Starkeeper gives him a small box. "This will show their approach. You'll get the hang of it, and your love will protect her."

He gives James the box, before continuing. "You will be able to fly and look around the old earth, but you must be diligent and vigilant. Remember, James, 'All that's left of us is love'."

"So, Philip Larkin was right? As well as Rodgers and Hammerstein?"

"Yes, indeed."

"Will you help me, Dad?"

"I would love to, but I am looking out for your mother at the moment."

"Is she okay?"

"She is older, James, and misses you terribly."

"So sorry, Dad." James breaks down.

His father, The Starkeeper, comforts him, before explaining. "Come on, I'll show you where they are. One day we will all be together."

They both smile.

**

San Francisco sits in early morning sun. Its light streams into a high bedroom window in a house at the top of a hill. James sits on the apex of the roof above. Inside the room, a gorgeous little girl wakes up.

Lucy Smith comes into her room, smiling. "What should we do today, Little Joan?"

Joan smiles as she thinks. "Painting."

Lucy laughs. "Okay, but should we go see the seals first?"

"Yes." Little Joan smiles and leaps out of her bed.

James smiles as he watches Lucy and Joan leave the house. He hovers as he accompanies them skipping down the hill. At the piers, Joan meets a little friend, and they smile and hug. The children run on the Pier and laugh at the seals, which bark back at them.

The mothers all chat.

James soars and swoops over the scene.

As the day wears on, Joan and Lucy paint pictures in the house.

As night falls, Joan gets ready for bath and bed as James sits on the same roof bay, looking at his 'starkeeper' warning box for any stray snakes of evil.

He misses his last life. He wishes he was down there making up songs. He still makes up songs. He often stands next to Lucy and tries to send her songs. He remembers how she used to tell him that songs were 'The Gifts of Ghosts'. He laughs as he remembers telling her that the theory was 'bollocks'. Now he sees he was wrong.

He looks at the traffic continually flowing over the Bay Bridge. He wonders about The Dog. He worries about the pollution. He worries about the world of men. He worries about all these things, because of Little Joan.

He still makes up songs.

He worries about Skulk Rock.

The Floating Ghost

I'm looking from a window and I can't see a tree
I'm in a desert city in the land of luxury
A woman in a fur coat is walkin' up the street
She got the light in her eyes but she can't see me
I am the floating ghost
That no-one ever knows
And I go places no-one ever goes

I arrive from the skies and I float away untouched
To the heart of the stars where all light is crushed
All the night time sounds - I conduct
I'm the genius that was always overlooked
Float over Mexico
Float over Idaho
I float anywhere I want to go
I am The Floating Ghost

I look down on this earth – from way up high
I don't understand – how I can fly
I got eyes so wide – there ain't no place to hide
You can lock your doors but I just float inside
I am the floating ghost
That no-one ever knows
And I go places no-one ever goes

Float in the summer heat
Float over Downing Street
I float in the places old ghosts meet

And I trail the Taliban
And I view the Vatican
And I piss in the Palace of Buckingham

Chapter 25
Ghost Radar

It's evening, and Lucy is reading Little Joan a story.

Joan is entranced.

Eventually, Lucy says, "C'mon, Little Joan, it's time for bed."

Little Joan stalls for time and asks, as she always does, "Can we see if the moon is out tonight, Mom?"

Lucy carries Little Joan to the window, because she always wants to see if the moon is there. That night, it is. It looks close too. It hovers over San Francisco Bay. James sits on the roof above and looks at the same moon.

Little Joan asks, "Are there people on the moon, Mom?"

"Nobody knows for sure?"

"I can see them, Mom."

"You better behave then, Little Joan. They are watching you."

Little Joan nods.

Lucy carries her over to bed. As she is tucked, in she suddenly remembers what she always remembers. "Mom, can we check the ghost radar?"

Lucy smiles and takes out her phone, and boots up the Ghost Radar app.

Little Joan asks, "Is our ghost there?"

"Yes. There he is, Joan, as always."

They see a flashing green light on the screen.

Little Joan looks a little apprehensive, so she asks. "Mom, it's not a scary ghost?"

"No, Little Joan. Only evil people get scary ghosts."

Little Joan smiles. "We're not evil, are we, Mom?"

Lucy smiles at her. "No, Little Joan, you are not a bad person, and you seem to have a Guardian Angel."

They stare at the Ghost Radar screen, and the flashing light on screen marks a big cross-kiss onto the screen. They both blow it kisses.

Ghost Radar

I got a phone with ghost radar
And man they are everywhere
There was one in the back of my car
When I was going somewhere

The darkness of the next world
Don't screen my sight
I'm on the 6th sense network
And my phone is fully charged tonight

Ghost Radar
I know where they are
There's 2 in my backyard
Switched on my ghost radar
Ghost Radar Ghost Radar

They don't need no tickets
They don't need no doors
They don't worry about traffic
And they don't need no cars

I heard it on the news today
A dead man got up and walked away
I'm sitting in a high window bay
As life and death – pass me by

If I'm lonely at night
Switch on my ghost radar
A ghostly light
Is never very far
Magnetic disturbances
talkin' to me....talkin to me..

Do you feel like you're never alone ?
Do you hear footsteps following you home ?
Maybe a dream you've always known
Maybe a mystery message on your mobile phone

Ghost Radar Ghost Radar
Ghost Radar Ghost Radar

Chapter 26

Lists Of Love

Lucy Smith is on stage with The Lowdown Dirtkickers. Mike Remo introduces her to the large crowd, and announces, "Our guitar player and songwriter, Lucy Smith, is going to sing this one for you."

As she moves to the mic, Lucy speaks to the audience. "You know, sometimes songs just appear from nowhere. It's like a ghost visits and gives them to you. All you have to do is write them down and sing them. This is one of those songs."

You know what they say? 'All That's Left Of Us Is Love'?". Well, make sure there's something left of you - and you will always stay in The Lists of Love. This song is for JIMMY ENGLISH."

The audience cheer and cheer and cheer. They too miss Jimmy English.

Lucy Smith looks across and behind at Mike Remo, Thunderman, and TheGnome. They smile and strike the Skulk Rock salute. The considerable audience does the Skulk Rock salute. The Lowdown Dirtkickers are top of The Skulk Rock Charts.

Lists of Love

I want to stay in the lists of love
Be there when push comes to shove
I'm a heart angel from above
And you are what I'm thinking of

I'll summon all the magic shadows tonight
All the tracks and tricks of the light
You cut a heart shaped hole in my soul
So I can never die, never even get old
And if blood might fall on England's green
Sands of time from across the sea
This is evil that could come to be
But I mostly just think of you and me

No need for a pension plan
Might be old but I was once a man
This is not a heart that love deserts
This is not a love that comes in spurts
As I finally admit defeat
My ghost will sniff your sheets
My dark desires cannot be destroyed
I'm gonna be touching you across the void

Time took these eyes and made them blurred
A passing year is just a four letter word
But time turns round and time turns back
All my dreams are still intact
You are nailed to my memory
Crucified across my heart
Time has been and time has gone
Of all I've seen you are still the one

The audience of SkulkRockers cheer. They know the truths of this world, as it carries on in all its ignorant glory outside the venue.

*****

PostScript:

Boris The Cranium has finally completed his unification theories. His mathematical ramblings show conclusively that there are parallel worlds to this one. Not many people believe him, though. They prefer to cling to their beliefs in good versus evil, and an 'afterlife' dependent upon the balance of each over a whole lifetime.

*****